Joining
the Rainbow

Bel Mooney

mammoth

For Kitty, Ruby,
Amala, Daisy and Luke.

Every effort has been made by the publishers to trace the owners of the copyright of the
material quoted in this book. If we have inadvertently wrongly attributed a quote,
we shall be happy to correct it in the event of a reprint.

The extract from *Cry, The Beloved Country* by Alan Paton is reproduced by kind
permission of the Late Alan Paton and Random House Jonathan Cape.
© Alan Paton. First published 1948 by Jonathan Cape. (Page 139)

The Prince in Waiting by John Christopher
© John Christopher. First published 1970 by Hamish Hamilton. (Page 166)

First published in Great Britain in 1997 by Mammoth
an imprint of Reed International Books Ltd
Michelin House, 81 Fulham Road, London SW3 6RB
and Auckland, Melbourne, Singapore and Toronto

Copyright © 1997 Bel Mooney

The right of Bel Mooney to be identified as the author of this work has been asserted by
her in accordance with the Copyright, Designs and Patents Act 1988

ISBN 0 7497 2817 5

10 9 8 7 6 5 4 3 2 1

A CIP catalogue record for this book is available from the British Library

Printed in Great Britain by Cox & Wyman Ltd, Reading, Berkshire

Contents

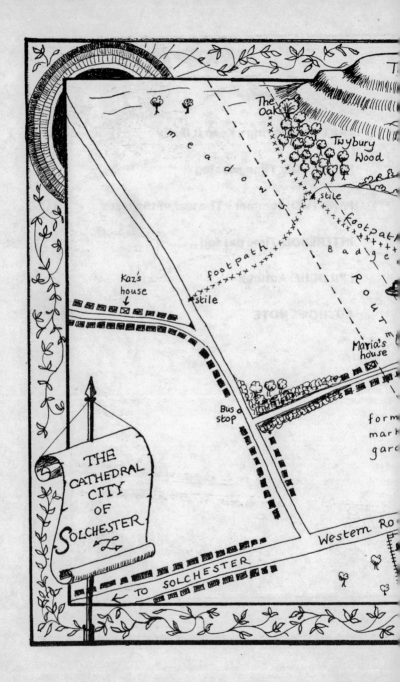

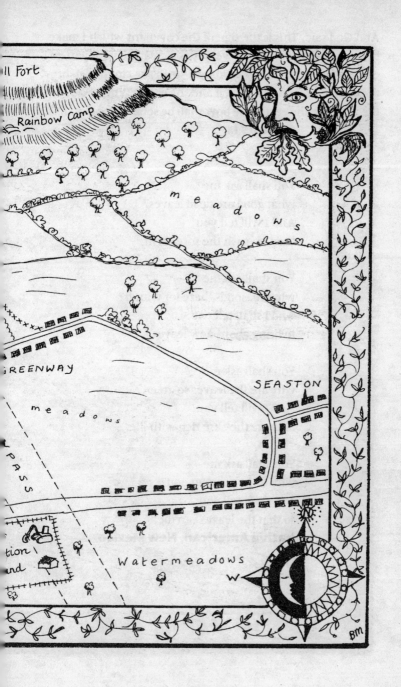

And God said, This is the sign of the covenant which I make between me and you and every living creature with you, to endless generations. My rainbow I set in the cloud, sign of the covenant between myself and the earth. When I cloud the sky over the earth, the bow shall be seen in the cloud.

Genesis ix

You shall ask me
what good are dead leaves?
And I will tell you:
they nourish the sore earth.

You shall ask me
what reason is there for winter?
And I shall tell you:
to bring about new leaves.

You shall ask me
why are the leaves so green?
And I will tell you:
because they are rich with life.

You shall ask me
why must summer end?
and I will tell you:
so that the leaves can die.

Native American, New Mexico

It was very dark. A bitter wind cut in from the north east, making the bare trees and bushes on the hillside shake and bow their heads, as if in terror of whatever threats the night might bring. A badger barrelled his way home, along the frosty brockway, to his sett. Small creatures sheltered in the lee of hedges, glad of the darkness which might protect them from death. Or else contain it.

Somewhere an owl hooted, calling back across the centuries to the time before time when men and women, afraid, retreated to the flat, bare top of the hill to build their settlement. Then, as now, the threat came from below; better to shiver high on the stronghold than trust yourself to the blackness of the valleys. On nights like this they huddled round their fires – listening – and prayed for morning to come quickly. Who knows what they worshipped, what belief gave them strength? All they knew was the power far older than themselves, which they heard in the cry of the wind and the shaking of the trees – a dark and ancient magic, which drew its strength from the core of the earth itself. Some- times it seemed a tree would detach itself from the ground and walk, a rustling green giant, across their dreams. There would be whispers in the darkness, or harsh cries of anger – and the shapes of the Mystery dancing in the blackness beyond the firelight. Then who knows what dark sacrifices were made, to propitiate the savage gods? Strange carvings on rocks. Blood on the leaves. Fear. There will be blood again . . .

The world turns. Legions came and went. Others built in the valley; over centuries the town spread out towards the hill, which, all the time, squatted across the landscape, dark and brooding. Holding the key to mysteries long forgotten. And the trees there growing taller, roots deep in the sacred earth, topmost branches tossing wildly in a winter wind. Uneasy.

One

'There's a sale on at Sami,' said Chris, pulling on Kaz's arm.

'I need new jeans,' said Sally, 'but Sami's too cheap. I want Levis. Gotta be Levis. I heard Debbie Mansfield's getting Calvin Kleins . . .'

'That's stupid,' said Kaz. 'She's spoilt rotten. They're all the same. You just pay for the label.'

'I reckon they fit better,' said Sally, shaking her head.

The three girls walked arm in arm down Solchester's main street. They stopped outside Sami, peered in the window then went inside. The shop was crowded, as if half the teenage girls in the city had chosen that Saturday morning to buy clothes. There was a pushing and a shoving, and a giggling babble of talk, which the girls joined in.

Kaz stared critically at her reflection in the mirror as she tried on a short leather jacket. Pale oval face, dead-straight dark blonde hair, which her mother said people would have killed for back in the sixties, blue eyes, and the pointy nose she hated. She ran a hand through her hair, tossing it back. 'Ugh, I've got a spot,' she said, pointing to her chin.

3

'Who hasn't?' sighed Chris.

'Debbie Mansfield,' grinned Sally.

'Yeah, but she's thick. I think I'd rather have one spot and not be thick!' laughed Kaz, replacing the jacket on the rail.

This was the Saturday routine, after the tedium of school. Shopping for a pair of leggings or some silver earrings; spraying on perfumes and smearing trial lipsticks on the back of their hands in Boots; pulling on velvet hats and giggling at the mirror. Then strolling around, nudging and smiling when they passed certain boys, ignoring others, chatting, laughing, chewing a hot dog outside the market – Kaz, Chris and Sally: best friends. Later they would go their separate ways because their parents insisted on a couple of hours' schoolwork. But only after they'd arranged the time to meet for the evening disco. The routine had the comforting familiarity of a favourite piece of clothing you just throw on without having to think.

Somebody was busking at the corner of a sidestreet. Kaz heard the acoustic guitar and recognised the words of one of her mother's favourite songs from the sixties. It asked mournfully how many times a man would turn away, pretending he didn't see. The sad old-fashioned sound blew by them on the slight wind, to be replaced, as they strolled on, by the delicate sound of a flute, with taped orchestral accompaniment, and then – more to the girls' taste – the rhythmic, echoing clatter of two steel drums. Buskers did well in Solchester on a Saturday, particularly when the pale sun promised spring.

Kaz Armstrong felt she wanted no more than this: she was getting on quite well with her parents, and she and Chris and Sally seemed to have formed a little rampart against the other girls in school. It made her feel secure. She even stopped worrying about her height. Her mother always said good things came in small parcels, after all.

Suddenly Chris stopped, dragging on Kaz's arm. 'Look! Something's going on down there.'

At the same moment Kaz and Sally heard the noise: a shouting from further along the street, where it widened to join the Cathedral precinct. The crowds were even thicker down there, swirling into a different pattern. Kaz saw banners and placards and police helmets. Then there was the strangulated sound of a voice yelling into a megaphone, words so distant and distorted they merged into a sort of fuzzy lament.

Kaz wanted to hear. 'Come on!' she said, pulling away, so that Chris and Sally were forced to follow.

Before the Cathedral's magnificent fourteenth-century west front a large crowd had gathered. The girls took their places at the rear of the crowd, then gradually wormed their way through until they could see what was going on.

The placards bore different slogans: NO TO THE ROAD, SAVE OUR HILL, NO BYPASS HERE and PUT THE EARTH FIRST. There were mothers with children, men in anoraks and green waxy coats, grey-haired women in voluminuous skirts or baggy trousers, people in their twenties looking very grim, teenagers in brightly coloured jumble-sale clothes, and amongst them, bizarre figures with long, matted hair, nose-rings and painted faces.

'Look at the crusties!' giggled Sally.

'It's about Twybury Hill,' said Kaz. 'That's near us!'

Chris laughed and dug her in the ribs. 'Look at that!' she whispered.

She was pointing at an elderly man with a bald head and a florid face, who was dressed from top to toe in the Union Jack. He had stitched bits of the flag all over his tweedy jacket and trousers, and he carried a huge banner that was more like a book. BRITISH LAND IS BEAUTIFUL, it read. CONSERVATIVES FOR THE ENVIRONMENT. The slogans were surrounded by newspaper cuttings pasted in an elaborate collage.

Kaz was fascinated as the bearded first speaker brandished a packaged sandwich and told them that it had been made in the north of England and transported to Solchester by road. 'Wasteful, polluting and ridiculous,' he yelled, throwing it into the crowd. Then he handed the megaphone to a girl of about eighteen, with thick red hair waving about her freckled face. She leapt up on to the bench.

'I just want to say one thing,' she yelled. 'They start work on Monday. They'll be cutting down the trees at the foot of Twybury Hill and clearing the way for this horrible monster of a road that's going to ruin our countryside . . .'

'I've seen her before,' whispered Sally. 'I think she went to our school.'

' . . . and we have to stand up this time and say NO! We'll go down there and we'll stop them working! We'll show them that we won't let the countryside be desecrated without a fight. The pollution levels in this area are already worse than anywhere else in the South of England.

If the government is worried about asthma in kids, how can they force road projects of this size through?'

. 'Because they don't give a damn!' somebody yelled.

'Oh yes they do!' shouted the red-headed girl, waving a fist in the air. 'They give a damn about all the businessmen who want their journeys to be quicker! They give a damn about the huge supermarket chains who send stuff up and down the country by road, and put the small shops and growers out of business! They give a damn about making money for the few and spoiling the land for the many – the land that's ours! The land that's been there for thousands of years!'

She was interrupted by a storm of clapping. 'Listen – I was born and brought up in this city. I know the fields of Twybury like the back of my hand – all my life I've flown kites on the top of the hill. Don't forget it's a special, historic place. Just look at the plans and see what this so-called bypass is going to do to that landscape. It'll be ruined – unless we do something to stop it. There's a choice: you can all go home and say, "It's too late," or "It's nothing to do with me." Or you can stand up and be counted – now! Join us on Monday! Help us stop the diggers! Take direct action to STOP THIS ROAD!'

'She's nearly crying,' whispered Chris.

'I don't blame her,' Kaz replied.

A middle-aged woman in a big black hat and a brightly coloured shawl stepped forward and took the megaphone. She paused briefly to put an arm round the girl's shoulders. She stepped up on the bench as if she was very weary, but her voice was strong. Kaz recognised her, too. This was Janey Morgan, a well-known illustrator of childrens' books, who lived locally and had once given a talk at the girls' school.

'You've all heard what Maria said, and I respect her views. I'm one of those who's been working for six years to stop this road. We did all the right things – wrote letters, spoke at the public inquiry – all that. We tried, we really tried. But they take no notice. They just do what they always intended to do, and all that pretence at democracy is a sham. I think they decided they were going to build this route years and years ago, and nothing anybody said would have made any difference! So this is our last chance to fight it by getting as much publicity as we can. You never know – someone might listen! But I just want to say this. Some of you will want to try to stop the work by taking action, but for the rest of you – don't give up, don't stop writing your letters! Write to the MP, the councillors, the Secretary of State for Transport! Honestly, it's still worth a try. Because we know we have right on our side. I'm looking forward to being a grandmother one day, and I want my grandchildren to inherit the landscape I grew up in. I don't want them to grow up in a Britain that's wall to wall concrete. Do you?'

There was a loud chorus of 'NO!' from the crowd. It made Kaz uncomfortable somehow, as if by not joining in she was being a coward, with no right to be there at all.

'Come on, let's go,' murmured Chris in her ear.

'I'm going to be late,' said Sally.

'Just wait a bit longer,' Kaz said.

'What for?' asked Chris.

'I . . . I want to see what happens.'

Now Maria and the bearded man who had spoken first stepped up to join Janey Morgan on the bench. They stood, the three of them so different, looking out over the crowd with an air of great determination. The two women linked arms, the man raised the megaphone to speak.

'NOW! We're going to have a peaceful walk right along the Western Road, and up to Twybury, to show you where the work is going to begin. We want you to look at the trees and the hedges and the meadows and think how quickly it'll all be gone – unless we *do* something! Are you coming with us? Are you?'

Then came a roar of 'YEAH!' and this time, to Kaz's amazement, she found herself joining in. There was a swirling movement in the crowd as the three leaders jumped down, and started the walk from the Cathedral precinct. Chris and Sally grabbed at Kaz's arms.

'What are you doing?' shouted Sally. 'You can't go with them.'

'Why not? It's on my way home – do me good to walk instead of getting the bus.'

'She's lost it!' grinned Chris. 'OK then, see you at half past seven – and don't get chatted up by weirdos!'

Kaz wanted to say something rude, but she was swept away by the long snake of demonstrators as it ribboned its way through the town. There was a carnival atmosphere: people were playing tin whistles behind her, and somewhere up in front there was the rhythmic tattoo of a drum. The placards waved like flags; the sun glittered on streaming ribbons attached to a pole. The policemen and women keeping a careful eye on events looked relaxed.

Yet it was not long before Kaz noticed something strange. When you were a part of the snake, you weren't a part of the rest of the world. Walking alone, wishing she had someone to talk to, she still felt part of this huge crowd of strangers, and different from the people passing by who gave them dirty looks.

And there were *very* dirty looks. Kaz simply did not understand why. Nobody was really doing anything wrong, except of course, sometimes getting in the way of the traffic. She supposed that was it. The world had its business to get on with – even on a Saturday – and anything that held it up even for a second was an irritant. Even so, Kaz thought, it couldn't possibly explain the hatred she saw.

As Kaz grew older, life became more and more confusing. She still took her old baby doll, Rosie, to bed (although she would have died rather than tell the girls in school). In the wonderful warm smell of Rosie's head and clothes she could comfort herself with the security of childhood, when all you worried about was whether there would be roast chicken on Sunday, and if your best friend would still want to be your best friend on Monday. But even that came later: childhood was Mum and Dad and bedtime stories, and playing games with your little brother, and believing in Father Christmas, of course, and the Tooth Fairy. It was all such fun; now Kaz was sometimes overwhelmed by a deep sense of sadness, as if Rosie was lost and she was wandering all over a bare, dark hillside looking for her, yet knowing that the little doll was gone for ever.

When you reached fourteen it seemed that everybody was at you. In school and at home you had to start taking work seriously, and be mature about things. Then, when you tried to be grown-up in choice of clothes, your parents told you off, and the school slapped more and more rules on you, about the colour of your tights and the size of heels and the kind of jewellery you could wear . . . And nobody told you *why*. When you watched the news at night, and saw people killing each other in Africa or parts of Europe, you couldn't begin to understand why either. Sometimes Kaz felt she had lost more than her beloved doll on the dark, wild hillside. She had lost herself, too.

'You're not dressed for a demo!' somebody said behind her. The voice was gentle, but faintly mocking too. Kaz turned round quickly, and was startled.

The smiling face was bright green, lips pink and rubbery in contrast. It was made even uglier by the daubed red lines marking the eyes, giving an impression of wildness. The creature wore a sort of crown of leaves and twigs that drooped comically round the green face, and it took a few seconds for Kaz to realise that she was talking to a boy. He was of medium height, but very thin, with long dark hair tied back in a ponytail. He was wearing an assortment of clothes that made him look half-jester, half-labourer: dark padded jacket, orange patterned kerchief, dirty yellow and black striped leggings and enormous muddy boots. The backs of his hands were painted green, but she saw that the palms and nails were caked with dirt. He smelt of woodsmoke on Bonfire night.

Disgusting, Kaz thought.

'*You* won't stop the diggers dressed like that,' he said, glancing down at Kaz's feet then back at her face, with an even wider grin.

'Who said I wanted to?' she retorted, feeling her cheeks flush as

11

red as his were green. She felt a fool, ashamed of her miniskirt, cropped jacket, shiny tights and black dolly shoes with the high, stacked heels which clearly amused him so much.

'It's the only thing to do,' shrugged the boy, still with that light, bantering note in his voice. His grey eyes twinkled at her from their rings of scarlet, contradicting the hideous hostility of the green mask.

'Who says so?' she asked, suddenly feeling furious.

'Why come then?'

'Just . . . just to see.'

'See what?'

'What – er – what all the fuss is about.'

'You live here?'

She nodded.

'So how come you didn't see before?' he asked.

'Where do *you* live?' she asked, instead of replying, because she knew she had no reply.

'On the hill, of course! We're the new Neolithic tribe – come to tell you locals to open your eyes. We're occupying the hill and we're gonna stop the road.'

'Just like that!' mocked Kaz.

'Yeah, right! Anyway, you didn't answer me – how come you didn't know about all this?'

Kaz shook her head, and started to mumble, 'Well, er . . .'

'Too busy shopping, I reckon,' he grinned, tapping her Sami carrier bag.

'What do you know?' Kaz shouted.

Some people in front started to chant, 'No more roads!' over and over again, and the words were taken up all around Kaz, more and more loudly.

He shrugged, as if he thought her too stupid to be worth a reply, then he gave a little mock bow and dropped back into the crowd.

Kaz tried to turn, but it was impossible. She was caught up in a press of people, a raggle-taggle army, which pushed her relentlessly onwards towards Twybury Hill, laughing, talking, singing, shouting. She stumbled in her silly shoes and suddenly wanted to escape.

Two

Twybury Hill was on the eastern side of Solchester, a long, flat hill, densely wooded on all sides. The place was a famous local beauty spot – an Iron Age hill-fort from which you could see for miles. People would picnic on the summit on summer days, and fly kites all the year round. It was a wild and beautiful place, with grassy ramparts mysterious at sundown, and stony hummocks and gulleys concealing the secrets of lives and deaths long gone, from the time the land was dark and wolves roamed in the dank valley mists.

The hill was famous for its wildlife – the old brockways where at night you could smell the sharp, hot scent of badger, and the hedgerows (thick walls of elder, hawthorn, blackthorn, hazel, bramble and dogrose) were safe corridors for countless creatures: mice, voles, shrews, rabbits and foxes. Thrushes, wrens, bullfinches, chiffchaffs, yellowhammers, blue tits, robins and dozens of other birds called to each other from the tallest hedge branches and the trees all around. And in spring, wild flowers and herbs were a promise of summer's butterflies: brimstone, tortoiseshell, large white, orange-tip, peacock, meadow-brown, common blue . . .

Kaz Armstrong knew it well. When she was nine months old her family had moved from London to a comfortable large cottage on the outskirts of Solchester, at a point where town and country met, and the landscape was dominated by the brooding presence of the hill, visible from the Armstrongs' back garden. When she was younger the whole family would go for Sunday afternoon walks in the meadows that sloped upwards, through Twybury Wood, gradually becoming the hill itself. Jamie was little then and could not walk very far without complaining and asking to be carried. Now he was eleven, and it was he who instigated the walks.

Kaz was already puffing. The march had turned left, off the long, long Western Road and up the old A02, which wound along beneath Twybury Hill, heading north. Kaz's house was down a little lane off this road, and when they drew near it, she looked at her watch, not knowing what to do. Her mother would be expecting her for lunch. She worried and got angry if ever Kaz changed her plans without letting her know. On the other hand, if she slipped off home for lunch she would miss . . . what? Kaz was not sure, but she knew one thing: this was at least interesting and *different*. It had cut into the usual Saturday routine like scissors through silk, and she realised she couldn't just go home. Not yet.

Five minutes after Kaz's turn-off point, the procession began to turn right, leaving the A02 behind. They were on the Twybury meadows now, crossing stiles and starting to climb very gradually upwards in the

15

direction of the hilltop. The meadows were studded with clumps of primroses and ragged daffodils nodded here and there. The air grew fresher as they climbed.

Suddenly, without any commands being shouted, people stopped, and the snake curled itself into a crowd again. Somebody was shouting up ahead, but although Kaz strained her ears she could not make out the words.

'What's she saying?' she asked the white-haired woman next to her, who was leaning heavily on a walking-stick.

'Can't hear, dear.'

'Just explaining the route of the road,' said a man in front. 'Where we're standing we'll be slap-bang in the middle of a dual carriageway with a central reservation. Nice, eh?'

'What, here?' asked Kaz in disbelief.

'Oh yes, lovey – didn't you know?' said the old lady, shaking her head sorrowfully.

Kaz looked around. The voices seemed to recede, so that it was as if she was standing on a high pinnacle, utterly alone. A kestrel was hovering in the distance, high above the fields, and for a second Kaz felt at one with it, poised at the still point between earth and heaven, threatening some tiny creature far below, but unthreatened by any other living thing itself. Or was that true? Maybe we are all part of a whole, she thought, so that if the small creature is no longer there, then the kestrel cannot eat and so must perish. She closed her eyes for a second, feeling dizzy, and seemed to feel concrete beneath her feet and hear the roar of cars and lorries . . .

But the roar was the crowd again, applauding the speaker. Kaz looked at her watch again, feeling a prisoner both of the people pressing all around, and of her mother's routines.

They had started lunch, of course, and her mother gave Kaz a reproachful look. 'We waited as long as we could without it spoiling. I do think you could be on time. It isn't much to ask.'

'Sorry, Mum.'

'You don't sound it.' Kaz's brother beamed at her from behind his spectacles, enjoying the fact that she was in trouble again.

'Shut up, Jampot.'

'Kathleen – just eat your meal without any more fuss,' said her father, frowning.

'I wasn't making a fuss, Dad! And please don't call me Kathleen,' said Kaz, sulkily picking at the plate of pasta her mother put in front of her.

'You change your name as often as you change your friends,' said Jamie.

'Has anybody told you you're the most annoying little boy in Europe, Fleabag?'

'Not the world?' said Jamie in mock horror.

Kaz decided it was more dignified to ignore her brother. 'There was a demonstration in town,' she blurted. 'That's why I was late. I wanted to see.'

'You didn't join it, did you?' asked her mother.

'No. Well . . . sort of. Just to see.'

'It was about the bypass – I saw a poster,' said Jamie.

'Oh, that old chestnut,' said their father, rolling his eyes to heaven.

'Why's it an old chestnut?' asked Kaz.

'Well, they were talking for donkey's years about replacing the A02 with a dual carriageway that'll go on to form a bypass for Seaston. There was a public inquiry two or three years ago; I wasn't very keen on the idea, but what can you do? It's going to happen now.'

'Shame, really,' said their mother in the tone of someone who is already thinking of something else.

'Those people this morning – they seem to think they can stop it,' said Kaz thoughtfully.

Her father snorted derisively. 'Fat chance. And I tell you what we want even less than the new road – a whole pile of troublemakers coming in from outside. These travellers ... local people don't like them. The whole thing is a waste of time and money, and the sooner they realise it the better.'

'Better for who, Dad?' asked Jamie.

Their father hesitated, forcing Kaz to hide a smile. Her brother was a funny, old-fashioned little boy, and a part of her was embarrassed by him. But the truth was, she really rather liked him, especially since he reached the age when suddenly he seemed to know a lot about volcanoes and toads and the mating habits of spiders. He wanted to be a scientist or inventor, and it was easy to see why. Jamie Armstrong and the public library were made for each other; each week he came home with a pile of books and regaled them all with tales of UFOs, crop circles, mountain lions, penguins and the whole universe of stars and planets. Her brother, with his funny, pale, freckled face, round glasses, and habit of wrinkling up his nose like a piglet, was well on the way towards becoming a true eccentric. She was protective of him, but oddly enough, sometimes felt that he was far wiser than she.

Their father ran a small engineering works, and considered himself a man of science and logic who could generally have the last word on most issues. He too devoured library books as though they were about to be banned and his resulting mine of general knowledge could give him an air of superiority that shut other people up. Sometimes, though, his eleven year old son would make a comment or ask a question that left him open-mouthed as a goldfish. Like now.

'For them, of course. Protesting is a waste of their time.'

'But if it's *their* time, and they want to do it, then what's wrong?' asked Jamie.

'Better for us, then,' said his father.

'Why?' asked Jamie.

'Because . . . well, frankly, they're just rather silly young people with no grasp on reality. Crying and moaning about what's inevitable does no good at all, and it takes up valuable police time.'

'Dad!' Kaz interrupted. 'You don't know what you're talking about! There were lots of old people on the march – easily as old as you – and much older. And nobody caused any trouble at all. The police looked just as happy as the marchers.'

Her father gave Kaz that look which says don't-try-to-pull-the-wool-over-my-eyes-because-I-am-much-older-and-wiser-than-you-therefore-whatever-you-say-I-won't-believe-still-less-take-seriously. It made her want to rev up and run all over the walls and ceilings of the house, smashing everything in her path, and then start throwing the tiles off the roof, not to mention bouncing up and down on top of his car . . . Instead she just said, 'I *was* there, father,' in as cool and contemptuous a voice as she could muster.

Jamie gave her the most subtle wink possible, took his glasses off, polished them on his sleeve, then asked in his most innocent, inquiring voice, 'So, just tell me, Dad, you said you didn't used to think this road was a good idea?'

'Well, no – when it was first proposed I thought it was the worst of two evils, really. OK, so the traffic is bad, but I didn't think ruining huge areas of Twybury and further on down was the right way to go about solving the problem.'

'Have you changed your mind?' asked Jamie.

'Not really – it's just that it's going to be built, and there's nothing to be done about it. That's the democratic process.'

'And is democracy everybody having a say?'

'Yes.'

'So those people Kaz saw in the town – they're having their say *and* what they're saying is what you used to say. Is that right?' He blinked inquiringly.

Kaz could not stop herself. She threw back her head and laughed – and her mother joined in. For a few seconds their father looked cross, and Kaz held her breath, dreading his anger falling on her smart little brother. Instead her father grinned suddenly, and reached out to ruffle Jamie's sandy fringe.

'OK old clever clogs, you've got me. Let me know when you're sending off your application for Mensa, and I'll just hide quietly.'

'What's Mensa?' asked Jamie.

'It's an organisation for geniuses, of course!' said his mother proudly.

'If you have to ask they won't let you join,' grinned Kaz.

'Of course I knew,' said Jamie.

That night her mother dropped her off at the Osborne Hall on the dot of seven thirty. Chris and Sally were already waiting. A long line of teenagers stretched past them, and Kaz felt that old sick feeling inside: the chilly hand clutching at her heart and then dropping down with a punch to her stomach. She always felt nervous; it was the boys, it was the loud music, it was the other girls, it was the darkness. And wanting to be pretty. Wanting to be liked. You always looked forward to the disco and it was never as you wanted it to be, but each week you dressed carefully and put on more than the usual amount of make-up, and went in the hope that this time it would be different.

There were always dreams, Kaz thought.

She was wearing a red miniskirt her mother had made her, and the new black top with the silver heart. Chris and Sally were both in black miniskirts and cropped tops – one orange, one bright pink. Kaz grinned and pointed. 'You clash,' she said.

'I saw Simon go in!' said Chris excitedly.

Kaz and Sally both made exaggerated faces and pretended to be sick.

'Ooooh, Chrissie! You can't still like *him*!' they chorused.

21

'Why not? He's nice!'

'He's nice looking, but so thick!' said Kaz. 'I think his head's a football under the skin and hair.'

'Who cares? He's a babe -- and I wouldn't want to *talk* to him!' grinned Chris.

'Oh gross!' groaned Sally. 'What are we going to do with her, Kaz?'

'Go in and have a laugh,' sighed Kaz, looking for a moment as though laughs were the farthest thing from her mind.

'What's wrong with you?' asked Sally.

'Nothing . . . Well, I went on that march this morning, and they took us to where the new road's going to be. It'll be really horrible.'

Chris and Sally looked at her, but Kaz could see they were not interested. Their silence was expressive as a shrug.

The girls were almost at the front of the queue now. They could hear the thud of music quite clearly. Kaz swallowed hard and tucked her arms through her friends' for courage – determined to forget, to have a good time.

But something inside her head added . . . *While you can.* A strange, unearthly, echoing voice, which rustled like leaves in the wind, lonely and eerie. Kaz shivered.

'Are you cold?' Sally asked.

She shook her head, furiously denying something she did not understand. Then at last they paid their money and walked into the dense, hot darkness of the disco, where the music would drive out thought – for a while.

Three

The Armstrong family finished Sunday lunch early. Kaz's mother had announced that Kaz needed to get in a proper afternoon's work, and a late lunch ruined the rest of the day. It was not that their parents were obsessed with Kaz and Jamie's schoolwork – or so they said. It was more that they had both worked very hard to get their qualifications, and insisted it was the only way to have choices.

Her parents were washing up, Jamie was drying, Kaz was putting the dishes away. There was still the delicious aroma of roast chicken in the air. Kaz made a pretence of taking a deep breath, then said casually, 'I feel like some fresh air. Does anybody fancy a walk?'

Jamie clutched his chest and staggered around, a little like somebody having a heart attack, then collapsed in a heap on the floor.

'Oh, very funny,' said Kaz.

Their mother smiled, and helped Jamie to his feet. 'Well, you can't pretend that physical exercise is your normal way of spending Sunday afternoon,' she said. 'In any case, love, haven't you got a pile of homework to do? I thought we'd agreed . . .'

'I've done it all – I'll show you,' said Kaz quickly. 'I got up early this morning, so it's all finished.'

It was true, but she knew her mother could not possibly guess why. The truth was, she had woken early, legs aching slightly from the dancing, but that was not what had woken her. She had a strange, leaden feeling in her chest, a miserable sense of something bad about to happen, which she did not understand. It had driven her from her bed to her desk to do her homework, because she knew in a flash that what she most wanted to do that afternoon was walk up Twybury Hill to the protest camp. The mockery of the boy with the green face had stung her. Yes of course she should *see*, she should *know*.

'I thought we could go up the hill, Jamie – just you and me,' she said. 'We haven't done it for ages. I could do with a walk – I'm so unfit.'

'You're sure you've done your work . . .?' Her mother looked dubious.

'Promise! Come on – I'll show you!'

'No – I trust you. If you say you've done it, that's good enough.'

Peter Armstrong was wiping his hands with a flourish, looking very pleased. 'Good! So we'll all go. It'll be a family outing – for a change.'

Oh no! thought Kaz.

Twenty minutes later they had crossed the A02 (almost empty on a Sunday), climbed two stiles, and were heading across the low meadows that rose gradually towards the hill. It was chilly. Spring was being as lazy as Kaz this year; thick grey clouds bunched on the horizon. Kaz's parents walked arm in arm, Jamie thrust his hands deep in his anorak pockets and strode ahead, examining the landscape all around him as he did so, like a bird on the lookout for food. Kaz walked quickly to catch her brother up.

'There's a kestrel nesting around here,' he said.

'I know. I saw it yesterday,' said Kaz.

'I'd love to be one,' said Jamie.

Kaz asked why. 'Well, you could see everything, and sort of be in charge of everything,' said her brother. 'Like, you could hang up there and see exactly where this new road's going to be.'

'The trouble is – you can't imagine it,' murmured Kaz. 'When we were all standing over there yesterday, somebody said that very spot would be a dual carriageway, with one of those things in the middle . . .'

'Central reservation,' said Jamie.

'Yeah, one of those, and I just couldn't visualise it at all. I mean, it'll sweep along there, and what . . . join the A02 further up . . .?'

Their parents had caught them up and overhead. 'Well, I could walk you through it; I did study all the documents at the time,' said their father. 'If we go to the top of the hill, I think I'll be able to point out the route.'

'I'm not sure I want to see,' said Kaz's mother gloomily. 'It'll be depressing.'

'No point in being depressed about something you can't change,' he replied crisply. 'We just have to learn to live with it. There'd never have been any progress if people couldn't do that. We'd be back in the Dark Ages.'

They walked on in silence, feeling the wind blow stronger on their faces as they began to climb, and the land change from meadow to rough grass. A silence seemed to surround you when you climbed Twybury that had nothing to do with actual noise, or the lack of it. It was an inner quietness; if you stopped and let your imagination leap you might just hear a badger breathe, the small dry cough of a fox, or the rabbit's high terror.

Kaz felt the silence now; it wrapped round her – but not in a comforting way. It made her uneasy. She did not know what she was supposed to do.

They came to a point at which the path split. The choice was between a steep, direct route to the summit, or the long and winding way up, along the bushy ramparts which surrounded the hill's flat top. In the past, before her laziness set in, Kaz used to prefer the first way; she was impatient and always wanted things to happen almost before they had begun. Today her energetic father did not even ask; he strode ahead, taking the smallest hummocks at a single step, heading straight for the top.

'I want to go the long way,' called Kaz.

'Come on, love! This'll do your little flabby muscles the world of good!'

'They're not flabby! No – I want to go this way. You come with me, Mum, and we'll meet them on the top,' smiled Kaz, knowing her mother would be glad.

Jamie and her father jeered, but climbed up without them. Kaz and her mother wandered peacefully along the side of the hill, where they were sheltered from the wind by the trees, the shrubs and the brow of the hill itself. Later Kaz was to think how strange it was that she should make that choice, as if the hill itself was telling her where to go. Had they gone straight up with the others they would never have stumbled across the Rainbow Camp.

The first sign was a flutter of colour ahead, in the bushes. Her mother saw it first and pointed. At the same time they heard the thin, clear sound of a pipe, the tantalising notes dancing up and down the scale in no familiar tune, but a wild sound, such as the great god Pan might have played, deep in some untamed wood.

'I wonder what that is,' said Kaz's mother.

Kaz's stomach gave a little jump: a mixture of curiosity, shyness and fear. She remembered the boy with the green face, and felt her face grow hot, despite the cool breeze.

'Come on, let's go back the other way,' she muttered.

But her mother was walking quickly ahead. 'Don't be so silly!' she called over her shoulder. 'I want to see what's going on.'

The scene that met their eyes as they came out through the straggly bushes, was extraordinary. The sheltered clearing in the lee of the hill was transformed into what looked at first glance like a refugee camp, and at second a gypsy fair. There was a circle of low tent-like structures, which appeared to be made from bent branches covered with tarpaulin. Some had little smoking chimneys sticking out from the side, reminding Kaz of pictures in storybooks, of underground homes for animals or elves, dark and warm and cosy. Here and there, between the tents, arches of twigs and branches fluttered with ribbons in all the colours of the rainbow.

There was a smell of woodsmoke and food. Skinny dogs chased

each other around the clearing, snapping in play fights. People sat round the huge campfire in the middle of the clearing, on an assortment of logs, old car seats and wooden pallets. Some were finishing a meal; others sat smoking and talking; a girl played a tin whistle; a tall, burly man in a fantastic tall hat decorated with feathers and bells, and wearing the oddest assortment of clothes Kaz had ever seen, danced dreamily on his own at the edge of the circle, his arms tracing balletic patterns in the air.

'Wow!' whispered Kaz.

'Quite a scene,' said her mother. 'Let's go over and be friendly.'

'No!' hissed Kaz, but she was already strolling over towards the camp and Kaz had no choice but to follow. For the first time in her life Kaz regretted her mother's easy friendliness. She was ashamed of herself for feeling shy . . . the truth was, it was more than embarrassment. These motley travelling people were *alien*, and she felt threatened by their presence on the hill.

The man in the fantastic hat stopped dancing and marched towards them. He held out a hand. 'Hello and welcome, beautiful people!'

Kaz was torn between wanting to run away and needing to giggle. The laughter won: it bubbled up from deep within her like a spring and would not be stopped. Close up, this man looked even more bizarre: he wore yellow and black tiger-print leggings tucked into orange socks and enormous black muddy boots. The leggings were held up by white braces over a purple T-shirt with a flower hand-painted on the front. This was topped by an old black tail-coat with satin lapels. When he swept off his towering hat in a theatrical bow, his shaven head looked pink and cold, and contrasted oddly with his thick stubble and moustache. A fringe of dreadlocks hung down from below the shaven bit, some of them decorated with beads and feathers.

He shook their hands, and Kaz was unable to hide her giggles. Grinning broadly, he announced, 'Laughter will save the world.'

'If only!' smiled Kaz's mother.

'They call me Colonel,' said the man. 'Welcome to the Rainbow Tribe.'

'Where are you all from?' she asked, looking around.

Their presence made little difference to the people round the campfire. One or two were smiling at them, but the rest went about their business. It surprised Kaz. Since she felt nervous of them she expected them to be nervous of strangers . . . even hostile . . . But the tin whistle's haunting tune had changed to a jig, and the atmosphere was peaceful and happy. Kaz began to relax.

Colonel waved an arm expansively, embracing hill, trees and sky. 'We come from everywhere,' he said.

'Why?' Kaz asked, surprising herself.

'Why are we from everywhere? Or why do we come here?'

'Both,' Kaz said.

The man replaced his hat thoughtfully. 'You asked two good questions in one, beautiful little person. We come from everywhere because we want to – people from every background making one family. And we've come here (he pointed to the ground emphatically) because needed. Wherever they start to attack the earth, that's where we go, to stop them.'

'As simple as that?' asked Kaz's mother. She sounded curious, but cynical too, and Kaz was afraid Colonel would take offence.

'It's never simple, but we have to believe,' he said.

'So you're going to stop them building the road?' asked Kaz.

'Of course,' he said, as if there was no doubt at all.

Kaz's mother shook her head. 'I wish you were right – but honestly, there was a public inquiry three years ago, we all wrote our letters, and did all we could. We know the government needs to build up a serious road network, and this'll be a through route to the south coast. Businessmen want it, and the people in Seaston think it'll get rid of the traffic through their village – so, what's to be done? You have to be realistic.'

He smiled gently, as if nothing in the world could ever cause him offence. 'Do we? A famous poet once said, "In dreams begin responsibilities." '

Kaz knew there was nothing her mother could say to that. She looked puzzled and uncomfortable suddenly, as if she wanted to go. But Kaz wanted to stay. She wanted to sit by the fire and listen to the tin whistle and be accepted. 'What will you do?' she asked.

'We've already started! Haven't you been down to Greenway Lane? They've already started taking out the hedges and they've knocked down two houses. We stopped the work for five hours on Friday, and we'll do the same tomorrow. Go down there and see. That's where the office is. And another small camp.'

'Greenway Lane is so pretty,' said Kaz's mother.

'Won't be pretty for long,' snapped Colonel, with a sudden change of mood. The man thought them blind and stupid for not seeing, not knowing – Kaz could see that. Perhaps he was right. Greenway Lane was a ten minute walk from their house, yet they had not even bothered to go along and survey the beginning of the destruction.

The tin whistle stopped. More people were staring at them now, and Kaz felt uncomfortable. She shivered in the chilly breeze, wondering what it would be like when the cold night wind was howling around the camp.

'We'll go and look, won't we, Mum?' she said.

'Good!' said Colonel briskly. 'Then, when you've seen what they're doing, you can help us. We need food, money, rope, matches, baccy, cigarette papers, torches, coffee and more money. And if you don't want to give us any of that, we need bodies to stop the diggers.'

Kaz was horrified by the man begging, and even more uncomfortable when her mother thrust a hand into her jacket pocket and brought out a pound coin and a fifty-pence piece. 'That's all I've got on me,' she said. He took it with a nod.

'All helps,' he said.

Just then someone emerged from the bushes on the other side of the camp, carrying a pile of firewood. The face was still smeared green; Kaz recognised the thin figure as the boy who had been so hostile to her on the march. Instinctively she moved, so that Colonel effectively concealed her from sight. She could not bear him to see her, in case he should berate them for coming to gawp at the camp like sightseers, then being charitable enough to contribute a couple of coins in conscience money.

Voices drifted from the top of Twybury Hill. She could see kites, but the angles of the land made their owners invisible, so it was as if the hill itself had sprouted a headdress of waving black wires topped by multi-coloured flowers. Then two figures stood on the skyline, looking down at them. The smaller one waved.

'It's Dad and Jamie,' said Kaz. 'We'd better go.'

'Nice to meet you,' said her mother awkwardly.

'Come back any time – come for a coffee,' said Colonel politely.

They nodded, then turned to ascend the ramparts of the hill fort. The tin whistle started to play again, joined by a guitar this time, in a lively folk rhythm. A girl started to sing in a high, sweet voice, but the words were indistinct, carried away by the breeze. Kaz longed to look back, but kept her face turned resolutely ahead to where her father and brother waited. She did not want to see those mocking eyes in the green face – but was sure they were watching.

Four

At breakfast the following Thursday Kaz told her mother, very casually, that instead of being collected by car she would take the bus home from school.

'I've been suggesting you do that since your birthday and you always said the walk from the bus stop was too far, Lazylegs!'

'Well, you're always complaining you have to drop your work early and dash round to get Jamie and then me in all the traffic so . . . I thought I'd give it a try. Looks like a nice day for a walk, anyway!' Kaz explained.

'That's fine, love – thanks!' said her mother with a smile.

Sue Armstrong designed birthday cards at home for a local manufacturer. She also managed to look after the house, garden and her family in an efficient way Kaz noticed and appreciated more and more as she grew older.

But the truth was, Kaz was not thinking of her mother's convenience at all. For three days she had been plagued by thoughts of the protest march, the hill camp, and the whole road project. She felt as if somebody had pulled out a brick at the bottom of her life, so that it was cracking dangerously. The nearest bus stop to their house was almost opposite the end of Greenway Lane, due south of Twybury Hill, where Colonel had said the work had already begun. Kaz knew this was sneaky, but the need to go and see for herself was like an itch that would not go away.

Lessons seemed to pass more slowly than ever. Kaz found herself wondering if she would ever get to love school again. These days she was restless, gazing from the window, dreaming of the larger world outside where people *did* things . . .

Greenway Lane was green and narrow, and led to the cluster of small houses and cottages that formed Greenway itself – not really a village proper now, just another edge of Solchester. Once this area had been famous for its market gardens. It was still a quiet backwater whose tall hedges protected it from the hum of traffic on the A02, and from which people could easily make the climb across meadows and up Twybury Hill. It was a popular place for dog walking, and children could ride their bicycles in Greenway Lane without danger. Kaz could not remember the last time she had been there, but thought how peaceful and pretty it was.

Suddenly the lane widened, and the atmosphere changed. On the right was a broad open area of green; on the left a half-demolished house, a huge digger, and a scene of chaos. There were the beginnings of long, brown scars in the earth where hedges and trees had been grubbed out. Piles of stones and brushwood in the background, some of them smoking, gave the air of a war zone. A little way from the demolition site was a house, which still looked inhabited, with a caravan parked in its garden. This was festooned with signs saying, SAVE TWYBURY, and TWYBURY ACTION GROUP. The caravan was surrounded by three or four tents, and the whole area was sectioned off with rope. About twenty-five people milled around in front, facing a line of men in yellow jackets and white hats. With a threatening grumble the digger moved forward a metre or so, then swung its enormous claw arm down into a patch of bushes and grass with a sickening crunch. As it did so the people tried to run forward, only to be pushed back roughly by the line of security guards. There were yells and screams.

Kaz drew in her breath as a lone figure broke through the cordon and raced for the digger. It was Maria – the red-headed speaker at the march on Saturday. She was almost on it when two guards brought her crashing to the ground, then dragged her by her feet back to the line. Her body was limp and bumped like a sack of potatoes. This angered the protesters even more, and two men made a break for it. They were faster, and outran the guards. As soon as they reached the digger it stopped and they clambered up over the caterpillar treads. A guard gave chase and caught the boot of one of the men, clinging on as though his job depended on it. There was a struggle, and more guards reached the digger. They finally pulled the man to the ground and piled on to him in a scrum. But the first of the two men, young and thin as he was, had made it to the digger arm and was shinning up like a monkey, his long dark hair swinging as he did so.

Instinctively Kaz cheered as a deafening chorus of shouts and whistles and strange high-pitched yelps erupted from the watchers.

She ran forward until she was on the edge of the crowd. She thought she recognised some faces from the Saturday march. There was the same mixture of ages, but the main groups seemed to be women in their thirties and forties and people from the hill camp. She squinted up at the digger arm on which the lone, dark-haired figure perched. He reminded her of the green-faced youth she had talked to, but this face was unpainted, so it was hard to tell. In any case, he was too high up. Kaz shuddered and closed her eyes; she hated heights.

Kaz was surprised none of the guards went up to bring the climber down, but it was probably too dangerous. The protesters stopped shouting and an odd calm descended. Some of the people were chatting to the guards. Maria walked slowly back to the caravan and went inside. A few women began to chant, '*The earth is our mother and we will take care of her*,' in a hypnotic, lilting tune, over and over again.

Kaz walked round the rear of the crowd and approached the office. Nobody took any notice of her. She was relieved she would not have to prove her right to be there, but also had a slight feeling of loneliness – since they were as one, and she did not belong. How she wanted to be a part of the experience – the belief – they shared. She envied it.

As she drew near to the caravan she saw, tacked on a large board, a map of the area, with the route of the proposed road clearly marked out in red. Beneath it was a skilful artist's impression of what it would look like. Kaz could pick out her own home, the top of the hill, the existing single carriageway A02 – and the route of new bypass. Involuntarily, she let out her breath, as though someone had punched her in the stomach.

'Awful, ain't it?'

Kaz looked up. Maria lounged in the doorway of the caravan.

'I didn't know it was going to be that size,' she said shyly.

'Where do you live?'

'Swinford Road.'

'Oh, just over there . . . Well?'

Kaz could see the girl was wondering why it was she had not done more homework. She felt guilty.

'Where do *you* live?' she asked, to change the subject.

Maria pointed at the half-demolished house, lying like a creature on the roadside, its guts exposed cruelly to the air. Strips of wallpaper fluttered in the breeze; splintered windows hung at the crazy angles of fractured bone.

'That's my house,' she said. 'The Department of Transport bought it – there's no choice, y'know – and now they're knocking it down. Only, yesterday Colonel and a couple of others spent the day on the roof, so they couldn't finish the job.'

'*That's* your house?' asked Kaz.

'Well, it was. Mum's renting something the other side of town. I live here now, and run the office.' She jerked a thumb over her shoulder at the interior of the tiny caravan. 'I'm Maria Donnell, by the way.'

'Kaz Armstrong.'

'Are you going to join us, Kaz?'

'I . . . I . . . don't know what to do.'

'*Do*? There's a million things to do. We need bodies for actions, and people to collect money and stationery for the office . . . When we set up the next camp in Twybury Wood there'll be tree-houses to build, and a base camp to set up, and we'll need rope and night supplies, especially buckets, and that's when the real food stockpile will be needed. There's some local people going to bring veggies – maybe your parents could too. All helps. Oh, and there'll be rotas for manning the office . . .'

Maria Donnell had the fervent look of someone who has seen the light and cannot understand why everyone else doesn't up sticks and follow the true path. It was attractive – yet daunting, too. Kaz felt as if she was backed against a wall in a harsh spotlight, with a stern voice booming, '*What did you do*?'

'I could help in the office . . . on Saturdays,' she said hesitantly.

Maria grinned broadly. 'Sorted!' She went inside, clearly expecting Kaz to follow.

Organised chaos reigned inside the caravan. Maria's sleeping-bag and some clothes were bundled in a corner, and every available bit of space was taken up with papers, leaflets, maps, books of cuttings, and legal documents. A copy of the local paper lay open on the table; Maria had clearly just been cutting something out when disturbed.

'I could do that,' said Kaz pointing to the paper.

'Sorted!' said Maria again. She immediately picked up the tele-phone and was soon involved in a complicated conversation with a lawyer. Kaz heard the word 'injunctions'. Maria pointed at the news-paper, as if telling her to get on with something.

She sat at the table, picked up the scissors, and surveyed the *Solchester Echo*. It was open at the letters page. Kaz read quickly. There were three letters, two in support of the protest and one against:

Why don't the smelly, long-haired hippies who have come to our area UNINVITED to waste tax-payers' money realise that they are far more of a pollution than the proposed road? Who asked them for their opinion on whether this much-needed road should be built to relieve the traffic problems of Seaston? They represent the lazy minority of stupid, scruffy, sentimentalist weirdos and are a disgrace to this country. The majority of us know that bigger and better roads mean progress, and progress brings jobs and prosperity. Ah, but the hippies don't want jobs, do they? No – they want to live off the rest of us whilst drivelling on about trees and badgers, and wasting police time. The sooner Rowley Construction takes the gloves off and kicks them out, the better for Solchester.

> *Yours sincerely,*
> *Harold Keridge,*
> *Seaston Road.*

'That's really horrible!' said Kaz.

Maria put down the phone and looked at her grimly. 'Oh, that's nothing, there's been far worse ones! And at night cars pull up here and we get abuse shouted at us. In the King's Arms they won't serve people who're obviously from the hill camp.'

'That's like racial prejudice!' blurted Kaz.

'Tell me about it,' said Maria.

Just then there was a burst of cheering from outside. Both girls ran out to investigate. The cab of the digger was empty, the little army of security guards was in retreat, and a man in a green hard hat was yelling something at the lone protester still perched high on the digger arm. Maria gave vent to an ear-splitting screech of triumph.

'He's telling Ash they're stopping for the day now,' she said, glancing at her watch. 'No point in them carrying on really. They need him to come down so the digger can get back to the main compound.'

Sure enough, the skinny figure started to edge down until he was helped by a forest of willing arms. He disappeared into the crowd, which began to swarm all over the machine.

'Come on!' Maria yelled.

Kaz did not hesitate. The feeling of elation was extraordinary. Close on Maria's heels, she jogged into the crowd, which parted to let them through. Then Maria was climbing up over the enormous caterpillar treads, and holding out a hand to Kaz; someone gave her a push from behind and she was up.

'*The earth is our mother and we will take care of her . . .*'

The chant was taken up, and Kaz joined in, relishing this new feeling of belonging, of sharing a tiny victory. As she sang she felt an arm snake round her shoulders in the briefest of hugs, and heard a voice say, 'Welcome!'

She looked round quickly. The boy who had climbed up the digger arm was right behind her, still with people patting and hugging him in congratulation. But he was smiling at Kaz. Without the green face paint he looked younger, and far less threatening. His thin face was tanned, the eyes as sharp as she remembered, but not mocking now.

Kaz did not know what to say. She wanted to justify her presence there, but there was clearly no need. She'd come along, she was sympathetic, she belonged – it was as easy as that. The boy winked at her, then glanced down at her heavy, laced shoes.

'Bit more sorted!' he said. 'You going to come up the hill for the party?'

'No, I've got to get home,' Kaz said shyly.

'Tomorrow then . . . come and join in the action.'

'Some of us have to go to school,' she retorted, thinking that he could have glanced at her dark skirt and sweatshirt and guessed it was regulation.

'I'm Ash,' he said, holding out his hand with a slightly theatrical flourish.

'Kaz,' she said briefly.

To her embarrassment the boy did not let go of her hand. 'Well, Miss schoolgirl, why don't you come up on Saturday afternoon? We've got some DA training.'

'What's that?'

'Come and see!' he yelled, just as a huge man with dreadlocks threw an arm round his neck, pulling him close in a rough embrace. Ash laughed aloud. People were yipping triumph all around them. Kaz started to giggle helplessly as Ash dragged her into the communal hug.

And it was at that moment that the photographer from the *Solchester Echo*, unnoticed by anyone, took his picture of the victorious protesters.

Five

Double English on Friday morning was Kaz's favourite. Mrs Robinson, who taught English, was also her form teacher, and Kaz thought that if she had to live with anyone in the world other than her parents, Mrs Robinson would be first choice. She was a perfectly ordinary-looking woman in her forties, who wore rather boring skirts and polo necks, and always the same plain gold hoops, but when she taught her whole face lit up. Her love of books and words transformed her into an enchantress who could make them do anything she wanted. Few of the girls bothered to play up in Mrs Robinson's lessons. Make a witty remark and she would cap it, but with cleverness not cruelty. She turned a blind eye to illegal things like nail polish, and was the only member of staff who respected Kaz's wish to leave the name Kathleen behind with her childhood.

However in English today Kaz fidgeted in her chair and glanced at the window, longing to escape even from this her favourite lesson.

It was all the fault of The Road (the phrase had already written itself up with capital letters within Kaz's consciousness). When she had arrived home the previous afternoon she had been forced to tell a lie.

'I was starting to get worried,' her mother said.

'Oh, I popped into the library to take a book back, and just got . . . sort of . . . looking around. You know how it is,' mumbled Kaz.

Kaz had felt guilty, of course – and was tempted, for a second, to tell her mother where she had been. But something stopped her. It was not so much the feeling that her mother would be unsympathetic; it was more that she wanted to guard her secret for herself.

That night she had been haunted by a dream more vivid than any she had known. She was being chased across a dark field by a gang of men in yellow coats and white helmets, who yelled obscene words at her. Heart thumping, breath tearing jaggedly from her lungs, she found the strength to run faster, even though the land became rocky and steep, and the wind howled from the top of the hill. The shouts behind her grew closer; it was as if the hot breath of animals scorched her heels. She had never known such terror . . . Just then the sky flashed and a thunderous voice cried, 'WELCOME!' Kaz looked around in panic, but there was no one there, only a massive oak tree, which tossed its gnarled branches in the air, as if to warn her pursuers to go back. They did indeed fall away, whimpering with terror, until she was left alone with the sound of the wind and the rustle of branches and bushes all around. And then there was a cracking noise, the bark of the tree splitting from top to bottom, as a strange being stepped out, walking stiffly. She caught a glimpse of a green face, thick tendrils curling around its head, leaves pouring from the sides of the terrible red mouth, and the twig-hands stretching towards her . . .

'Aaah!' she screamed, sitting up in bed and feeling sweat trickle down her sides.

Now, remembering that dream in school, Kaz shivered. The whispers of the girls as they looked at the sheets Mrs Robinson had given out, the distant sound of a games whistle, and the tinkle of the piano from the school hall . . . all faded, so that Kaz felt she was both there and not there. She wondered what they were doing at the camp, or in the office . . .

Mrs Robinson's voice broke into her reverie. 'Well, Kaz Armstrong, I can only assume you were reading an improving book so late into the night your eyes got tired.'

'What?' said Kaz.

'You haven't even looked at it!' the teacher said.

'Oh . . . yes, sorry,' muttered Kaz as she turned over the photocopied sheet on her desk.

'Right, now I know you're *all* with me I want you to read this through to yourselves, and then I'll read it aloud.'

Kaz read slowly, taking a deep breath as she did so, because each word incised itself on her brain.

First they came for the Jews
but I did not speak out –
because I was not a Jew.
Then they came for the communists

but I did not speak out –

because I was not a communist.

Then they came for the trades unionists

but I did not speak out,

because I was not a trades unionist.

Then they came for me –

and there was no one left

to speak out for me.

After a couple of minutes Mrs Robinson read the piece aloud in her lovely deep voice. 'Now, there's lots to discuss there. The poem was written by a priest, Pastor Niemoeller, and he was a victim of the Nazis. But what I want to ask you is this: *is* it a poem or just a series of statements? I called it a poem, but is that right, do you think?'

Some of the girls shook their heads.

'It doesn't rhyme,' said Chris.

'Yes, but I think we've learnt that poems don't have to rhyme, haven't we? And in any case, not all things that rhyme are poems! Think of those verses inside birthday cards – verses, or doggerel, they are, but not poems. So – who thinks this is a poem?'

Kaz shot up a hand, followed by about three-quarters of the class.

'Why is it a poem, Kaz?'

'Because . . . Oh, I don't know really. You can't say why, you just know that it is.'

'You have to try and say why,' Mrs Robinson coaxed.

45

'Well, it's . . . saying something really special, and saying it in a very short way, and I always think of poems like that.'

'Good! I think you said that well. Poems are *economical* with language – even long poems. But tell me what you mean by something special.'

'It's about prejudice, isn't it?' said Kaz.

'Sticking up for people,' said a voice behind her.

'Not being a coward,' someone else joined in.

'It's saying you have to treat other people's problems as your own,' said Kaz.

'Stand up and be counted,' somebody called out.

'It's saying, we're all – like – victims, and so we have to speak up for each other, even if we're scared,' said Kaz.

Mrs Robinson was nodding approval. 'Yes, it's saying all those things, and yet when you said them like that, you weren't saying a poem, were you? So what makes it a poem? What do you notice about the *way* it's written?'

'It sort of repeats itself,' said Kaz.

'What do you mean?'

'Well, the way it's written it gives the same situation over and over again, and you just imagine this weedy, cowardly little man watching as they took people away, and not daring to speak up . . .'

'Could be a woman, Kaz!' smiled Mrs Robinson.

'You said it was written by a priest!'

'Yes, but he's not actually writing about himself, is he? He was a brave man who certainly did stand up for his beliefs. No – he's writing about what we call a universal situation – and that is another thing which makes it a poem, I think. It's about the kind of oppression that's happened all over the world, isn't it?'

'Still happening now,' called out Kaz.

'Yes, you're right. Now, girls, I want you to write me something along these lines . . .'

She was interrupted by a chorus of groans, but held up a warning hand to quell them. 'Don't moan at me. It's a waste of energy. I want you to write something for me which expresses something you really feel strongly about, long or short, poem or story, I don't mind. It could be about something that's happened to you, or about something happening somewhere in the world, like Bosnia. All I want is for it to be *serious*, and for you to try to use repetition to make a point, like Pastor Niemoeller does here, if you can. But don't worry if it comes out very differently. Just *care* about it. All right?'

There was a muffled no from one or two desks.

Kaz felt gloomy; she liked writing but there was always such a gulf between the leaping words in your heart and the pathetic little things that limped their way on to the page. How could you write anything as good as that priest's poem? It was impossible. For that matter, how could you put what he said into practise in your own life? It was all very well to talk about standing up for your beliefs, but when you are fourteen you care too much what people around you think. You want to be popular, not brave.

The girls clattered out of the classroom. Deep in thought, Kaz did not feel like talking at all.

'Shall we meet by the bus station at eleven tomorrow?' asked Chris.

'Mum says I've got to tidy my room in the morning – so why don't we make it two instead?' suggested Sally.

'Fine by me – my mum's been nagging too. Is that OK, Kaz?' asked Chris.

Kaz hesitated. Ash had invited her to the camp on Saturday afternoon, and she realised now that she wanted to go more than anything. If you did nothing to fight something you believed to be wrong, were you not being as cowardly as those the priest had written about?

'Er . . . Oh, I won't be able to. My mum said I've got to stay in with Jamie while they go shopping,' she lied.

'Boring!' grinned Sally. 'I want to buy my jeans. I've still got some birthday money left.'

'I'll help you choose them,' said Chris.

'Can't wait for Saturday night, can you, Kaz?' said Sally. 'I really like Simon, and he said his mate fancies you.'

'Which one?' Kaz asked, trying to sound like her normal self.

'The one with the fair hair. He wore baggy jeans last week. One earring – you know – posse kid!'

'Yuk, I don't think so, somehow,' said Kaz shortly.

She took the bus again and ran along Greenway Lane. When she reached the camp the place was almost deserted, but there were shouts coming from beyond a clump of trees and she saw security guards in the distance. What was going on? She knew she dare not go and see.

Instead she ran to the caravan, hoping Maria was inside. Panting, she paused at the open door, suddenly shy because a stranger lounged by the table. He was about eighteen, she guessed, with a round face stippled by reddish stubble, and with a blue bandana round fair dreadlocks. His eyes were small and grey, and instinctively she mistrusted the way they looked at her. There was no warmth in his gaze.

'Can ah help you now?' he asked in a thick Scottish accent.

'I . . . I was looking for Maria,' Kaz said.

'She's on the action,' he said laconically, jerking his head in the direction of the distant sounds, 'so ah'm in charge.'

He blew out smoke with a self-important air Kaz disliked. She was about to leave when he jumped up, skirted the table and squatted down on the caravan step, a few centimetres from her. She started back.

'What's your name?'

'Kaz.'

'I'm Dougie.' She had no choice but to shake his hand. 'What d'ye want Maria for?'

'I was told – I wanted to know – someone said there was some sort of training tomorrow . . .'

He burst out laughing, and Kaz felt her face grow red. 'Och, so you're going to turn yourself into an eco-warrior, are you?'

His silly, high-pitched giggle irritated Kaz. She was sorry she had come.

'All I want to know is the time and the place,' she said coldly.

'Och, I'll take you,' he grinned.

'I don't need to be taken anywhere, thank you,' said Kaz.

He shrugged. 'Suit yourself. It's at two tomorrow, up at the hill camp. And ah'll be there!'

'So what? That's enough to put anybody off,' Kaz retorted and turned on her heel. As she hurried home she wondered why someone as unpleasant as that was allowed to join the protest. He did not seem to fit in.

When she got home her mother was in the kitchen and Jamie was watching television. Relieved, Kaz collapsed on the sofa and lost her mind in the programme.

She did not look up when her father came in the room, but both Armstrong children jumped in surprise when he strode across the room and snapped off the television set.

'What are you doing?' Jamie protested.

'I want to know what *you* are doing, young lady,' said her father, glaring at Kaz.

'I'm watching TV. It's Friday night, and I need to relax, and I can do all my homework tomorrow morning,' said Kaz, amazed at his expression. 'Don't get stressed out, Dad, everything's OK.'

'No, it is *not* OK!' he shouted, slapping the top of the television set with his newspaper.

'What's Kaz done, Dad?' Jamie asked.

Their father held up the front page. Jamie got up for a closer look, but Kaz saw in an instant what had sparked her father's rage. The blood rushed to her face.

'Well, Kathleen? What have you got to say?'

'I . . . I . . . don't know,' she mumbled.

'What do you mean, you don't know? I want to know what my daughter is doing on the front page of the *Solchester Echo* with her arms round a bunch of hooligans!'

'She hasn't got her arms round them, Dad,' said Jamie.

'They're not hooligans,' said Kaz.

Their mother came into the room. She had her arms folded as if she were angry, but her eyes were upset and worried.

'Kaz, have you been playing truant?' she asked.

'*No*! Of course not! I just went along after school. To see,' she finished lamely.

'So you told me a fib. You said you were late because you'd gone to the library,' said her mother very quietly.

'Oh, that was only because I . . . I didn't know what you'd say.'

'I should think you didn't!' shouted Kaz's father. 'I should think you had enough sense to know we wouldn't want you hanging around with a bunch of useless thugs. Like this!'

He jabbed his finger at the large photograph, which showed Kaz in the middle of a scrum of smiling protesters. Two people were embracing her – one a tall, older man with a mass of dreadlocks, and the other a slight teenager with dark hair caught back in a ponytail. The headline screamed, *Protesters laugh as taxpayers pay.*

The finger jabbed again. 'Well?'

'Well what?'

'I'm waiting for your explanation. How long have you been involved with that bunch?'

'I'm not involved, Dad! I mean . . .' Kaz stopped and took a deep

51

breath. 'Look, I only went along to see where they had started the work. I mean, we live here, don't we? Shouldn't we show an interest? You're always moaning at me and saying I'm getting too keen on boys and clothes and discos. Don't you want me to show an interest in the environment?'

'Of course we do, darling,' said her mother. 'And it's good to belong to things, and sign petitions, and all that. But not to join in with *that kind* of protest! It's breaking the law, for one thing. And dangerous.'

'I didn't join in; I just went along to see, and they stopped the work because the boy in the picture climbed up the digger arm, and I was talking to this girl called Maria – she used to go to our school apparently *and* she was a real star! – and then she ran over to the digger, and everybody was really pleased, and I climbed up after her. Everybody was singing and acting crazily, and that's all that happened. There was nothing wrong with it, can't you understand? It was like a party!'

All that came out in a blurt, and when Kaz had finished she was panting. She could see that her parents were surprised at her vehemence; they had never seen her like this before.

'I don't want you going there again,' snapped her father.

Kaz flopped down on the sofa, suddenly exhausted. 'I don't know why, Dad. If you all came with me down Greenway Lane you could look at the map of the route, and meet some people, and you'd end up knowing a lot more about it. Wouldn't that be good?'

'Have they got a map up? I'd quite like to see that,' said her mother.

'I told you all – nothing can be done! We looked at maps years ago, and marked the route we thought they should choose, and now the damn thing is happening. And that's all there is to it!' Kaz's father slapped the arm of the chair.

'Is it?' asked Kaz sulkily.

'Yes! And I forbid you to go anywhere near those people again. Do you hear me?'

Kaz said nothing.

'Kathleen – do you hear me?'

'Peter, don't shout,' said Kaz's mother, in that worried, soothing voice Kaz knew well. All Kaz wanted to do was bury her face in her mother's breast and cry: I don't know what I think. I want to be involved with the protesters. I hate seeing the trees bulldozed. I wish the world was an easy place . . .

Instead she stared at her father coldly.

'You'd have to be deaf not to hear you. Maybe I need a hearing aid.'

Six

Saturday morning in the Armstrong household was a flurry of activity. A general tidy-up was the rule; sometimes Kaz wondered what would happen if you didn't bother, but when she tried that with her own room she soon hated the chaos even more than she hated her parents' irritation.

On this particular Saturday, Kaz's parents woke to the sound of the vacuum cleaner, and looked at each other in astonishment. They pulled on their dressing-gowns, crossed the landing and stood at the door of Kaz's bedroom. Then they stared at each other in shock. Kaz was on her knees, cleaning under the bed with the long, snake-like attachment. All the bits and pieces that normally littered her floor had been put on the bed, ready for sorting through. The dressing-table was already a newly dust-free zone, with little bottles and ornaments in military rows.

'Good God!' said Kaz's father quietly.

'Sweetie . . . what's got into you?' her mother called over the sound of the cleaner.

Kaz unfolded herself to show a face shiny with exertion and virtue. She switched off the vacuum cleaner.

'Oh, hello!' she said as casually as she could. 'I thought I'd make an early start.'

'But it's . . . seven forty-five!' said her father, staring at his watch in disbelief.

'I'm sorry I woke you,' said Kaz.

'Oh, we were already awake, we . . .' her mother began. 'Hang on – I'm not having *you* trying to make *us* feel guilty for having a tiny lie-in on Saturday!'

'I'm not! I just couldn't sleep, so I thought I'd make a start. I'll get this done and get my homework out of the way, then I can spend this afternoon in town with Chris and Sally.'

'Good girl,' said her father, as he stifled a yawn, and turned back to bed.

Her mother stood for a few seconds looking at Kaz in a way Kaz could not quite fathom. The look made her uncomfortable. Sometimes she felt that her mother could see right through to her soul. At last she simply asked if Kaz would like a boiled egg for breakfast and turned away. But there were unspoken things between them.

Just before lunch Kaz changed from her blue jeans to an old black skirt, then to black jeans, then back again to the blue jeans. Footwear was a problem, but luckily she had only recently abandoned a pair of hardly worn DMs because her taste mirrored her friends', and they suddenly wanted to wear clumpy high heels.

'I thought you told me you'd grown out of those!' her mother said.

55

'Oh, only a bit. They're coming back in . . .' Kaz mumbled.

'Where'd they go out to?' asked Jamie.

'All her footwear makes her look like Olive Oyl, with little thin stick legs,' laughed her father.

'Thanks, Dad! That makes me feel really good about myself!'

'So what are you doing this afternoon?' asked her mother, as they all sat down to jacket potatoes, beans, bread and cheese.

'Meeting the girls, I told you,' said Kaz, with her mouth full.

'So you did! Well, I can give you a lift into town. I want to pick up that curtain material I ordered.'

'I was going to take the bus,' said Kaz, praying she would not blush.

'No need! I'm going anyway.'

'I wanted to go soon. I said I'd meet them at two,' said Kaz.

'That's fine. It won't take a minute to clear up. We'll leave at ten to two.'

'But . . .' Kaz began.

'Honestly, love, it's fine.'

Kaz's heart was thumping so loudly she felt they must surely all hear. She had planned to leave at one thirty, to leave plenty of time to walk up the hill and be there before the start of the meeting Ash had mentioned. What now? What if her mother, walking around the centre of Solchester, bumped into Chris and Sally?

Her mother dropped Kaz in the centre of Solchester at two. Kaz doubled back, half-walking, half-running, to the bus stop. Each second she thought she would bump into Chris and Sally, or someone else from school. Or else her mother would forget her cheque book, be forced to drive back home, and would see Kaz getting off the bus at the start of Greenway Lane – so she would be caught out in *that* fib.

The bus seemed to take for ever to arrive. Kaz looked over her shoulder. It was so unfair. She was made to feel like a criminal, when all she wanted to do was what she had planned. What made it worse was that all the time a stupid little voice inside her was whispering, *They weren't fibs, they were lies and this is what you get for telling lies!* Kaz wished it would shut up and mind its own business.

It was half past two by the time she stood near Greenway Lane, gazing up at Twybury Hill. She made her way along to the Office Camp. It was deserted apart from a woman in her fifties, with streaky grey hair in a bun, who was pinning fresh information on the notice-board outside the caravan, and a few local people who were gazing in undisguised dismay at the beginning of the clearing work.

Kaz returned the woman's friendly wave, and hurried on, cutting up behind the caravan, where she knew there was a footpath to the top of Twybury Hill. Soon she was crossing the ancient brockway and following the track beneath an old hedgerow, starred here and there with early spring flowers, pink and yellow and blue. There was a curious sharp scent in the air she could not identify, and unfamiliar birds carolled wildly in trees she could not name.

It was so strange, Kaz thought: you lived in this world, you were a part of it, you walked around on the surface under the lid of sky with the terrifying, endless universe of space beyond – and yet you went through your life in a state of ignorance about all the creatures and the growing things which shared with you the precious oxygen. Oh, you learnt some things in biology, of course: how the digestive system works and why leaves are green and how seeds are carried, and that was all interesting. But what did it *mean*? Why was it men could build bombs, and concrete the land to build highways and superstores, and yet if there was an earthquake those men might feel the same fear as the smallest creature trembling beneath a tangled hedge?

Kaz slowed her pace a little, looking around her in a way that was new. For reasons she did not understand she suddenly felt close to tears.

The well-worn footpath approached Twybury Wood. Kaz skirted the trees as the path curved round, and suddenly stopped dead in her tracks. This landscape was familiar, and yet she could not remember ever approaching it from this direction. Ahead of her a gnarled oak tree stood as if barring the path, its branches twisted into fantastic shapes by centuries of wind. There were strange growths on its trunk, like petrified fungus, and you did not have to stare for long to imagine a face in those cracks and fissures of bark.

Somehow Kaz *knew* this tree. She was convinced that if she were to pass it, no matter how quickly, it would stealthily uproot itself with a silent shower of soil, and pursue her to the end of time. Kaz stared at the tree, and the tree stared back at her. She knew it did: each leaf an eye watching . . .

WELCOME!

Kaz shook herself. She listened to the birds and the slight rustle of breeze in the leaves of the ancient oak, but that was not what she was hearing. Inside her heart, her mind, in the current of her blood, the voice boomed again, WELCOME. Just as it had . . .

With a gasp she remembered her dream exactly – that it was not the tree itself which chased her but a leaf-crowned creature, which lived inside the tree, and which was looking at her now from its protection of bark.

'Who are you?' she whispered.

The world seemed to have stopped breathing. Even the noise of the birds had ceased, and the leaves of the oak were still. Kaz listened, not knowing what she expected, but suddenly aware that she did not feel scared any more.

'I . . . I think . . . I know you,' she said softly, stretching out a hand to touch the gnarled trunk.

She held her breath and closed her eyes. It was as if the whole universe was compressed into the small patch of rough bark trembling beneath her fingers. She opened her eyes, and was sure, her face very close to the bark, that another face was gazing out at her, wearing an expression of infinite sorrow.

Then a sound of voices broke the spell, and she raced on, leaving the oak behind her.

There was a flat area beyond the Rainbow Camp, just before the huge earthworks rose up, which was crowded with people. They sat quietly, whilst a small woman with long black hair stood in front of them, talking and gesticulating just like a teacher. As Kaz drew nearer she noticed that most of the ones sitting down were panting slightly, as if they had just been running around.

It was impossible to approach the group without being seen. Kaz felt exposed and self-conscious.

'That was good,' the woman was saying. 'What you have to remember is that security won't be as fluffy as you've just been . . .'

She broke off as Kaz made a little slinking run to squat down on the edge of the group, and waved a greeting at her.

'Hi . . . and welcome!' she said. 'I'm glad you could come. I'm Skye, and I'm just running through some basic principles of non-violent direct action.'

Kaz knew her face was red. She attempted a smile, and ducked her head down, thinking how pleasant it was always to be welcomed. For a few minutes she did not hear anything of what the young woman was saying. The scene itself was too interesting: the curious mix of people, some young with matted hair and rings in their noses, some obviously students, some older in waxy coats and with uneasy, self-conscious expressions – as if to say, I never thought I would see the day when I would be doing this!

Then, the leader herself looked like no teacher Kaz had ever seen. She was about twenty-three, small with a tanned, pretty face, and dressed in a ragbag assortment of garments: grey and blue striped leggings, a multicoloured patchwork coat, and a scarlet Arab scarf. The huge battered boots looked far too big for her, and their broken laces trailed. Her long, dark hair was caught here and there into tight rainbow hairwraps, some ending in tiny bells. She looked like a gypsy.

'All right,' she said. 'The important thing to remember is to keep it fluffy at all times. We're not about violence – this is non-violent direct action, and if you let yourself get tricked into being angry, and doing something that's even a little bit violent, you're just as bad as them. We are peaceful people. We'll stop this road by peaceful means.'

'What if you get thumped by a guard like I was yesterday?' a man shouted.

'We've got cameras. If there are witnesses we can charge them with assault. But if you thump him back they'll have you arrested. You have to resist all temptation. You have to be better than they are. And don't forget, some of these guards aren't wicked guys – they're doing it because they need a job. We haven't got a quarrel with them, our quarrel is with this government's road-building programme!'

At that, there was a cheer. Kaz looked round, excited. She could see Maria, Colonel and other familiar faces. There was no sign of Ash, but Dougie lounged at the side smoking, with his mocking expression.

'OK, now, we're going to divide into two, down the middle right there. You lot on the right can be the guards and you lot on the left are going to try to run past them. Don't forget, you can duck and weave, and put them off by yelling. Since you've got conviction on your side you'll always get through and stop the diggers, OK? Keep it fluffy!'

Everybody got up and began milling around. Kaz was on the 'side' of the protesters. The two groups formed themselves into long lines and faced each other. When Skye blew on a whistle, Kaz's side began running across the clearing, whilst the others stood firm. There was a lot of laughter as the two sides met, and Kaz found herself easily caught by a burly man in his thirties, who pushed her back. The small defeat inspired her. She ran back a bit then dodged along her own line, determined to look for a weak link. She found it in two women, who were doing their best to stop a young man from breaking through. Kaz took the chance and ducked between them. She raced on behind the line of 'guards', her heart thudding.

She was through! Kaz Armstrong, who had always been bad at games, had broken through! In triumph she started to laugh out loud, and skip instead of run . . . *Crash*! Suddenly the grass and Kaz's nose were making a close acquaintance. A pair of arms gripped her tightly, pinioning her down.

'Ow!' she yelled, although she was not hurt.

'Not so easy, is it?' said a voice in her ear.

The arms released her, so she could twist round and sit up. Ash sat back, grinning at her.

'The first lesson is, keep it fluffy. The second is, don't slow down once you're through because they'll be coming after you!'

'You hurt my elbow,' frowned Kaz, rubbing it.

'I didn't hurt it, the ground hurt it when I brought you down,' he said. 'Hey, you gotta get some knocks and bruises when you do direct action. It's all – like – part of the deal.'

'I'm not going to do it,' said Kaz, feeling cross.

'Why not?'

'My dad's said I've got to keep away from here.'

'What's wrong with the guy? He got problems or something?'

Kaz felt defensive. She hated her father's attitude, but that was for *her* to say, not someone else.

'No he hasn't! He just . . . doesn't understand, that's all.'

'So he wants the road to be built?'

'Not . . . really.'

'So – why doesn't he fight to stop it then? And if he won't, why do you have to do what he says?'

'Because he's my father, of course!' shouted Kaz, scrambling to her feet.

Behind them the lines were reforming, under Skye's instructions, but suddenly Kaz did not want to play the game any more. She wanted to go home, where it was safe. Kaz and Ash stood staring at each other, dislike on both their faces. Kaz went to turn away.

'So if Daddy told you to kill somebody, would you obey him, then?' demanded Ash, holding her there with the dark force of his gaze. 'Like – if you were Germans and he was a Nazi killing Jews, would you think he was right just 'cos he was your father?'

'Of course not! That's stupid,' Kaz hissed, hating him.

'No it's not, it's logical,' he insisted.

'What about your parents, then?' asked Kaz. 'How come they let you live here and do what you like? How come you're so lucky? Are they road protesters too, or what?'

Ash stepped back a pace and shrugged. His face grew hard, as if someone had suddenly dropped a mask on it from on high. 'I'm one of the lucky ones,' he said. 'I ain't got no parents, have I?'

Kaz felt as if all the blood in her body was pounding in the veins of her cheeks. 'I'm sorry . . . are they dead?' she said quietly.

He turned abruptly and walked away from her, ignoring the question. Kaz looked round. Behind her there were cries and laughter as the direct action practice went on. Skye was shouting to everyone to sit down. There was the same party atmosphere Kaz remembered from her first visit to the Office Camp.

Ash had disappeared into a clump of trees and bushes. She found him sitting with his back against a tree, smoking.

'I'm sorry,' she said.

'What for?'

'Saying that – about your parents.'

'It doesn't matter. Forget it. Isn't it time you went home? Your daddy might come looking for you and find you with the terrible wicked travellers, and stop your pocket money!'

Embarrassed and offended, Kaz wanted to do just as he said and run home. But instead she squatted down on a little hummock of grass in front of him.

'What's the matter?' she asked. 'What have I done to you?'

He looked at her sadly. 'I told you, forget it. It's – like – you live on another planet.'

'I'm here, aren't I? We're under the same tree. Breathing the same air . . .'

'Yeah, yeah.' He inhaled deeply and leant his head back against the tree-trunk as if he were bored.

'For God's sake, Ash!' Kaz said loudly. 'Stop being like this! If I said something to hurt you I'm sorry. I guessed your parents are dead, and it must be so horrible . . .'

He looked at her sharply. 'You don't know anything at all, Kaz. Like – *nothing*!'

64

'How can I know if you don't tell me?'

He stared at her for what seemed like a very long time. Then he relaxed a little, shaking his head sadly. 'Listen – you live in a nice house – right? And you've got two nice parents and nice brothers and sisters . . .?'

'A brother. He's eleven,' Kaz said.

'Right! Well, me, I got nobody at all – except them. That's my family.' He pointed across to where Skye stood with a small group of people from the camp. The afternoon sun was low now; the breeze was very chilly.

'That's . . .' Kaz began. She wanted to finish with the word 'awful' but realised that would be hurtful. How could she get it right? 'When did your parents die?' she whispered, determined to find out.

To her horror, Ash leant forward and took hold of one of her hands. He held it loosely, staring down at her palm as though he would tell her fortune. Her hand looked tiny and white in contrast to his – hard and engrained with dirt. He was smiling faintly, as though his thoughts were miles away.

'You want to know the story of my life, Kaz?' he asked softly at last, still looking down.

Kaz hesitated. 'Sort of . . .'

He stood up abruptly, making her jump, and hauled her unceremoniously to her feet.

'OK – well, why don't you come to our party tonight, and then I'll tell you.'

'What party? Where is it?' asked Kaz nervously.

'Here of course! At the camp. You'll be very welcome – you know that, don't you? We make everybody welcome. But I wonder if you'll come, little schoolgirl Kazzie? I bet you don't dare!'

Seven

Kaz always looked back on that afternoon as the turning-point. When she walked home, knowing in her heart that she would have to meet the challenge of that dare, the child inside her made an unwilling step towards being an adult.

She knew that on the surface it is foolish to do something wrong simply because somebody dares you. And if she went to the party on the hill it would be wrong because she would deceive her parents. But there was a mystery about Ash, which mirrored the mystery she felt on Twybury Hill, and somehow she was convinced that she would understand if only she had the courage to discover.

She was astonished at her own daring, and it was all she could do not to let her voice shake as she told her mother, very casually, that she was going out with her friends to the disco as usual. On her way back home from the hill she had telephoned Chris from a call-box, and said that she was being forced to babysit Jamie whilst her parents went out for a meal.

Chris groaned. 'Well, you'll miss out on Simon's mate,' she said.

'Still, Sal likes him.' Kaz stifled the thought that one of her best friends suddenly seemed very young.

Then, after a short pause in which neither of them seemed to have anything to say, Chris asked her about the photograph in the *Solchester Echo*. 'I couldn't believe it was you!' she said. 'My mum was quite shocked.'

'Why?' asked Kaz, feeling her stomach tense.

'You know – you being involved with that lot.'

'Chris, for one thing I'm not involved with anybody, OK? For another thing, they're not "that lot". They're just . . . people.'

'They look weird to me. My dad says they're loonies.'

'Look – let's not get into this now, OK? I've got to go. See you Monday – be good tonight! Bye!'

When she put down the phone, Kaz stood staring at it for about five minutes without moving.

Teatime dragged. The noise from the television set grated on Kaz's nerves and she dreaded her father asking her awkward questions. But why should he? Kaz told her parents that Sally's mother was picking her up from the end of their road, and that Chris's father would drop her off at ten thirty as usual. And so there was nothing to worry about.

Except clothes. Her normal disco uniform of miniskirt and skimpy top would hardly do for a party on Twybury Hill, and yet if she set off in jeans and boots her mother would suspect something. So, feeling uncomfortably shifty, Kaz shoved jeans, a thick sweater and DMs inside a plastic carrier bag. She hesitated for a moment, then added a torch and an Indian scarf patterned all over with suns and moons. She tied the top of the bag and crept out of the back door whilst everyone was watching the news. She hid the bag in the hedge just by the front door, went back into the house, and watched the hands of the clock crawl round until seven.

And all the time it was as if she was watching someone else do all these things. Just two weeks earlier, if anybody had told Kaz that she would be setting off down the lane – stopping to pull on her warm clothes – along the footpath, across the meadows and up Twybury Hill, alone and in the gathering gloom of evening, she would have laughed in disbelief.

There was a pale moon rising, and the first suggestion of stars in the sky. No wind disturbed the trees; the evening seemed even a touch warmer than usual. An owl hooted nearby – but to her surprise, Kaz found that she was not nervous. All she could think was, Will Ash be friendly?

As she approached the Rainbow Camp she heard the sound of the tin whistle again, accompanied by singing, sweet and high. Now she did feel nervous, and hoped she would see Maria or Skye and be made welcome. Above all she hoped Ash would realise she had come to show she was sorry about his parents, not just to rise to a dare like a silly schoolgirl.

The scene that greeted her was like something out of the Middle Ages, as if she had stumbled back in time. Two fires were burning in the clearing, lighting the tarpaulin tents. A large cooking pot was suspended over the smaller fire, a delicious savoury smell drifting on the smoke. Two girls squatted nearby, still chopping and throwing vegetables into the stew, while a man poked about in the hot ash at the edge of the fire, turning potatoes. Around the larger fire people were sitting, many with faces painted in green, red and yellow patterns, as if they were members of some primitive tribe. The man with the tin whistle swayed in time to his own music, and a girl with a shaven head sang words Kaz could not catch. She stood shyly in the shadows beyond the firelight until a voice behind her made her jump.

'Welcome, beautiful person. Tell me your name.'

'It's Kaz!'

Kaz turned, and there were Maria and Colonel smiling at her. The relief was instant. Without further words Maria linked her arm and drew her forward into the circle.

'Everybody! This is Kaz – she's going to help at the office when she can. She goes to my old school – poor thing – so we've got to be nice to her, as if we wouldn't be anyway! Anyway, Kaz, that's Kit . . . Steve . . . Rob . . . and Ian . . . and Harmony. Next to her is Julie and her baby, Wim. Then Indra . . . and Ben . . . and Olly . . . and . . .'

The names went on, becoming a sort of chant in Kaz's ears. She smiled a general greeting, then stood, not knowing what to do until someone made room for her on a log. Casually she let her eyes travel round the circle of faces, wondering if she had missed seeing Ash. But there was no sign of him.

After a while a tall, skinny man with a beard, who reminded her of pictures of John the Baptist, settled down with a didgeridoo, his cheeks puffing out comically as he coaxed out the most extraordinary, haunting sounds. Kaz loved it. She closed her eyes, breathing deeply as she listened to the strange, echoey music and allowed pictures to pass across the surface of her mind, like a light show: a lake in moonlight . . . a silver disc glowing in the heart of the universe . . . the shadow of a bird's wings . . . golden liquid pouring . . . waterfalls frozen in winter . . . trees drenched by silver rain . . . an owl crying in the darkness . . . a tree walking, walking after centuries of stillness . . . a face in branches, a face *of* branches, smiling and whispering a welcome . . .

A voice close by her ear whispered, 'You came then.'

Kaz blinked and pulled herself out of her daydream, almost sorry. Ash had squeezed himself on to the log beside her, and was smiling as easily and openly as if there had never been any harsh words between them.

'Here – I got you some food,' he said, offering a bowl of strange-looking stew, with a white plastic spoon stuck in it.

'Donga mush,' he said, by way of explanation, as Kaz peered dubiously at the steaming pile of beans and vegetables. 'It's good. Here, taste!'

It *was* good. Ash said they were short of plates so he and Kaz would have to share. For a while they ate in relaxed silence. When the bowl was empty Ash stretched out his legs. 'That's better,' he sighed. 'Now I'm going to get a beer. Do you want one?'

Kaz shook her head.

'Somebody's brought some cans of Coke, would that do better? This is a celebration, see, so you've got to have something.'

'What are we celebrating?' asked Kaz.

'It's Skye's birthday, and later on she and Colonel are gonna be handfasted.'

'What's that?'

'Come and I'll show you.'

A little way away, at the edge of the clearing, someone had constructed a bower out of branches, which had been decorated with coloured ribbons, more branches, and paper flowers. Inside, candles burned, and Skye sat cross-legged, wearing a velvet cloak over the clothes she had worn that afternoon. She was attended by two other women, one dressing her hair with a coronet of flowering twigs, and the other painting her face with little white stars.

'She looks lovely,' Kaz whispered. 'So what's happening?'

'Handfasting is like your marriage – only it's much older. When a man and woman decide they want to be together we have a handfasting ceremony, when somebody else from the family says the words and ties their hands together. Make fast – see? They have to vow to stay together for a year and a day.'

'Is that all?' Kaz asked.

'Well, they can go on longer if they like – plenty do!' He grinned.

'It sounds lovely – when will it happen? Can I watch?' she asked.

'I reckon it'll be too late for you,' said Ash.

They stood for a while, watching Skye, then turned away. More and more people were arriving – including some faces Kaz recognised – people who lived locally. 'I hope nobody spots me and tells my mum and dad,' she said – then stopped abruptly, expecting him to tease her. Instead he just nodded.

'Let's go and sit by my bender and get some peace then,' he said.

He picked up the drinks then led her to one of the smallest tents, and explained how he had made it from bent branches. Inside it was hung with old bits of rug and scraps of fabric, making a snug cocoon, a pile of bedding at the end. Outside was a piece of carpet to sit on, and a little rusty lantern, which he lit. They sat cross-legged, facing each other.

'Well?' said Ash.

'It's lovely!'

'I don't mean this!'

'Well what?'

'Why did you decide to take me up on my dare?'

'You know why – you said you'd explain things. About your family.'

'Oh – that.'

There was an uncomfortable silence, and Kaz was sorry she had raised it. 'You don't have to,' she said at last, desperate that things should not be spoilt. The tin whistle had joined the didgeridoo, and the sound they made together seemed to contain all sadness. Kaz shivered.

He stared at her, until she grew very uncomfortable and longed to escape.

'Hard to know where to start,' Ash said at last.

'What about at the beginning?' Kaz made her voice deliberately light.

'OK, so I was born in Worcester seventeen years ago, and now I'm here with my family – will that do?'

'If that's all you want to say,' said Kaz, disappointed.

'It's all I *want* to say. Whether it's all I *need* to say is another matter,' he sighed, and stared down at the little pouch he wore round his neck, twisting it round and round.

Puzzled, Kaz said nothing. There was a long silence. Then at last, because he showed no signs of breaking it, she plucked up the courage to ask, '*Are* your parents dead?'

The face he turned up towards her hardened as he shook his head. 'Oh no, they're not dead, though they might as well be as far as I'm concerned.'

'Ash – that's a terrible thing to say!'

'Yeah – well, terrible people, ain't they? Like I said, you don't know much, Kazzie, and I don't blame you. It's better not to know too much, believe you me.'

Shocked, Kaz said nothing. She knew he would speak, and yet she was afraid now what he might say.

'I feel like two people sometimes. I'm Ash, and this is my family, and we're all about saving the planet and peace and love. And I'm really Kevin – yeah, that's my real name – from Worcester, and my dad was a complete git who used to beat up my mum, and me for that matter. Then he walked out when I was six and after two years my mum's boyfriend moved in with us. Now *him* – he made my dad look like a plaster saint! He was something else, that Larry – he was probably the worst human being in the universe and I still dream of seeing him buried . . .'

'What did he . . . do?' whispered Kaz.

'Do? What didn't he do. He got drunk the whole time and took it out on my mum, and then when he wasn't drunk he took that out on her too. He put her in hospital twice, but she *lurved* him, see. She loved him more than anything – stupid cow! She loved him more than me. The best time was when he was in the nick for three years, because we had a bit of peace. I was, what, eleven then, so I was fourteen when he got out and that's when the worst times started.'

'Why?'

He shook his head. 'Don't make me talk about it, Kaz, it's too much for me. Don't even ask, OK? He had this friend . . . oh, never mind. Anyway, all you need to know is that I kept running away, and then they put me in care.'

'She gave you up?' Kaz exclaimed.

'More complicated than that. Look – she didn't want me, OK? She didn't believe me when I told her what him and his friend tried to do to me – she didn't wanna know. I had to get out.

'I was hitching and I was picked up by these guys with a trailer who lived on the road. They were brilliant – just took me along. It was – like – having your eyes open for the first time. They were into so many good things . . . So I left poor old Kev behind there in miserable Worcester, and started again. These people, they were all into trees, and so some-body called me Ash. I reckoned it was better to be called after a beautiful tree than walk around for the rest of my life with some sad name my stupid rotten parents had given me . . .'

His voice tailed off, as if tired. Kaz had absolutely no idea what to say and felt ashamed for her stupidity and lack of sensitivity. Tears filled her eyes; she wiped her nose on her sleeve. Somebody was roaring with laughter by the fire and she wanted to jump up and stop them, because laughter was wrong in a world which could treat someone so cruelly.

'Don't feel sorry for me, Kaz,' he said, looking up at her at last. His eyes were bleak.

'But I *do*,' she whispered, her voice breaking.

He shook his head. 'There's lots here with stories like mine. The older ones, like Colonel and Skye, look after us. But we get people who are – you know.' He tapped his head, then went on. 'There's nowhere else for them, see? We've had some nutters join us, I'm telling you – but we're a community and so we do our best to take care of them. What else can we do? Anyway, most of them – they're great. Up here, we look after each other, and because we're trying to do something *big* . . .'

'Stop the road?' asked Kaz.

'What else? Because that's so important we can forget how different we all are and it gives you – like – a feeling that you matter.'

'You do matter,' whispered Kaz.

'Not to my mum, I didn't, did I?'

Kaz thought of her own home, where at that moment her parents were watching television maybe, or chatting, or reading, or maybe playing Monopoly with Jamie, or even watching a video . . . and all the time thinking that she was at the disco with her friends.

'I'm lucky,' she gulped. 'Because I know you say I'm Daddy's good little girl and all that, but my parents are really quite cool. I mean . . . they're lovely, and they're . . .'

'I'm sorry – I didn't mean it,' Ash said, swigging the last of his beer. 'It's only because sometimes I meet someone, a girl like you, and I know you're worlds apart from me, and . . . I suppose . . . I'm jealous. Not that I don't like it here . . .'

'Course you do!' said Kaz enthusiastically, hating the doubt in his voice. 'It's lovely.'

People had started to dance by the fire now – black figures making fantastic shapes against the hot orange light. Kaz remembered all the Bonfire nights she had ever known, and thought that none had been as exciting as this.

'Here – a present.' Ash pulled something from his pocket and held out a balled fist.

She held out her hand, and he dropped something in it. She looked down and saw a friendship bracelet woven in all the colours of the rainbow.

'For me?'

'Who else?'

'But – why?'

'Because.'

'Oh – it's nice,' she said, aware how words were so hopeless at expressing her feelings.

'I love rainbows,' Ash said dreamily. 'When I was a kid I used to imagine the pot of gold at the end of the rainbow – you know – like you read about? I'd think of finding it, and being rich, and then I could buy myself a big house and live on my own – away from her and Larry and the lot of 'em. Then one day I thought, suppose the rainbow doesn't end at all? Suppose the ends just go on, so that it joins up beneath the earth, and it's a beautiful great circle of light and colour? On and on. You know?'

'The rainbow joining,' said Kaz.

'Yeah – and it's all light down there, all the time, under the ground. Like – that's *the real* gold. And when we can't see the top bit, because there's been no rain, the bottom bit is still always there, in the earth. You *know* it's still there.'

'The diggers – they could break it up,' said Kaz softly.

'Right!'

'You've got lots of things you believe in, haven't you, Ash?' she asked.

He leant forward to fasten the bracelet on to her wrist. 'Haven't you?'

Kaz examined the bracelet. It was a little rainbow, going round and round her wrist, made from lots of strands of colour woven together like all the complexities of life. She ran a finger along it, and saw her mother in the red, her father in the blue, Jamie in the yellow, and Ash in the green . . . All together, going round and round her wrist . . . all together, if she could make it happen.

She looked up and found him staring at her with those intense dark eyes, a small smile on his lips.

'Are you glad you told me?' she asked.

'Yes,' he said simply.

'It's good to be open,' she said, looking at her watch. 'Listen, I can stay for another half an hour, then I have to go home. Shall we go over by the fire?'

'Let's go and sing,' he grinned, pulling her to her feet.

Kaz felt as if she was floating. The music, the laughter, the smell of woodsmoke and food, the dancers like members of a tribe, torchlight red on painted faces . . . She let her limbs move freely, all self-consciousness gone. But she kept looking at her watch, so that in the end Ash called her Cinderella.

'When the clock strikes your rags will be turned to proper clothes!' he joked.

At ten she said she had to go. He insisted on walking part of the way with her, although she protested that she was perfectly capable of looking after herself. When he asked if she had the right to stop him going for a walk in the moonlight she laughed and said no. They set off in a companionable silence, shoulders hunched against the chill of the spring night. Kaz felt more at one with the world around her than she had ever been in her life. In the distance she could see the lights of the city, and thought of all those people, curtains drawn, watching television, who were unaware of the great dome of sky above.

WELCOME!

She seemed to hear the rustle deep within her mind. Yet it was all around her too . . .

'Yes, the hill did make me welcome,' she said aloud.

'What?' asked Ash.

'Nothing. Just a dream I once had . . . I'll tell you about it some time.'

'OK.'

They did not speak again until they reached the stile which led to the flat meadow by the road. There Kaz stopped and retrieved the plastic carrier bag containing her silly dolly shoes.

'Don't come any further,' said Kaz. 'I'll be fine, honestly.'

'Will you come up again? Come and see us tomorrow,' said Ash.

Kaz clutched the bag to her chest. 'I'll see,' she said. 'There's some things I've got to sort out at home.'

'You do that,' he said, with no trace of sarcasm in his voice. 'See ya.' Then there was the gentlest of touches on her shoulder as Ash turned and loped away into the darkness before she even had the chance to say goodnight.

Eight

Something important had been decided on the hill, Kaz knew that. She drifted in and out of sleep, and always the knowledge woke her up, just as it sang to her in the liquid cries of birds at first light. She knew what she had to do. There was no alternative. But it still scared her.

The kitchen was filled with the smell of bacon, sausages, tomato and scrambled eggs. The atmosphere was easy and sloppy-Sundayish. Jamie was flicking through a wildlife magazine, their father was setting the table, their mother was dishing up. Kaz felt as if she was about to be executed.

She pushed the food around her plate, took a few mouthfuls, then laid down her knife and fork.

'Listen,' she said. 'I want to talk to you properly about something – you two, I mean.' She held up a hand when her father opened his mouth as if to speak. 'Dad – I want you to hear me out. Don't let your breakfast get cold, but just listen to me. Jamie can be the referee and see I'm not interrupted. Because I want to tell you the truth and I want you to treat me like a grown-up – OK?'

Anxiously her parents nodded. Then Kaz drew breath and told them about her fibs, and how she had gone to the party on the hill, and why. She tried to describe her feelings when she went on the march, and tried to convey how she had changed. At last she told them the story of Ash's life, and it was at that point that her voice wobbled.

'You see, Dad, you can't lump people together and call them names, like you did. All those people, they're all different, like my schoolfriends are all different, and it's not fair if you don't realise that. It's like being a . . . a . . . racist, or something.'

'I think that's right,' said Jamie, taking off his glasses and rubbing them on his sleeve.

'Oh, you do, do you?' said Kaz's father, staring at his son. Kaz's mother looked as if she was waiting for the explosion. It did not come. Calmly he went on eating. Then he looked at Kaz and said quietly, 'So what next?'

'I want you to come to the Office Camp with me today, and maybe Maria will be there and you can meet her. We can look at the map and read the leaflets, and stuff. Then I want us – as a family – to walk some of the way the road's going to go, and up to the other camp and hopefully meet some people. Mum already did, last week, but it's different now. Because I'm going to get involved and you can't stop me. I'm fourteen now, and old enough to know when I think something matters. You should be pleased, because I want to take it seriously – I do! I mean – this planet, it's for us, me and Jamie and people our age. People your age have already mucked it up, and it's us who have to go on living on it, you know . . . when you're dead.'

Her father stifled a grin. 'Are you killing us off then, Kaz?'

'Don't be silly – you know what I mean!' she said, amazed at his reaction.

'Well, darling, I think you put your case really well,' said Kaz's mother. 'You *were* wrong to lie, but brave to come clean so soon. It could have gone on and on, couldn't it?'

'I couldn't have stood that,' said Kaz.

'No, you'd have got in deeper and deeper . . . So look, I don't know what you think, Peter, but I vote we at least go with her – just to see.'

Kaz's father nodded.

'Hooray!' shouted Jamie, rolling up his magazine and hitting Kaz on the head in his old annoying way.

'So that's sorted!' cried Kaz, with a grin so big she thought her face could split.

'Don't you mean sorted *out*, dear?' asked her mother.

'No – I mean *sorted*!' said Kaz.

That was, she thought much later, more true than she realised. Her father was looking at her in a new way, no longer his baby, his little girl, but a person with ideas and feelings he had to respect. She found herself thinking, as they set off for their walk that afternoon, I owe this to Ash.

When they emerged at the brutal clearing of Greenway Lane, Kaz's parents stopped simultaneously.

'My God!' said Kaz's father.

'It was so pretty before,' said her mother.

At that moment a police car, which had been parked down the lane, drove off past them, but the Armstrong family was too absorbed to notice.

For the first time in her life Kaz felt in control. She led the way to the caravan, waving casually at the group of people who were sitting around the campfire, although they were all strangers. Maria was with them, talking intently, waving her hands as if trying to make a point – but when she saw Kaz she stood up and came over.

'Hi!' she said.

The tension Kaz had noticed on her face disappeared immediately as she made an effort to impress Kaz's parents with her knowledge. She pointed out on the map where the road would become six lanes wide, where it would be raised up on concrete stilts, what trees and hedges would be lost, where there were more houses to be demolished, and so on.

'Didn't you get amazing A level results a year ago?' asked Kaz's mother, 'I'd have thought you'd be at university now. On your way to some brilliant career.'

Maria shrugged. '*This* is what I'm doing, and you can call it a career if you like!' she said, waving a hand to encompass the caravan, the camp and the destruction all around. 'I don't see much point in doing anything else at the moment. Why get a degree when the world you know is being ruined for ever? What's the point of joining the system which thinks money and speed is more important than the planet?'

'What's your answer to that, Dad?' asked Kaz.

'Get yourself a degree and try to change things from that position –

when people will listen to you,' said her father, folding his arms in the way he did when he was about to have a good discussion.

'Oh, they listen to me now; they think I'm a real nuisance!' grinned Maria, pulling at the fat plait that lay on her shoulder. 'I could show you newspaper cuttings . . . Look, you may be right, and maybe in two years' time I'll decide to go and study law so I can really take them on. But for now – they bulldozed my house, and they're ripping into these fields I've known all my life. What am I supposed to do? Read Dickens? No – I want to jump on diggers and stop them for as long as I can. I don't know how *anybody* who lives around here can sit back and let them get away with it.'

Jamie was watching Maria with an expression of dazzled admiration. He took off his spectacles and polished them vigorously, his face pink.

'That's what I think, Dad!' he said.

'Oh, you do, do you?' said his father.

'So – are you going to help us?' Maria asked their mother, who looked suddenly flustered.

'Go on, Mum!' said Jamie.

There was a collecting tin on the rickety table that stood outside the caravan. There was a label stuck to it which said the money was for THAG. Kaz's mother asked what it stood for.

'Twybury Hill Action Group,' Maria explained. 'Somebody wrote to the paper and called us thugs. So I wrote and said we're not thugs, we're thags!'

Kaz's father hesitated, grinning despite himself. He fished around in all his pockets, pulled out a five-pound note and stuffed it into the tin.

'Thanks,' Maria said, in a tone that said, Is that the best you can do? But her smile was winning.

As they walked away, Kaz's father said, 'That is one very self-confident young woman. You'd call her arrogant if . . .'

' . . . She wasn't so nice,' finished Kaz's mother.

'I don't know if she's nice or not nice,' said Kaz slowly, 'she's just . . . just . . . convinced she's right, and so she makes you feel the same way.'

'I think she's right,' said Jamie.

They walked on in silence. Then Kaz's father stopped and consulted the poorly copied map he had picked up from the Office Camp. He looked around as if seeing the place for the first time.

'Now . . . according to this map, where we're standing is where it will start to widen into six lanes, because there'll be slip roads off both sides . . .'

'No way!' squeaked Jamie. 'This is the brockway, where all the badgers have always lived.'

'And right down there will be the roundabout. I must say I didn't think it would be a split level one. It'll look like something in Los Angeles.'

'So huge!' breathed Kaz's mother.

They were all silent as they walked on slowly, but Kaz felt no sense of triumph. She wanted the bypass not to be true. When at last they approached the old oak tree she felt tears in her eyes; she wanted to run forward, throw her arms round it, and weep. She stared, and for a second it was as if the whole world had stopped turning and was waiting . . .

'But for what?'

For death and destruction, unless we rise up out of the darkness . . . to face the dark . . .

'Who?' asked Kaz, knowing as she did so that this was inside her head.

I am in the tree, I am in the hill, I am beneath your feet, I am in the rain . . .

'But why?'

Because I have always been, since before time . . .

'I do know you, I saw you in a dream.'

There is a darkness coming, and the sound of screaming, and crashing, and there will be blood on the hill. But they will never destroy me. When the last patch of green is covered with grey, and the sun dies, then I will awake, and push, and heave, and break through into life once more . . .

'But we can rise before that! We can fight! We can, we CAN!'

. . . A darkness coming . . .

Kaz was not aware that her family was standing beside her, wondering what she was looking at. Her mother said, 'Are you feeling all right, love?'

'What? Oh yes, sorry! It's just that sometimes when I come up here, I . . .' She stopped.

'What?'

'Oh nothing.'

'Go on, love,' her mother encouraged.

' . . . it's like I hear the tree talking to me. It's so weird, Mum!'

'I think trees can talk,' said Jamie. 'I mean, we don't know they can't, do we? So if we don't know, we might as well believe it's true.'

'Not very scientific, son,' said their father.

Kaz looked at her little brother with affection, as she fingered the rainbow bracelet on her wrist. 'You're great, Jamie, you know that?'

'Come on, Kaz, you've got to introduce us to your friends,' said her father, striding ahead.

Now they were nearly at the Rainbow Camp, Kaz's heart was sinking. She felt shy and uncomfortable again, dreading seeing Ash, wondering if she had betrayed him by telling her family about his life. Then she imagined the people in the camp just getting up, wandering about dishevelled, some with hangovers, dirty hair, pierced noses . . . and realised how bad it would look. She wanted to go back – but it was too late.

A part of her hoped that Ash would not be there, but another part wanted to see him. She also hoped that Skye would be around – calculating that since she was about twenty-three and very pretty, with a pleasant voice, no nose-ring and perfectly normal long hair, her father might like her.

There was something magical about Twybury Hill, Kaz decided, because in answer to her unspoken wish, Skye wandered down the path towards them. She looked bleary and dishevelled, and stared at

Kaz for a moment as if she did not recognise her. Then she said hello, in a vaguely troubled voice.

'Is . . . something the matter?' asked Kaz nervously. 'I was going to take my family to see the camp. Is that OK?'

'What? Oh . . . if you like. We just had a meeting.' Skye shook her head slightly and ran a hand through her hair.

'Sounds a bit businesslike!' said Kaz's father heartily, making Kaz cringe.

'Yeah, well something bad happened, and we had to talk about it.'

'What?' Kaz asked, feeling gloomy. This was not what she had imagined.

Skye sighed. 'Last night, or early this morning more likely, somebody set light to a hut down near the Office Camp, where the security guards keep a lot of stuff. Obviously we're being blamed, and that kind of thing doesn't do us any good. Not very fluffy . . .'

'Fluffy?' asked Kaz's mother.

'It means non-violent. Peaceful,' explained Kaz.

'Anyway, Colonel and I called a meeting – tried to get to the bottom of it. Nobody knows anything about it at our camp, but then there's new people arriving every day. Maybe somebody thinks that's the way, but we have to tell them it isn't. It looks so *bad* . . . oh, I don't know. I'm going down to talk to Maria about it now.'

As they walked on Kaz felt she was in for a lecture and a total ban when they arrived home.

The rainbow ribbons were fluttering in the slight breeze that blew from the top of the hill. The camp looked rather messy and dreary.

Then, to Kaz's horror, a green-faced creature with dark hair in a pony-tail, and tendrils of young ivy hanging down from the leafy coronet, appeared in front of them.

Oh no! Kaz thought. Why on earth has he put on his face paint at this time of the day? Stupid fool – what are they going to think? For a wild second she thought of pretending that she did not know the bizarre apparition.

'Hello, Kaz,' said Ash.

She introduced her parents and Jamie, relieved that Ash's voice, at least, was perfectly civilised. She could see that her mother was determined to be kind, but what of her father? His eyes were fixed on the leafy crown, but he said nothing.

'I like your green face paint,' said Jamie.

'Thanks, mate!'

'We met Skye . . . there's been a problem,' blurted Kaz.

'Yeah, some git thinks sabotage will persuade people that this road is a bad thing. Stupid destruction – *and* polluting the air!' He shook his head vigorously, so that the hanging tendrils waved in front of his eyes.

Kaz's father was staring at him. Suddenly he exclaimed, 'You're a Green Man!'

'What's that?' asked Kaz and Ash at the same time.

'You mean you dress like one and you don't know what it is?' laughed Kaz's father. 'Well, that's incredible! The Green Man's a kind of mythical figure, going back to before Christianity. You see him carved in churches, sometimes in stone, sometimes in wood – a man with leaves sprouting from him, sometimes coming out of his mouth as though he's being sick . . .'

'Yuk,' said Jamie.

' . . . and he's a sort of nature god, I suppose. You find him in France too. It's interesting that the priests let the people carve him in the churches, because really he's a pagan spirit. I suppose they didn't dare stop it!'

Ash grinned, his mouth very pink next to the green, and said, 'Well, I've spent most of my life getting things wrong without meaning to. Now I got something *right* without meaning to! You know – like – I just did this because we're all about being green, saving the planet. Now you tell me I'm a mythical pagan figure – a real Green Man – and I'm right into that! Wow!'

He was shaking his head in such a comical way, mocking himself, that they all burst out laughing. Kaz turned her rainbow friendship bracelet round and round on her wrist, and breathed a silent thank you to the air.

Ash led the way to his bender. Kaz's father was quite interested in its construction. Jamie crawled inside and Kaz's mother started to chat about cooking facilities with a young woman who walked by carrying a string of onions. She explained that local people donated food every day, and Kaz's mother promised to bring up some supplies.

The atmosphere was becoming more friendly and relaxed by the second, then somebody tapped Kaz on the shoulder. She turned round to see Dougie grinning at her, and her heart plummeted.

'These yer folks?' he asked.

'Yes,' said Kaz shortly.

'Maybe you'll bring 'em along on the next action,' he grinned. 'We need bodies to throw at the diggers!'

Shut up! Kaz thought.

Jamie was standing next to Dougie, staring at the thick ropes of his blond dreadlocks with open curiosity. 'I'd like to do action,' he chirped.

'Good!' crowed Dougie. 'We'll show ye what to do.'

'I don't think that would be a good idea at all,' said Kaz's mother coldly.

'Why not?' asked Dougie, folding his arms. His tone was aggressive. 'Ye're never too young to start. The wee ones – they can run between the guards' legs!'

'Don't be stupid, Dougie,' said Ash.

'Who're ye callin' stupid?'

'Well, you're the one who said it didn't matter that some stupid git fired that hut last night! *That's* pretty stupid!' said Ash angrily.

'Och, it was only the pixies,' said Dougie with an unpleasant grin. 'The wee pixies get up tae all sorts. And they'll no stop, either!'

'What do you mean?' asked Ash, suspiciously.

'Ah mean tae say – there's all this talk about keeping it fluffy, but me – ah think it's time we kicked a few heids.' He stopped in fake concern and put a hand over his mouth, looking at Kaz's mother. 'Och ah'm sorry, there's no way tae talk in front of nice people like you!' Then he shambled off, still grinning.

'I think it's time to go home now,' said Kaz's father angrily.

Kaz looked at Ash miserably and said goodbye. He walked with them to the rainbow arch and said his farewells politely, but a shadow had fallen over the day. It was all Dougie's fault. Kaz hated him.

'There's obviously something wrong there,' said her father.

'What do you mean?' asked Kaz.

'That yobbo we just spoke to is clearly one of the irresponsible ones. How many more are like him? Nobody seems to be in charge . . .'

'They're not like that,' protested Kaz, 'they don't have leaders.'

'Nonsense,' said her father crisply. 'You have to have organisation, you have to have people in charge. Otherwise things happen – like that fire. Or worse. Honestly, love, I don't want . . .'

'What about Ash and Skye – didn't you like them?' Kaz interrupted, desperately.

'Oh, I suppose they were fine. But . . .'

'And Maria! She's really bright, isn't she? You can't say she isn't responsible!'

'No . . . I suppose . . .'

He did not finish. Kaz caught her mother's eye, and saw in it a warning.

'Let's discuss it over tea,' said her mother gently, tucking Kaz's arm through hers.

'*I* liked them,' said Jamie. Kaz gave him a grateful smile.

Their father strode ahead. Kaz and her mother and brother followed at a much slower pace, not talking. Dougie had just confirmed all her father's prejudices. Nothing could make him be fair now.

She saw him climb over a stile into the large meadow, then stop and greet a man whom Kaz thought she vaguely recognised.

ho's that, Mum?' asked Jamie.

)h, what's his name . . .?' She screwed up her face in the effort to remember. 'Um . . . I know! Melvin Douglas. He's from Seaston — a farmer, I think. And if I remember rightly, he's on the Seaston Parish Council. He's forever writing to the paper. They were all passionately in favour of the bypass, Jamie, because they think it'll get rid of their through traffic.'

As they approached, Kaz heard her father say, 'Well, it's a very complicated issue.'

'No, it's not!' said Melvin Douglas. 'It's an open and shut case, and anybody with half a brain can see it.'

'Sorry, I don't think it *is* that easy. You'll get even more pollution floating over to Seaston when this road is built because the traffic'll double. They've admitted that.'

'Won't be going through our village, will it?' growled Melvin Douglas.

'No — but what about the poor people who live along Greenway Lane? Their lives are ruined.'

'You don't make an omelette without breaking eggs.'

Kaz's father sighed. He hated clichés. Kaz opened her mouth to speak but was silenced by her mother's fierce nudge.

'You been up there?' asked the farmer, pointing. 'So what do you think of them smellies, then?'

'What do you mean?'

'Them crusties on the hill! Come to tell us we don't need this road.

Should mind their own business and go back to the holes they came from, evil bastards!'

There was a short silence, then Kaz's father said lamely, 'Oh, I . . . don't know.'

Kaz was horrified and ashamed. She thought of Pastor Niemoeller's poem about speaking up for people, and felt sick. She had to say something, even if her parents grew angry. She opened her mouth, but no sound came out.

Melvin Douglas went on in a loud voice. 'I won't tell you what I think in front of the ladies . . . but this I will say: they're on the common land which we own – us Seaston farmers, I mean – and we're going to get them off. Damn nuisances, they are! Living like animals, setting fire to things! They need serious treatment, that's what they need! If I had my way we wouldn't bother with the law at all . . .'

'Really?' said Kaz's father coolly, standing a little taller. 'What would you do?'

The farmer leant back on his heels and folded his arms. His face grew a shade redder and he laughed maliciously. 'Obvious! We should be allowed to nail them to the fences and *shoot* them – like the vermin they are.'

Kaz heard her mother draw in her breath. Tears sprang into her own eyes, and she felt weak. There was a long pause. A thrush sang its heart out nearby.

'Shall I tell you what I think?' said Kaz's father slowly, at last.

'Go on then!' grinned the farmer.

'I think what you just said *stinks*. I think it's utterly *disgusting*. Do you understand? And if that's a view which your people in Seaston hold, then I know which side I'm on. Is that clear?'

Kaz's father turned his back on the farmer and held out his arm for Kaz to link. She took it proudly.

'Come on, team,' said her father, 'let's go home.'

Kaz screws up her face in concentration. She is writing. The lamp on the table in her room makes a yellow pool; her hand wants to move by itself.

At first it is just her name, written over and over again in curly script. That is who I am, she thinks: Kaz Armstrong – and none of them can take that away from me. It is so lonely when they won't speak, and you feel you are the only person in the universe. Mrs Robinson sees and understands but she can do nothing. Mum and Dad know, because I told them, but they can't do anything. Ash and the others dismiss it – because they're only really interested in their own way of life. But for so long I wanted to be part of the crowd, and now the crowd has left me. Or else – I have moved on and left the crowd behind . . .

What can I do? I don't fit in anywhere.

Kaz scribbles her name in lines, and studies it, because it proves she exists. Then she closes her eyes again, and thinks of what they are supposed to write. It's impossible! Everything seems impossible: a waste of time trying. Everything is being destroyed.

'You have to fight it, Kazzie,' Ash is saying, inside her head.

Kaz watches her own hand again. It has stopped and she wills it to move. There is a long, long pause, as she closes her eyes and imagines she is deep in a rainforest, dark and wet, hemmed in by trees so tall there is no sky – only the green darkness, wrapping her round. She skulks in this rich gloom, like a small wild creature, waiting for the hunter.

'Kaz, you're the only person not to have handed in your homework. I must say I'm disappointed in you.'

'I can't do it – I've got nothing to say.'

'Everybody's got something to say, Kaz.'

Somebody called out, 'She's too busy protesting!' and they all laughed.

In her imagination, deep in the green gloom, Kaz hears that deep, echoing voice again. It no longer says Welcome. Sometimes it roars at her, sometimes it cries, sometimes it booms the question, why? over and over again, driving her mad. Yet she knows she heard it before she was born; she knows it is the voice of the earth itself, calling to her.

Always on the hill, she feels its presence. It . . . or he? He is in the hill, she knows that. He is a sharp damp smell of undergrowth, he is a pattern of lichen, he is the swirl of a bole and the encrustation of decay on a dead tree. He is a skeletal shape against the night sky, and the owl speaks for him, sadly. He is the leaves.

First a smell, and a sound, then the sense of a presence all around. A spirit, a green spirit, who has entered through her eyes. A man who walked the hill centuries before, terrifying its first dwellers,

98

warning them to be careful – not to despoil what does not belong to them.

Kaz is sometimes afraid, but now she is used to the Green Man. Sometimes, when she sees the diggers grub out the hedges, the earth and the small trees, she has a violent fantasy. The engineers and security guards are swarming all over the ancient hill, with their horrible engines of destruction. Suddenly a hairline crack appears in the ground. Nobody sees it. The earth shakes, and it widens. A sliver, then a chasm, dust flying all around, a groan as if the earth itself were giving birth . . .

Somebody thinks that maybe there is an earthquake – but not here, not in their half of the world! What is that rumbling and shaking, beneath their feet? The chasm spreading apart, like a scream. And at last, with a sprouting of leaves and a flash of the terrible red mouth, he pulls himself up, towering over them all – the giant Green Man, bellowing in rage like King Kong, and holding a miniature crane in one hand, a digger in the other, as roadbuilders, guards and machines alike fall into the pit.

He howls in triumph and pain.

Kaz laughs aloud, though shocked by her own wish to destroy them. They have almost made her as bad as them . . .

This isn't helping at all. There is homework to be done, and the only thing in her mind is the road and the Green Man, and the war between the two.

Wars spread over the land as the centuries passed; battles fought on the hills, stench of blood as the wounded pile into churches, the weeping of mothers and wives as they pick through the battlefields for the dead bodies of their men. On and on – houses crumbling, kings and queens dying, customs changing.

Why?

Time passes, the seasons roll by endlessly. Change increases, making men and women dizzy as the twentieth century at last trails its bloody cloak across the world, and humankind reaches new heights of arrogance.

Why?

The genius of the race which produced Shakespeare and Mozart and all the rest, is turned to nerve gas and the hydrogen bomb and the evil technology of the concentration camps and the passion for profit which stuffs anything and everything into its poisonous mouth . . .

Why?

And all the time, through the centuries, almost unnoticed, his face, carved in stone and wood, stares down, from the emptying churches – leaves on his head, tendrils are his hair, branches pour from his ears, his mouth. Sometimes his image is sad, a small bird sheltering in his hair. Sometimes it is fierce, promising punishment one day to those who only think of now, and will hand on to future generations a ruined earth.

WHY?

The Green Man does not change, although people have forgotten him. He forces his way up with the daffodils in the windowbox in the heart of the city; he lurks in the weeds which penetrate the stony wasteland. He is the wounded bark of the old tree in the park, in which boys have gouged their names and dirty words. He watches with grief as the forests are cleared and the air is poisoned, leaving people (stupid, stupid people, he thinks) gasping for breath.

He is in the branch tap-tapping at the bedroom window in the storm.

He calls from the small things on the nature table in school.

When the front door closes on him, he becomes its very wood; he follows up the stairs, stands by the bed, magicking images of earth's pain like a slide show – and asking all the time, why?

Kaz closes her eyes and listens acutely to that familiar voice inside her brain. She is not afraid any more. She knows that the spirit which haunts her is good – as long as she listens to him. Now it is as if he is telling her what to write, and she allows her hand to move across the page like a spider, as if guided by the unseen force.

Outside, in their garden, an owl hoots mournfully, giving her its wild companionship. Another screeches like a soul in pain. She writes:

Conversation

Man said to Monkey,

'I am powerful and clever,

I know what to do and say,

I am going to rule for ever –

So bow down and obey.'

Monkey said,

'Hear these stories of woe.

See man's heart is made of lead.

Am I lying?

No.

'Dolphin swam freely, loving all,

Not knowing what fate would have in store,

He followed the tuna as they swam south,

The nets spread wide like an open mouth,

And swallowed the creatures of the deep . . .

In the supermarket the tins are cheap.

'The rainforest was a beautiful place,

Animals prowled leaving not a trace,

Birds swooped high above the trees,

Snakes would slither through fallen leaves,

Until the day when the trees crashed down,

And the roar of the fire was the only sound,

And all that was left was blackened ash –

So the lush green leaves were turned to cash.

'The harmless rabbit, wild and free,

Man hurt so it could no longer see,

Dropping chemicals in its eyes,

Into its fur rubbing lotions and dyes,

Until its nerves were screaming with pain –

All so commerce could gain and gain.

'The seagull soaring, high and swift,

Landed on a wave's white quiff,

But the clear blue sea,

Slicked slowly black,

And the creature of air,

Floated dead on its back.'

Man replied angrily,

'Monkey, Monkey, can't you see

That your life belongs to me?

I am the master of the earth,

Your value to *me* is your only worth.

I decide what is right and wrong.

You must do as I say, sing my song.'

Monkey sighed and said,

'One day, maybe, Man will learn,

To rule the earth wisely, he must earn

The friendship of nature, the love of life –

Or the earth will strike back

Like a sharpened knife.'

Nine

Three months passed, March warmed through into May, and the life of the Armstrong family settled into a pattern none of them would ever have dreamt. Kaz thought one day she would look back on this as one of the happiest times of her growing-up. The Road dominated their conversations. They bought the local paper and scoured it for correspondence and controversy, of which there was plenty. Kaz's mother took food to the protest camps and designed posters and leaflets. Her father was on a committee to organise a petition demanding that work on the road be halted on legal grounds. Jamie helped his father, although he was forbidden to go anywhere near the camps or the works. Kaz promised not to go near the works during the week, on condition she was allowed to go to the Office Camp on Saturday mornings. She promised faithfully never to join in direct action.

The change in Kaz's father, especially, was remarkable. He read as much as he could about transport and the environment, he wrote to local councillors, he studied the system of public inquiries. And, of course, he lectured Kaz.

105

'You have to do the work, so you can support your emotions with facts,' he told her, waving a finger. 'The trouble with half the protesters is they just shout slogans without understanding how complicated it all is. It's not enough to blow tin whistles and beat drums. All it does is alienate public opinion . . .

'To read the papers you'd think the only people against this road are travellers and students. What about people like me? I pay my taxes, I live in this country, I've got a right to speak my mind. Then you get these stupid politicians calling us all rent-a-mob. It's partly because of some of your friends, Kaz! I mean to say – why have they got to paint their faces?'

Kaz had no answer. A part of her agreed with him. But one day, for fun, she had sat by the campfire whilst Skye carefully painted her face in an intricate pattern of green and white. A mask. Kaz had looked in a scrap of mirror and laughed, hardly recognising herself. She loved what she saw. It was somebody powerful, not just a schoolgirl. For a second she heard ancient drums beat in her blood, tribal rhythms, which made her forget herself, so that she could do anything . . .

'Oh, Dad,' she said softly. 'You always used to say it takes all sorts to make the world. Well, it takes all sorts to make a protest too!'

'But what about all this sabotage?' he asked, looking worried.

'It's not our side, Dad! Skye thinks security guards are doing it to give us a bad name. Or else it's somebody working undercover, paid by Rowley Construction.'

'Is that likely?' asked her mother.

'Anything can happen. Ash and the others say it's a war,' said Kaz.

It was just as well she had her family's support, for at school there was none. She, who had always been quite popular, found herself a creature set apart. Some girls would not speak to her and even Chris and Sally treated her as if she was slightly mad. The road issue split Solchester in half, just like civil wars did throughout history – sometimes setting brother against brother. Kaz sensed bitterness and prejudice all around her. One girl in school, whose father worked for the electricity board, was forbidden to speak to her. Chris and Sally's parents thought she had 'gone wild' and said that her parents should know better. Kaz's friends did not hesitate to tell her this, making the excuse that they thought it best to be honest.

'I don't want to know, thank you very much,' Kaz said angrily. They shrugged, turned away and were cooler than ever. The days of shopping arm-in-arm and giggling outside the disco had disappeared. Without Chris and Sally school was a bleak place.

The teasing had begun the week after Kaz's picture appeared in the *Solchester Echo*. There were arguments, and Kaz lost her temper. A week later she wrote to the *Solchester Echo* to protest over a particularly nasty piece of reporting she thought was an outright lie. It took pride of place on the letters page. There was more teasing. It grew worse after Mrs Robinson had read out her poem to the class. Kaz was pleased her English teacher liked it, but groaned inside because she knew what the result would be.

Debbie Mansfield started the persecution. She called her Monkey. The name stuck with a large section of the class, although Chris and Sally and her own little set did not join in. Then, when the *Solchester*

Echo reported the first tree houses in Twybury Wood, the name took on a new significance.

'Will you be going up the trees, Monkey?'

'Any banana trees over your way?'

'Will the hippies teach you to swing from branch to branch, Monkey?'

'That's why she's called Armstrong. Monkeys have to have strong arms, see?'

Kaz knew it was best to be dignified, to be silent. She could manage it when the insults were directed against her, but when the girls sneered at the people in the protest camps, calling them smelly crusties and dirty hippies, she could not bear it.

'It so happens they try very hard to keep clean – *you* try it, when you have to walk miles for water, and when it's been raining, so there's a sea of mud!' she shouted. 'Anyway, my mum lets people come and have baths at our place, so there!'

They gaped at her.

'You're joking, Monkey!'

'Phew – must have to get the disinfectant out!'

'Scrape the dirt off the bath with a trowel!'

'Your mother's obviously madder than you, Monkey.'

'When's *she* gonna have her nose pierced, then?'

'What's wrong with people?' Kaz asked her mother later, wiping tears from her cheeks. 'You would think I was waiting outside the primary school gate selling drugs to little kids, the way they treat me! What's wrong with saying we shouldn't build more roads? What's wrong with saying we need more buses and that trains should be cheaper? I don't understand, Mum!'

Her mother was painting with her usual placid concentration. She was working on a card which showed old teddy bears on a shelf, with some leather-bound books behind them. Kaz loved her mother's designs; they reminded her of a time of lost innocence. At last her mother looked up. 'People are afraid, love. What we're saying makes them uncomfortable. It's like they've got two halves to their souls; the green side and the black side. Just now the black side has the upper hand.'

'Sometimes . . .' Kaz began.

'What?'

'Nothing.'

'Were you going to say sometimes you wish you'd never got involved?' Kaz nodded. 'Well, if it wasn't for you none of us would be involved – and I'm glad we are!'

'Are you really?' asked Kaz.

'Yes I am,' said her mother loudly. 'When this road is built . . .'

'But they won't build it, will they?' wailed Kaz.

Her mother sighed. 'Yes, love, they will in the end. They've got all the power, all the money – and the law on their side.'

'What's the point in us fighting, then?'

Her mother put down her brush. 'Look, love, we're getting attention in the national papers. You have to make people ask whether these big roads are the answer, and the only way to make them think is to cause a fuss. Anyway, when it's built people will look at it and realise we were right. In a few years' time it'll be choked with traffic, and there'll be fewer buses even than now, and the trees will be gone for ever. Maybe then people will wake up, and ask why they let it happen.'

'Not much choice, is there?' said Kaz.

'Not really.'

'And at least we've tried to do our bit,' said Kaz.

'You have to,' said her mother. 'After all, you've only got one life, pet, and you might as well use it to stand up for what you believe.'

Kaz jumped up and flung her arms round her mother's neck. 'Oh, Mum – you're so lovely,' she said, loving the warm smell of her mother's skin, which always carried her back into the safety of babyhood.

Ash had become a regular visitor to their house, and although Kaz was now at ease with most people at the Rainbow Camp, and loved Skye especially, Ash was her particular friend. In school Kaz thought about him too much of the time, but the thoughts compensated for her loneliness. She liked his sense of humour, and his thin brown face, and the way he would sit for hours at their old piano, picking out beautiful melancholy tunes.

'Where did you learn?' she asked, amazed by his skill.

'Oh, I went to this posh music school, didn't I? They invited me to play with the best orchestra in the country, but I said I had to save the planet instead!' He burst out laughing when he saw her expression. 'Don't be daft – who'd have taught *me* the piano?' He shifted the mood into something fast and jazzy.

Once she found her mother just sitting in the armchair watching him play. Her eyes were suspiciously bright. Later, when he had gone, Kaz asked her why. She just shook her head and said, 'Some of these young people – especially Ash – they're just lost souls really. I wish I could turn the clock back, and rescue them all, so they'd have a proper chance in life.'

'Nobody ever cared for Ash – before we did,' said Kaz.

'That's not true – he says his family's on the hill, and he's right,' said her mother. 'They'll be his family, most of them anyway – people like Skye and Colonel – long after he's forgotten us.'

'Don't say that!' said Kaz.

'Oh, sweetheart,' said her mother. 'I don't want you getting a major crush on Ash, do you understand?'

Kaz felt her face flame. 'Don't be stupid!' she yelled. 'I mean, Mum, that's a really stupid thing to say!' And she rushed from the room, slamming the door behind her.

Ten

The trees were the important thing now. They were the ramparts of the new hill fort. Fresh recruits arrived each day at the camps, not just the hangers-on, but climbing experts who knew about trees, and how to colonise them. The campaign seemed to move into a different gear. There was a new seriousness in the air. Perhaps it was desperation.

'You'll have to learn to climb,' Ash told Kaz, proudly showing her the harness strapped round his body, with the metal fasteners that would be clipped to ropes in the trees for safety. Kaz shuddered and shook her head. Just the thought of the top branches waving in the breeze, with all that air below . . . made her feel slightly sick.

In three months, despite all the efforts to halt the work, Rowley Construction had made progress on the road. Greenway Lane was now unrecognisable, except for the pocket handkerchief of the Office Camp which clung on there, like a limpet on a rock face. The diggers gouged their way across the foothills of Twybury. Metal fences went up to keep out the protesters . . . Centimetre by centimetre: hedges gone, small trees plucked up with no trouble . . . On and on, a spreading sea of mud, until Twybury Wood was in sight.

'Trees are such a . . . a . . . big symbol,' said Ash, like a war veteran explaining tactics. 'They know that once the trees have gone there's nothing left to fight for. So the sooner they're cut down the better for the developers.'

They were walking down from the Rainbow Camp towards Twybury Wood. Suddenly Kaz stopped. Ahead of her, right at the edge of the clump of trees and overhanging the path, was her oak, which, she believed in her heart, contained the spirit of nature, the Green Man himself.

'My tree!' she cried out, grabbing Ash's arm.

'Yeah?'

'I didn't think it would come up this far!' said Kaz.

'What you on about?'

'The road, silly! It won't spread across to this bit, will it?'

'Course, they're going to take out the whole wood! The road stops over there, but they need to have access, don't they? All the trees will go, but it's OK – they're going to be planting lots of weedy little saplings in neat little rows, to make up for the massacre!'

'They can't cut down my oak,' said Kaz in horror.

'They can – and they will. Unless we stop them,' said Ash grimly. 'I tell you what, Kazzie, I'll make you a promise. *I'll* defend your tree. So help me God.'

He held up his hand, like someone taking an oath in court, and smiled. Then his smile faded, but he went on staring at her, with a curious intensity – as though something had been said that he did not fully understand. They looked at each other in silence for a few moments. Then Ash pulled Kaz to him, and held her tightly, his chin resting on her head.

Kaz thought the din of her heart must deafen them both. She could feel him trembling, like a leaf in a breeze, and knew that she was too. Her face was buried in his T-shirt so she could hardly breathe, but she knew that if she looked up he would kiss her. And whilst a part of her wanted that to happen – so very much – the rest of her was afraid.

'Little Kazzie,' he whispered into her hair.

'Yes?' she mumbled.

'I really like you, you know that, don't you? But you're only a kid, really.'

At that Kaz broke away, her face red. 'I'm not a kid!' she said indignantly. 'And I don't want you to treat me like one!'

He was looking at her with an expression of great sadness. 'Kaz, my last girlfriend was nineteen,' he said.

'Who was talking about girlfriends anyway?' said Kaz, making a superhuman effort to sound light and cool.

'Nobody was, Kazzie,' said Ash. 'I just thought . . .'

'Don't think too much, you'll hurt yourself!' Kaz retorted.

'OK, OK,' he said, twisting his face into a grin.

They walked on in silence. Twybury Wood was a scene of frantic activity. The base camp consisted of a large bender surrounded by chaotic piles of equipment: tarpaulins, plastic sheets, buckets, coils of rope, a sack of potatoes, plastic bags of clothing, and large water carriers. Four or five tree houses had already been built. Hammering filled the air as work progressed on the largest. Parallel ropes passed from tree to tree, and here and there people edged their way across these walkways, attached by harnesses and swaying in the breeze. Kaz felt dizzy just looking at them.

'Are they safe, Ash?' she asked fearfully, glad to have something to talk about.

He clearly felt the same, because he grinned. 'Course they are! Come and meet Mark – he's brilliant. He's a tree person from the Green Network. A serious climber, this guy, I can tell you. He's in charge of the training.'

They walked over to where a man about Kaz's father's age, bearded and thickset, was standing by the base camp, thoughtfully passing a length of old rope through his hands, as though testing it for quality.

When Ash introduced them, Mark did not smile at Kaz. He asked her, with great seriousness, if she was going to live in the trees. When she shook her head he appeared to lose interest, so that she felt young and silly.

'I get sick – I hate heights,' she protested.

He heard the note in her voice, and smiled at last. 'Sorry, love, I get a bit obsessed. We need as many as possible in the trees, see. This is the key to it all. The longer we can hold out, the better.'

'We'll hold out for ever,' said Ash enthusiastically.

'It'll be hard when they bring in the cherrypickers,' said Mark.

'I know that,' said Ash impatiently. 'But we've learnt a lot since last time. I tell you, they won't get us down.'

The older man shook his head. He gazed up at the branches with a look in his eyes that made Kaz shiver – as if he saw things that were invisible – and said, 'Sometimes I think . . . sometimes I reckon it'll take somebody getting killed before they realise what they're doing.'

'Don't say that, man,' whispered Ash.

Mark ran a hand through his beard, and appeared to shake himself back into the present. He looked fierce. 'Whatever happens, we'll put up a good fight.'

'Yeah – right! We'll be ready for them,' said Ash. He threw back his head and yelped a long cry, not of joy, or triumph, but of war.

In the silence that followed, a strange, unexpected gust of wind rippled through the trees, making the branches shake; it seemed to Kaz that the small wood itself was trembling, as she was, at the threat which hung over it. And somewhere deep within her mind she heard the low groan of pain from the hill, echoing through the very ground at her feet. Or was it merely the distant *crump* of the diggers?

Eleven

Kaz was wearing her green and yellow Save Twybury Hill T-shirt when she left the house and hurried down the road to the Office Camp. It was her turn for telephone duty and she did not want to be late. Cars roared past, and vans, and lorries big and small. She found herself brooding that before she had become involved with this protest she had never *thought* about traffic. It was just something you moaned about when it was heavy – a part of life. Now she saw how many cars carried just one person. She felt the vibration from the lorries transporting goods for supermarkets, stores and manufacturers pass right through her body – all necessary, her father said, but all horrible and polluting to Kaz.

Suddenly there was a harsh noise of hooting, which made her jump. A battered old red Ford Cortina sped by, and Kaz had a sense of young faces grinning and making signs . . . then it was gone.

Stupid boys, she thought.

At last she crossed the road and turned into Greenway Lane. At that moment she heard a car behind her, and the tooting and loud laughter. The same Ford Cortina pulled over in front of her. All the doors were thrown open, and four youths jumped out. They stood facing her. Kaz felt her stomach plucked with fear.

'Well, well, well – what have we here?'

'It's a little road protester!'

'Yeah, I've seen her with the crusties. Wonder if she smells too!'

'Go on, Darren – have a sniff!'

'You must be joking! Might catch something!'

In the same second Kaz glimpsed white helmets inside the car and recognised the faces too. She had seen them on the other side of the line. These were four young security guards.

There was nothing fluffy about dealings between the two sides now. The good humour of the early days had evaporated completely; increasingly it seemed as if the guards just came for a punch-up. They appeared to hate the protesters and lost no chance to use violence.

She tried to walk on, but found the way barred. The four men who faced her were boys really; she guessed the oldest could not have been more than twenty. They looked thuggish, with very short hair and big boots, and were grinning at her like a cat grins at its prey.

'Excuse me, please, I want to go past,' she said, in her most polite voice.

'Oh, *excuse me*,' sneered the one they called Darren, mocking her accent.

'She's quite pretty really – you reckon, Tel?' said the tall one.

'Yeah, I like 'em young,' grinned Tel.

'Most of the women up there look like a tree fell on 'em,' said the smaller one.

'With a bit of luck lots of trees'll fall on them!' said Darren, and they all sniggered.

Kaz was furious. 'That's a horrible thing to say!' she shouted. 'Do you want somebody to get killed?' She clenched her fists at her sides.

'Ooohhhh,' said the tall one, pretending to be afraid.

'Watch out, it's angry. It might bite!' said Tel.

'Not if you bite it first,' said Darren. 'You said you like them young. Go on, she looks quite juicy to me.'

Kaz felt sweat trickle down her back. She tried to keep her voice calm, as she held out her hands in front of her, palms upwards, in a gesture of peace.

'Look, I've got no quarrel with you guys, I know you're only doing your job. Come on, just let me go past.'

'Oh, ain't that nice of her – she knows we're only doing our job,' sneered Darren. 'Well, you know what my job is today, little girlie? It's stopping people like you giving people like me a hard time, get it?'

He stepped forward and jabbed a finger in her chest. Kaz shrank back, more afraid than she had ever been in her life.

'Nice T-shirt,' grinned Tel, plucking at her sleeve. He was staring at the design on the front, which showed Twybury Hill, with a big sun rising behind it. But he was also staring at Kaz's breasts.

Kaz felt her face blaze, and she folded her arms tightly for protection.

'Hey – we could do with one of those, stuck up in our hut!' crowed Darren.

'Like those stuffed animal heads!' laughed the tall one.

119

'Wanna be a big game hunter, Tel?' said Darren, nudging him.

'Little game hunter, ya mean!' whispered Tel, throwing down his cigarette and grinding it underfoot.

'Get it off, then, darlin',' said the small one.

'No! Leave me alone!' pleaded Kaz, stepping back. But there was a stone wall behind her, shadowed by a tall hedge, and the four guards were spread around her, so that it was impossible even to run back the way she had come.

'Look – we're gonna leave you alone, as soon as you've given us your T-shirt. Not much to ask, is it? We want something to hang up in our hut, just to prove we caught one of the animals, like. An' you wanna go home to Mummy. So just get it off, and then you can go, OK?'

'No!' shouted Kaz, hunching her shoulders and gripping her own body with her hands.

'Well, I'd better help her off with it then,' grinned Tel, stepping forward.

'Yeah, go on . . . whooo-hooo,' chorused the others.

Kaz felt his hands on her arms, trying to make her unfold them. She ducked her head, cringing back against the wall, paralysed, too frightened even to kick out, tears starting . . .

'GET YOUR HANDS OFF HER!'

There was the sound of running feet. A small head with flying beaded hair butted Tel away. He staggered backwards, cannoning into the tall one. They collapsed in an ungainly heap, swearing loudly. A burly figure in a top hat grasped Darren and swivelled him round into an armlock before he even had time to utter one curse.

'So, you pick on teenage girls, do you?' yelled Colonel, jerking Darren's head back with his free hand. 'Well, why not take on someone your own size?'

'Aaagh!' gurgled the guard.

'You're just cheap fascist bullies!' shrieked Skye, fists flailing at the two youths who lay at her feet. They were too shocked even to fight back. The fourth one tried to run past and escape, but he had not reckoned on Colonel's speed. His spare hand shot out and grabbed the smaller guard by the arm. The momentum of his flight made him crash around, straight into Darren – *clunk*.

Both started to struggle then, but Colonel held them with a strength that amazed Kaz.

'Listen, if I ever see you lot go anywhere near Kaz or any of the girls on the protest I shall personally rip your arms off – is that understood? IS IT?'

As he spoke he tightened his grip on both, making them groan. Tel put a hand out to raise himself, but Skye was too quick for him; she kicked it away, so that he collapsed again. His friend was too sensible to move; he just lay there, gawping at Skye, unable to believe that this little gypsy-like creature with beaded hair and rainbow clothes had dared to land a punch on him.

Darren and the other one looked terrified now, grunting as Colonel increased the armlocks. At last Darren gurgled, 'OK, mate – OK,' and Colonel released his hold so quickly both guards staggered.

Skye darted to the car and plucked a couple of helmets from the rear window shelf. She put one on, and threw the other one to Colonel.

He took off his top hat and donned the security helmet, looking stranger than ever – feather-trimmed dreadlocks and heavily silvered ears sticking out beneath the white plastic. He used his own hat to sweep to the ground in a mocking bow at the guards.

Relief made Kaz's tears flow freely. When he heard her sobbing, Colonel's face went dark again. 'I changed my mind,' he hissed. 'If I hear any of you lot have done anything like this again, I won't rip your arms off, I'll rip your *heads* off – OK?'

The guards retreated to the car. By the driver's door Darren turned, and Kaz saw through the mist that he was looking at Colonel with a sort of awe.

'I thought your lot was always on about peace and love and all that hippy rubbish,' he said. 'So how come you learnt an armlock like that?'

'In the Falklands War, matey,' said Colonel. 'I was a squaddie fighting for me country – just like I'm doing now! So . . . *don't* mess with me. Do yourselves a favour, friend, and put the word around!'

Kaz's eardrum was tortured by Skye's yip of triumph.

When the sound of the red car died away, Kaz leant on Skye, and Colonel put an arm round them both. Skye used a corner of her sleeve to wipe Kaz's face.

'I was so scared,' sniffed Kaz. 'If you hadn't come along . . .'

'Don't even think about it,' said Colonel.

'Was that true? Did you really fight in the Falklands War?'

'Yeah,' growled Colonel. 'But don't you go spreading it about. My army past isn't something I'm particularly proud of.'

'He's so daft,' giggled Skye, 'because he thinks people don't know. And his nickname's Colonel and he organises everyone!'

'Do you want us to take you home, pet?' Colonel asked, ignoring his girlfriend's teasing.

Kaz longed for the safety of her home. But she said flatly, 'I'm supposed to be on telephone duty.'

'That's my girl!' said Skye. 'The fight goes on, despite apes like that lot.'

'They'll never give you any hassle again,' growled Colonel.

He went to pick up the two carrier bags of shopping they had abandoned by the roadside. The three of them continued along Greenway Lane to the point where the chaos began. They stood silently for a few minutes, viewing the war zone.

Hard-core temporary road surface was flanked by tall metal fencing. There were piles of smoking vegetation, and mini-mountains of bricks. Away to the left the new road slunk its way up and along the foothills of Twybury; down to the right it broadened out into a vast, excavated gully that would be crossed, in time, by concrete bridges over the four-lane highway. Down that way too, in the distance, was the main works site, where all the machinery was kept and where the construction firm had all its offices. A Land-Rover full of senior security guards was parked about ten metres from where Skye, Colonel and Kaz stood. Near them was a van bearing the logo of a television company. The whole area was swarming with vehicles, guards and people.

The tiny Office Camp sat in the middle of all this, facing eviction but clinging cheekily to existence. Kaz and the other two ignored the hostile stares of the men in the Land-Rover and walked on. But just as they drew level to the Land-Rover Kaz became aware of a video camera trained on them from the back, following their every move.

'They're filming us!' she whispered to Colonel, clutching his arm.

He shrugged. 'Yeah, that's Wray's Security. They always use them.'

'What for?'

'To make a record of everybody involved in the protest, of course – for later use. They press charges against protesters. Hold them responsible for delaying the work – all kinds of legal stuff like that. All on *their* terms, of course.'

Skye said, 'They've got enough footage of us, man, to put up for the Oscars!'

Both of them were still wearing the white plastic security helmets. Colonel turned to face the Land-Rover and the camera. He took off the helmet and held it out as a beggar might hold out a hat, and shouted, 'Got any change, mister?'

The doors of the vehicle opened, and five men got out. These were all men in their thirties and forties, and the only one who had the mean and thuggish look of Kaz's persecutors was the one with the camera. He wore a spotted blue bandana under his white helmet and went on filming all the time.

The oldest, wearing a green hat over his greying hair, came across to them with a pleasant smile on his face.

'Hello, Skye – how're you doing today?' he said.

'Oh fine, Jim!' she replied airily, to Kaz's amazement.

'Been busy?'

124

'We'll be busy as long as you're here.'

'Goes the same the other way around,' he smiled.

'Ah, but just think how much nicer it would be if you all gave up and went home, and let the earth grow back,' she replied in a gentle teasing voice. 'You can't want all this, Greenhat Jim. You're a local man, aren't you? And haven't you got grandchildren? This can't be the world you want for them.'

Jim shrugged and said quietly, 'To tell you the truth, love, I don't much go for it. But what can you do? It's progress, isn't it? And since they've got the go-ahead to build it, we're here to see they can go about their lawful business. It's as simple as that.'

'Progress!' spluttered Kaz.

'And while we're on the subject of the law . . .'

'You were, we weren't,' Colonel interrupted.

' . . . those helmets you're both wearing are the property of Rowley Construction. So I'd like to know where you got them, if you don't mind.'

'Oh, we were just bringing them back to you,' said Skye innocently. 'Four of your nice young men were so busy harassing this child they left their car door open. I mean, *anyone* could have stolen these! They could have got into *completely* the wrong hands! Lucky we were there to pick them up and keep them nice and safe. Here!'

With exaggerated care she took the helmet off, and removed Colonel's as if it were the coronation crown. Then, holding the plastic hats one in each hand, upside down like bowls, she made a little bow as she handed them over.

'May God bless them and all who fight in them,' Colonel intoned.

Kaz giggled, and Jim could not help smiling either. The other three men looked relaxed and amused, but the man with the video camera had a stony face. Skye pranced over to the lens, struck a glamour pose with her hair swept up in one hand and said, in a silly American accent, 'I wanna be a star! Don't you think I'm bee-autiful?'

The Wray's Security man stopped filming, looked her up and down contemptuously, and muttered, 'I wouldn't say so.'

'Ah, but *I* would, Bandana!' said Colonel, without smiling, as if daring the man to be rude again. 'Come on, girls, we got more important things to do than talk to this lot.'

'Yeah, like living on state handouts, causing trouble,' said the man, spitting on the ground.

'OK, OK, back in the van,' said Jim, giving him a warning look. The Land-Rover doors slammed, and the men drove off.

Maria was standing by the caravan, giving a television interview. 'Who are they?' whispered Kaz.

'They're a documentary crew – making a short film about the road. Good, isn't it?' replied Skye.

The reporter was a young woman with a carefully made-up face, hair in a sleek short bob, and the kind of clothes that had never before been seen on a protest site. Her face was set into an expression of careful concern. She asked Maria what was the general plan for the protest, and her tone was as smooth as honey.

'Do you *really* think you've got any chance of stopping this road, Maria?'

'Of course we have! We'll fight them every inch of the way,' she replied.

'When you say "fight", what do you mean?'

'Isn't it obvious? We're fighting against the destruction of the countryside we love, and we're fighting for the things we believe in – better public transport, clean air for children to breathe – all the things I've told you about already!'

'And do you think anything goes – to achieve those ends?'

'Yes!'

'Including . . . breaking the law?'

'Er . . . yes,' said Maria, growing very red. She hesitated, and the reporter waited.

Then Maria blurted, 'I mean, they're breaking the laws of nature doing this, so . . .'

'It doesn't matter if you break the law to fight them?' asked the neutral voice.

'No – it doesn't!'

'Thank you very much.'

'Cut,' said the woman with the clipboard.

'I hope you won't use that last bit,' mumbled Maria, looking worried. 'I don't want to look – you know – too wild, or anything.'

'You were great, dear,' said the reporter, absent-mindedly. 'Now, Alix, don't we need to film some action?'

The woman with the clipboard glanced round to where Skye, Colonel and Kaz were standing watching, with a mixed group of about twenty people from the hill camp and local protesters. 'What about it?' she said, in a bossy tone.

'What about what?' asked Colonel.

'Direct action. We need some shots.'

'We're not performing animals,' said Colonel angrily.

Skye laid a hand on his arm. 'Don't bother getting worked up. Look, let's just do what we usually do and it doesn't matter if they film it. With a bit of luck they'll get the guards' usual violence, and then people will know what it's like.'

He hesitated for a moment, shrugged – then broke into a run towards the digger. Everyone else followed. Skye gave out her strange wild yips, as she threw herself against the first guard she met like a small wave. He pushed her back easily. But there were only six or seven guards by the digger, and they were easily out-manoeuvred. It took two to hold back Colonel, and Skye, Maria and some of the other women were extraordinarily fast. Kaz watched as they darted past the guards and threw themselves on the ground in a line in front of the digger, which had to stop.

Kaz was standing by the television crew, and heard the director say, 'This is great!' She felt uneasy, as if she was just a voyeur on the sidelines, with no commitment to anything at all.

For a few minutes everything was peaceful. A guard was on the phone calling for reinforcements. The others stood smoking, knowing they could do nothing without help. The digger driver looked bored. Then there was the sound of an engine and the Land-Rover returned. At the same time a line of about twenty-five security guards came running from the direction of Rowley's main compound. The guards nearby grinned, and threw away their cigarettes. One thickset young man yelled at the protesters, 'Now we'll have you!'

'Shut up, Meathead,' a protester shouted back.

'Why don't you scum go and get yourselves jobs?' he snarled.

Kaz could bear to stay still no longer. She ran.

'Go for it, Kaz!' shouted Colonel.

She saw the outstretched arms of a guard, taken by surprise, but swerved to avoid him. In a minute she had flung herself on to the line. Skye and the person next to her made a space, then they all linked arms tightly again, waiting to be moved.

The unwritten rule was that two guards had to move each protester, without using unnecessary force. In return the protesters would make no attempt to struggle, just make their bodies a dead weight that was hard to move. The ritual was played out every day, but recently the security firm had been losing patience. Some of the guards were very rough. Kaz knew that, and her heart thumped. 'Hold on to me as tightly as you can,' whispered Skye.

The new wave of guards was upon them like a line of troops. Kaz found herself in the middle of chaos, as hands reached out, and people screamed. There was a pushing and a shoving, a crushing and a crashing, a tangle of arms and legs as some guards lost their balance, and others lost their tempers.

Kaz saw Maria, who was on the end of the line, hauled off by her arms and legs. A man yelled as Meathead jerked his head back viciously by his long hair. A heavy workboot crushed Kaz's foot, so that she cried out in pain, and nearly let go of Skye.

'Watch it!' shouted Skye angrily, as the guard, a huge man with a moustache, ignored what he had done, and reached out to disentangle them. Kaz felt the man on the other side of her let go as he was hauled off. She wrapped her other arm round Skye, so that they were face to face.

'Come on, you . . .'

'Leave . . . me . . . alone,' Kaz panted, as she felt her fingers being lifted. 'Owwww!'

She kicked out sharply, forgetting the rules. Her boot connected with the man's shin, and he cried out in pain. As he jerked back his head his helmet fell off. That was the final straw. His face went scarlet with rage.

'Right, you little . . .'

She and Skye were surrounded. Red hot pain shot up her arm as her fingers were bent back, and her hands were torn away from Skye. Her foot was crushed again. She flopped back on to the ground, expecting another guard to come behind and lift her carefully, as they were supposed to do. But the guard with the moustache grasped her ankles and pulled her along. Her head bumped on the ground. She felt her T-shirt dragged up, and desperately used her hand to hold the front down. But her back scraped along the stony soil. All the time the screaming and shouting was in her ears . . .

Yet there was a part of her that stood outside, and rose above the anger, pain and fear. She could see the mottled blue, white and grey of the sky above, and it was as if everything was in slow motion – the noise receding, the people tiny – as her spirit rose up above the chaos.

She thought she heard the Green Man roar, *What are you doing? What are you doing? What are you doing?* as he felt her pain.

'What are you doing?' yelled Colonel, breaking free and rushing over. The guard let her go, letting her legs crash down, and retreated to his friend before Colonel reached them. Kaz lay shocked for a moment, before Colonel helped her to her feet.

'Yeah, you pick on little girls, don't you?' he shouted to the line of guards.

'Tell them to stay at home, then!' came the reply.

Panting and dishevelled, Skye ran across to where Jim was standing with the other senior men by the Land-Rover.

'Did you see that? Did you see that?' she shouted, almost in tears.

'See what?' he said.

'What he did to that girl!'

'All I saw was people trying to disrupt the lawful building of this road,' he said shortly, and turned away.

'Bandana' thrust the video camera in Skye's face, grinning broadly. 'You got dirt on your ugly little face,' he sneered.

Kaz limped to the caravan step and sat down. Her back, head and legs hurt badly. Dispirited the tattered little batallion of protesters dragged themselves to sit by the campfire behind the caravan. Colonel went and put his arms round Skye, and they stood, not moving, as if giving each other strength.

'That was great stuff!' said the television director enthusiastically, as the digger resumed its maddeningly monotonous *crump, crump, crump*, and Kaz could no longer see the scene for tears.

Twelve

'They trick you into saying things you don't mean,' said Maria miserably. She pulled at her fat red plait so hard it must have hurt. 'I mean, all it takes is for me to be saying it doesn't matter if we break the law, and then they can all point the finger and say, yeah, they're the ones doing all the wilful damage.'

'So what?' said Dougie.

'You know so what!' said Skye, impatiently. 'It's no good if all those people in their houses think we're a bunch of criminals, is it? Hey look, Maria, maybe they won't use it . . .'

'Oh, they will,' said Colonel.

The work always stopped at one on Saturdays; the peace was welcome. Despite the warmth of the day they all sat round the fire behind the caravan, for comfort. Ash and a group of others had come down from the hill, feeling guilty about missing the action. So much time and energy was being concentrated now on establishing the tree colony that there were rarely enough people at the Office Camp. He heard what had happened to Kaz and hugged her.

'Look at it this way, you're a real eco-warrior now,' he grinned.

Hearing him, Kaz decided not to mind her bruises. She looked around the large circle of faces, and thought how extraordinary it was that so many utterly different people could be brought together. There was a lady in her seventies called Cynthia, who walked with a stick, sitting with her daughter and granddaughter, talking to a man with a shaven head. Famous Janey Morgan was deep in conversation with Harmony, a tall, big-boned woman with severely cropped hair who had arrived to join the tree people. She spent much time making exquisite little drawings of trees, with quotations and messages around them. Mark, the climber, sat whittling at a stick with his knife and saying little. There were others, come from near and afar, some of whom Kaz knew and liked, others who intimidated her.

Kaz reached out and patted Maria on the shoulder. 'Honestly, it'll be fine. You were brilliant. You're always brilliant,' she said.

'Thanks, Kazzie – and you're not so bad yourself. Did you all see her? The way she ran?'

'I thought that hulk was going to explode when she kicked him,' giggled Skye.

'Proper little fighter!' laughed Colonel.

'Keep away from me, d-don't hurt me, please,' stammered Ash, holding up his hands for mercy and cringing away in mock terror.

'Me? I'm ultra-fluffy!' protested Kaz.

Skye called them to order. This was supposed to be a strategy meeting. 'Right!' she yelled, rattling a stick on a tin can. 'We got to talk about tomorrow. Maria's made a suggestion . . . go on, tell them, Maria.'

She stood up. 'Well, there's been all this stuff in the paper about bits of sabotage here and there, and that pit they found, with spikes in it . . . OK, so I'm proposing a peaceful demonstration, top secret, for tomorrow. We'll get in touch with all our supporters, then meet here at two. It's a quiet walk down to Rowley's compound, and we'll bring lots of ribbons, coloured paper, and things like that – greenery too, if you like – and decorate their metal fence. Then we'll just stand in a silent vigil along the fence, with banners demanding that the earth be left in peace. No noise. No action – see?'

She sat down. There was a little flurry of enthusiasm, then Dougie said flatly, 'We couldn't do any action even if we wanted, since – haven't ye noticed? – they don't work on a Sunday.'

'You know what I meant,' said Maria sharply.

'It's important they don't find out, because then there'll be police there, and right away it looks like trouble,' said Skye.

'Och, I don't see the point – decoratin' a *fence*,' said Dougie, swigging at some cider.

'Public relations, man!' said Ash.

'Stuff yer public relations,' was the reply. There was an uncomfortable silence.

Maria's face was scarlet, and her look should have turned the Scot to stone.

'I think it's a great idea,' said Kaz brightly.

'I'll make some banners tonight,' said Janey Morgan.

'OK – I'll do them with you,' said Harmony. And so it was settled.

When Kaz arrived home she found, to her relief, that her parents were busy gardening. She waved so that they knew she was back and rushed upstairs to wash and change. Then she went back downstairs, walking slowly, because her whole body ached.

Jamie had newspapers all over the dining-table. He was studying the instruction booklet for his chemistry set so keenly that he did not notice Kaz come in.

'How's the mad scientist today?'

Her brother's glasses glinted, catching the light as he looked up, so that for a second Kaz could not see his eyes.

'Busy!' he said. 'Why are you moving all funny?'

'Shhh, don't tell them. I got a bit bruised – but it's a secret, OK? Just look . . .' She pulled up her T-shirt at the back and showed him the scratches. Then she told him what had happened that morning, and this time she could see his eyes widen with a mixture of excitement, fear and admiration.

'He might have really hurt you!' he cried. 'And if he had I'd have . . . I'd have . . . I'd have found him and really shown him!'

Kaz smiled. 'Yes, oh Superjampot, but I have to inform you he was about six foot two and built like an elephant's bottom. Looked like an elephant's bottom, too!'

'Phooh,' said Jamie, holding his nose, and they both laughed.

When her parents came in from the garden Kaz was lolling in front of the television.

'It's a beautiful evening, you vegetable,' called her mother. 'Come outside and see what we've been doing. My pots are going to look wonderful.'

'Oh, I'll go out later,' moaned Kaz, not wanting her mother to see her move. She always noticed everything.

Sure enough, her mother sat down beside her and said, 'Where did you get that bruise on your arm?'

'Oh, I tripped over,' said Kaz. 'Maria and them – they were sorting out the camp, and I was helping move some stuff – people had brought lots of food supplies in, and there was no room for it, and then some new people arrived and there was a bit of chaos . . . and I fell over. My clothes got a bit dirty too – I'm sorry, Mum.'

It sounded lame, and Kaz knew it. Her mother just laid a finger on the black and yellow bruise that spread over Kaz's forearm, then reached for her other hand, where red marks ringed her wrist by the rainbow bracelet.

'Mmm,' she said. 'That's all right.' She gave Kaz that look which said she was deeply suspicious.

At teatime Kaz told them all about the plan for Sunday, and announced that she would, of course, be going on the march.

Her father sighed. 'What *is* the point of it? Honestly, love, I think your time would be better spent doing some schoolwork.'

'I'll do it in the morning!' snapped Kaz. 'Unless you want to get your whip out and chain me to my desk and make me work all day. Wouldn't surprise me at all!'

'Kaz . . .' warned her mother.

'Well, it just gets on my nerves the way people keep asking the point of things! What's the point of protesting against this road? What's the point of breathing?'

'To keep you alive,' said her father dryly.

'Yes, well, the road protest's about staying alive too! If we don't have the guts to keep saying something is WRONG – even if the world doesn't listen and even if it goes right on as it was – then we might as well stop breathing!'

'We're all on the same side, darling,' said her mother gently.

'Yeah, well sometimes he doesn't sound as if he is,' muttered Kaz.

'Sometimes, Kaz, you only choose to hear what you want to hear,' said her father wearily.

There was a silence, during which her mother looked worried and her father looked pained. Kaz stared at her sandwich.

Then Jamie said, 'Mum? Dad? I want to go on the march with Kaz.'

'Oh,' said their mother.

'No,' said their father.

'Great!' said Kaz.

To Kaz's surprise, it did not take her very long to convince her parents. She told them again that this was to be a peaceful walk, that Janey Morgan was making banners, that it would be fun decorating the fence around Rowley's compound on a sunny Sunday afternoon when there were hardly any guards around and the atmosphere would be carnival, not confrontation.

'*Please* let me go with Kaz!' said Jamie.

'Well . . . I don't see that it will do any harm,' said their father slowly. 'Whether it does any good is another matter.'

'He wants to feel involved, Dad. He cares about it!' said Kaz.

'I know.'

'Why don't you both come too?' said Kaz. 'We'll make it a family outing!'

Her mother laughed, relieved the atmosphere had lightened. 'Oh, I gave up marches in the seventies, love! We'll get on with decorating the garden, and you can go and decorate a fence. Tell you what, I'll get out lots of crêpe paper and ribbons for you to use. That's my bit!'

These days, Kaz was content to spend the evenings at home. That night she went to bed early to read the book her father had recommended – *Cry the Beloved Country*, by a South African writer, Alan Paton. At first she had not liked it; she persevered simply because her dad had looked hurt seeing it face down, open at page five and gathering dust. There were bits she skipped, but gradually the story of apartheid in South Africa had gripped her. She had sat with her parents when Nelson Mandela was released, after years and years in prison, and though she had not fully understood then, she had been moved by the tears in her mother's eyes. This novel was the story behind it all, and the strange thing was, she found increasing relevance to her own life. She took a pencil and marked a line next to one passage:

> *Cry, the beloved country, for the unborn child that is the inheritor of our fear. Let him not love the earth too deeply, let him not laugh too gladly when the water runs through his fingers, nor stand too silent when the setting sun makes red the veldt with fire. Let him not be too moved when the birds of his land are*

singing, nor give his heart to a mountain or valley. For fear will
rob him of all if he gives too much.

She stood by her bedroom window gazing out at the dark garden. She could hear the wind in the trees, and imagined them all, sleeping in their benders or the tree houses. Ash would be in his tree house . . . she wondered what he dreamt of, there amongst the young oak leaves, in the chilly darkness. Did he ever think of his mother, and that terrible stepfather? Of course he did. Tears came to Kaz's eyes and she clenched her fists, wanting to kill them. How could they treat a child like that? For that matter, in South Africa how could they treat a whole race like that? No wonder you looked out of your window and heard the whole earth howling.

On Sunday afternoon Kaz set off promptly after lunch, with Jamie in tow. Jamie carried a plastic bag full of streamers of crêpe paper and some ivy from the garden wall. Soon they joined groups of people, heading for the Office Camp. As soon as he spotted them, Ash jumped up from the caravan step and came striding over.

'All right, mate?' was his surprised greeting, when he saw Jamie.

'He really wanted to come. Mum and Dad only let him come because I told them it's going to be a peaceful march.'

'When are we starting off, Ash? Will it be soon?' Jamie asked, hopping from one foot to the other, then taking off his glasses to rub them on his sleeve. Kaz looked at her brother fondly.

Ash grinned and told him the procession would set off in about ten minutes' time, leaving the Office Camp and walking slowly down across the wasteland towards the Rowley compound on the Western Road.

Janey Morgan and Harmony were distributing banners, decorated with doves and leaves and rainbows, and bearing slogans like, HEAL THE EARTH; HEAL THE PEOPLE, PEACEFUL PEOPLE; PEACEFUL PROTEST; LOVE THE MOTHER EARTH. Kaz seized one to carry. The site was like an ants' nest; the tiny area was thronged with about seventy local supporters, together with around fifty people from the camps.

Ash put an arm round Kaz and pulled her close in a hug which left her breathless. 'You're feeling good, aren't you, Kaz?' he said.

She nodded, not minding that her cheeks were pink. He added, 'I can tell, see – because you *look* so fantastic!' He pulled playfully at one of her tiny plaits, and she jerked her head away, feeling dizzy.

'*You* look too straight, Ash – you should have painted up!' was all she could say.

The procession started off, headed by a huge green caterpillar made of cardboard, papier-mâché and wire, beneath which six sets of legs kept time. Skye and Colonel had painted their faces white and decorated themselves fantastically with crowns of leaves and flowers; in fact everybody seemed to have made an effort to dress up for the event. Small children chased each other. Some people were even dancing as drum and tin whistle set the pace. It was a party on the move.

'Keep with me, Jamie,' called Kaz.

'OK – so who's being straight now?' teased Ash.

'Anybody'd think I was a little kid,' grumbled Jamie, swinging the

141

plastic bag so that it hit her. But his crossness was not real; and the plastic bag was filled with paper and leaves . . . Nothing, thought Kaz, could mar the magic of the day.

The leisurely pace meant that it took them about thirty-five minutes to come within sight of Rowley's compound. A crane dominated the valley; beneath it tall chain metal fences lined the road, protecting the rows of yellow diggers, the other equipment and the sprawl of office Portakabins. The vast compound had once been water meadows which stretched down from the road to the river. When the dual carriageway was finished this would be the site of the split-level roundabout linking the old roads with the new, and carrying the traffic south of Seaston.

The procession stopped abruptly, so that Kaz bumped into the person in front of her. The whistles and drums stopped.

'What's happening?' piped Jamie.

An eerie silence enfolded them for a few moments. It was broken by cries of astonishment that turned swiftly to anger.

'I can't see!' wailed Kaz.

'What's happening?' cried Jamie again.

'How would I know? I'm not a giant!' snapped Kaz.

Ash was dodging, craning his neck, and as the crowd of people fanned out, he gaped with amazement and horror.

'The place is swarming with security guards – and police!' he said.

'How come? Why?' breathed Kaz.

'Come on!' said Ash, grabbing Kaz's hand and starting to worm his way to the front.

'Jamie! Follow us!' she yelled.

At the front of the procession Mark, Skye, Colonel and Janey Morgan stood arguing with a police inspector. A long line of security guards stood guarding the wire fence and gates of Rowley Construction and they in their turn seemed to be guarded by five or six policemen.

'Why won't you let us near?' asked Janey Morgan, controlling her indignation. Her voice was middle-aged and middle class, and the police officer was respectful.

'Mrs Morgan, we were advised there was likely to be a breach of the peace, so . . .'

'But this is a peaceful procession! All we want to do is decorate the fence!' came from Skye.

'I'm sorry, we can't allow you near. That fence is the property of Rowley Construction,' said the policeman patiently.

'Yeah, and whose side are you on?' asked Colonel bitterly.

'We don't take sides, we are just here to see that the law isn't broken,' said the policeman.

'How on earth did they know we were coming?' whispered Kaz to Ash. He shook his head, and the face he turned towards her was dark with rage.

Now Mark was attempting to reason with the policeman. 'Look, Inspector, couldn't a couple of the little kids just go through and tie one of their banners to the fence? It wouldn't do anybody any harm, and it'll make them happy.'

'Yes, and we'll just make a line along the roadside, and hold our peaceful vigil like we planned,' added Skye.

Several of the security guards were sniggering openly. From behind

143

them Jim appeared. He stood by the inspector, who turned and whispered in his ear. It was obvious the policeman thought that Mark's request was quite reasonable, but the senior security man shook his head.

There was a murmuring from the crowd. Somebody passed in a car and made hostile, jeering noises. Nearly every guard was grinning now. All the time three employees of Wray's Security moved their camcorders to and fro, to and fro over the faces in the crowd.

'Sorry,' said the inspector. He did, in fact, look genuinely regretful. 'I think the best thing would be for everybody to go home.'

'We've got a right to protest!'

'We're not hurting anybody!'

'What happened to freedom?'

The crowd swarmed about with increasing restiveness. Suddenly remembering Jamie, Kaz looked around desperately for her brother, but could not see him anywhere. She was about to tell Ash when something struck her shoulder, and she was pushed aside so roughly she almost fell. Somebody was storming through to the front like a whirlwind, shoving people aside, shouting terrible abuse. She caught a glimpse of heavy blond dreadlocks and burly shoulders . . . Dougie. He was up at the front, screaming like a madman.

'We don't have to put up with this – DO WE?' he yelled.

There were answering screams of 'No,' and 'Fascists!' from all around. But Colonel and Mark each laid a hand on Dougie, to try to calm him down.

'Chill!' hissed Colonel.

'Keep it down, OK?' warned Mark.

'*I say we should TAKE 'em*!' screamed Dougie.

'NO!' shouted Skye and Janey Morgan. But it was too late. Dougie stormed his way through the guards, taking them by surprise. He was shinning up over the fence before anyone could reach him. A hand reached up for his foot, but his heavy boot sent the guard flying, so that he crashed back into his mates, and they swore.

Now Dougie was clinging to the top of the fence, screeching, 'Come on! Come on!' Other men began to run about, throwing guards and police into a panic. As if from nowhere a press photographer appeared behind the cordon of guards, dancing about, and snapping all the time. By now Dougie had dropped down inside the compound and had grasped the fence with both hands, shaking it furiously, so that it made a jingling din that was as high and hysterical as his screaming. 'Come on! We can tear down the fence! ALL OF YE – COME ON!'

It takes seconds for the mood of a crowd to change. Older women called out, 'NO!' and 'Keep calm!'

Mark was shouting, 'Fluffy! Keep it fluffy – remember?'

Skye was darting here and there like a tiny insect, waving her hands and trying to quieten people down. But Dougie's cries were the alarms of war. As guards from inside the compound rushed up to him, and pulled him to the ground in a flurry of fists, the crowd's growl of rage turned into a roar – and there was chaos.

Banners preaching peace and love fell to the ground. Children screamed. A policeman's helmet was knocked off. A man in a black, sleeveless leather jerkin tried to climb the fence. As the vast bulk of the procession attempted to turn back and leave the trouble behind, others were pushing forward, causing a log-jam. Cars screeched to a halt to avoid panicking people . . .

Kaz tried desperately to cling to Ash, but he was pushed away by the movement of the crowd. She screamed his name, but he took no notice – perhaps he did not hear. He seemed to be rushing for the fence too . . . and Kaz's heart was filled with dread. Terrified she looked around for her brother, but all she could see were flailing arms and legs. Her cries of, 'Jamie! Jamie!' were lost in the screams and shouts.

'Keep it calm!'

The earth is our mother, and we will take care of her . . .

'We're about peace, not violence!'

'Get the fence! Get the fence!'

'Fascists! Police state!'

'Don't rise to them! Don't be the same as them!'

'*Jamie!*'

Kaz glimpsed him between the legs. And as she struggled to push her way towards her brother it all seemed to happen in slow motion. The people around him were all trying to push their way back, but Jamie was paralysed, looking around in a panic for Kaz. He seemed to sway in the press of bodies, then fall. Kaz saw him crash to the ground, and the little shiny arc his glasses made as they flew through the air. A foot smashed them into splinters, the very second that Jamie's forehead struck the kerb. Kaz felt both a crashing and breaking inside her chest.

'*Jamie!*'

Ash reached him first, coming out of nowhere to crouch over the boy's still body. People stood back. Calm seemed to swoop down like a bird and silence the screams in that part of the crowd. And when Kaz reached her brother the first thing she noticed, with a little cry of anguish, was that he still clutched his plastic bag full of ivy leaves and streamers of multicoloured crêpe paper.

Thirteen

'It wasn't . . . meant to be like that,' sniffed Skye.

'It never is,' said Kaz's father coldly, his eyes narrow.

'Look – you have to understand that it wasn't anybody's fault. Especially not Kaz's,' said Mark.

Watching in dumb misery, Kaz saw that Mark's voice was most persuasive. Exhausted from crying, bruised, depressed and afraid, she was glad he was there, on her side.

'She promised me she'd look after him. She gave me her word,' said her father grimly.

'None of us could have known. It was gonna be so . . . beautiful,' said Ash quietly.

'Huh, a beautiful riot!' snorted Kaz's father.

'None of us wanted it that way,' said Mark with quiet dignity. 'And I know you know that really.'

'Well, somebody wanted it that way,' he replied.

'Who tipped them off? How did they know?' asked Ash helplessly.

'Maria and I think the office phone is bugged,' said Skye.

'Yes, but . . .'

'Could have been anybody,' said Skye unhappily. 'That's the trouble – everybody's got their own idea of how we should play it.'

'Exactly. And that's where the irresponsibility comes in,' said Kaz's father angrily.

Her mother came into the room. Her face was white and tired, but she smiled. 'He'll be fine,' she said. 'I've put a dressing on his head, and he's stopped shaking. It was just a shock. He'll sleep well, and tomorrow he'll have a sore head, but he'll survive.'

Kaz burst into tears again. 'Its – all – my – fault,' she sobbed. 'I should . . . I should . . . I should . . .'

'Hey,' said Mark, 'how could you have known that was going to happen? You couldn't hold his hand like he was a little kid, Kaz!'

'It was all that Dougie's fault – I hate him,' cried Kaz.

'Oh, he's all right really. He just loses it from time to time,' said Mark.

'He's *not* all right!' said Kaz's father crossly. 'That's one of the problems with you people – you won't come out and criticise each other. You won't make a judgement! Well, you have to make judgements in this life! You have to see when something, or somebody, is just plain wrong.'

'Dougie . . . he's got a lot of problems,' Skye persisted stubbornly.

'Yeah, and he makes a lot of problems,' said Ash.

'He's been working hard, and he's a good climber,' shrugged Mark.

Kaz's father clicked his tongue with irritation. There was an uncomfortable silence. Kaz wished Mark and Skye had not tried to defend Dougie. As far as she was concerned it was his fault Jamie was very nearly concussed.

'I'm . . . I'm . . . s-s-sorry, Dad,' she sniffed.

Her father looked at her. He knew in his heart that she could not be blamed, and he hated to see her so miserable. Besides, his son was safely tucked up in bed . . . He threw out an arm and said, 'All right, missy – come here!' It took a second for Kaz to perch on her father's lap, one arm round his neck. In that instant she almost wanted to suck her thumb.

When she looked around the room she saw Mark, Skye and her mother smiling broadly with relief. But on Ash's face was an expression she could not fathom. Was it envy and wistfulness that made him stand up suddenly, and say it was time to go?

The following day's *Solchester Echo* carried a huge front page picture of ugly, enraged protesters, with flying fists and dreadlocks, a policeman looking young and frightened without his helmet, and the headline, *PEACEFUL PROTEST*? Kaz arrived home from school to find Jamie and her mother studying it indignantly.

'It's just not fair – they don't tell the *truth*!' moaned Jamie, looking very young and vulnerable without his glasses, a large pink plaster on his forehead.

To Kaz's surprise her mother wrote to the paper making the point that the presence of the police and security guards that Sunday had simply served to turn a peaceful celebration into a confrontation. Following that there was a spate of letters agreeing and disagreeing with her. Some of the letters were very nasty. Stung by one insult, she wrote again, saying that many local people were proud to count some of the protesters as their friends, and were grateful to them for their courage. Kaz felt proud of her mother – even though it made her isolation in school much worse.

'Your mother's as bad as you,' sneered Debbie Mansfield.

'Who cares about a few stupid old trees anyway?' said Debbie's friend Jackie, who happened to live in Seaston.

'My dad says they'll clear all the hippies off the hill pretty soon, and good riddance,' said another of the gang.

'Why don't you *say* anything, Armstrong?' jeered Debbie, grabbing Kaz by the arm and digging her fingers into her flesh. Kaz took a deep breath, determined not to be goaded.

'Oh, you know me,' she drawled, 'I'm just into *peace*.' She looked down pointedly at the other girl's hand. Debbie removed it – with reluctance – and Kaz just turned away. As usual Sally and Chris said and did nothing.

Fourteen

June came with a gust of bitterly cold wind and leaden skies. The *Solchester Echo* reported the lowest temperatures for fifty years. The shop windows in Solchester were full of floral dresses in pastel colours, shorts and swimsuits, whilst people scurried past, huddled beneath their umbrellas.

Jamie mooched about the house, moaning that he could not go out, or skulked in his bedroom with his chemistry set. Sometimes Kaz felt she did not know her little brother any more. Jamie started to act very strangely. It was Kaz who noticed it first, although soon her mother asked if she noticed anything different about her brother.

'Like what?' Kaz asked.

'Well, he's much moodier than he used to be . . . almost rude to me sometimes. It's not like him.'

'All kids are rude to their mothers,' laughed Kaz. 'Sorry, Mum!'

'Oh, you know what I mean. What do you think?'

'Well,' said Kaz, serious again, 'he acts like . . . he's somebody with a secret.'

'What secret could he possibly have?'

'I dunno,' shrugged Kaz. 'Maybe it's just the road.'

'Like the rest of us,' sighed her mother.

The camps had turned into swamps. At the Rainbow Camp water poured off the hill and into the benders, and no fire would stay lit. At least the people in the trees were off the muddy ground. But rain dripped off Ash's plastic roof and soaked his sleeping-bag, and most of the others slept in the same damp and chilly conditions. It was miserable. Kaz's mother turned out cupboards and drawers to find old socks and sweaters and blankets, and telephoned all of her friends for more of the same. She collected food too, and so did many other local people – but despite all these efforts morale was very low. And all the time the diggers went on working, and the brown scar crept closer and closer to Twybury Wood.

One afternoon, just after five, Colonel, Skye, Mark and Harmony trudged along the road, and knocked on the Armstrongs' door, asking if they could bathe. Kaz's mother smiled at the bedraggled quartet and threw the door open. Before entering they stood at the threshold, painstakingly unlacing boots that were caked with heavy mud, whilst the rain ran down their necks.

Safely inside, Colonel murmured, 'I don't think much of your neighbours, Sue.'

'What do you mean?'

'Oh, some old bat just shouted something rude at us.'

'So what?' shrugged Mark. 'You should be used to that by now.'

'Anybody would think we look weird or something,' said Skye with a grin.

Kaz surveyed her friends. From the outside . . . well, yes, three of them did look strange. Mark looked like a bearded scoutmaster on a climbing holiday, but pretty Skye in her muddy, gypsy clothes and burly Colonel with his feather-trimmed dreadlocks were certainly likely to frighten old ladies. Tall Harmony, cropped head and lime-green leggings (sticking out from a tasteful black dustbin liner with holes cut for her head and arms), might have the same effect on old gentlemen. Yet to Kaz they were . . . normal. Just people she liked. Increasingly nowadays she puzzled what words like normal meant. In South Africa it was normal to despise black people, in Nazi Germany it was normal to persecute Jews . . .

'You look great,' she said.

'Little sister, have you had your eyes tested recently?' asked Harmony, pointing to her mud-streaked face with such a comical look they all burst out laughing.

'I give it another two weeks, then they'll send the bailiffs to evict us from the trees,' Mark said, suddenly serious.

'What will happen?' asked Kaz.

'Oh, the under-sheriff comes . . .'

'Wow, does he have a star and a gun?' asked Jamie.

'Not that sort of sheriff! No, he's usually some kind of solicitor. When the court serves the notice of eviction, he and his bailiffs have to see that we go.'

'No chance!' said Colonel stoutly.

Mark sighed. 'Well, sooner or later . . . But I reckon we can hold out for much longer than they think. The tree camp's really sorted now . . .'

'Will you go in a tree, Skye?' asked Kaz's mother.

'No, I hate heights,' said Skye, shaking her head with horror at the thought, 'so I'm ground support. When they move in on us we have to see they keep getting fresh water in the tree houses. That and coffee – and cigarette papers!'

'Did you hear about Ash yesterday, Kaz?' asked Mark.

Kaz felt herself go pink. 'What about him?'

'He was in the old oak – he's made a great little house there – and you know it's right by the footpath? Well, a couple of security guards are walking along, off duty, and Ash calls down and offers them a smoke. Heart of gold, has Ash! So they stop, and these guys are OK, you know? One of them, Dave, tells Ash he's been unemployed since he left school, about four years, and this is the first job he's been offered. The same with the other one, Danny. But they can't stand security – it's bad money and they hate the attitude of most of the other guards . . .'

'You know, like, it's Punch A Protester A Day,' added Skye.

Mark nodded and went on, 'Anyway, these two get really into talking to Ash, and he shows them his tree-house, and they give him a can of beer, and at last he asks them if they can face going on with the job? He says he knows they need the work, but should you do *anything* for money? You should have heard him, going on about principles like some philosophy lecturer! In the end Dave and Danny say they're going to pack it in and join us!'

'You're kidding?' said Kaz's mother.

'Wow, that's brilliant!' said Jamie.

Kaz knew she was pink with pleasure, and did not care who saw. Her friendship with Ash was one of the strangest, richest experiences she had ever known. When Jamie asked her once – in that maddening little brother way – if she wanted Ash to be her boyfriend, she answered loftily that she thought of him as a very good mate, or a big brother. But she knew that was not really true.

Harmony, Mark and Skye had all showered and were sitting waiting for Colonel to finish, when the doorbell rang.

'Go and see who that is, sweetheart,' Kaz's mother said to Jamie.

He jumped up and returned a few moments later looking puzzled. 'It's that man, Mum, the one we saw on the hill ages ago. He says he wants to speak to you. He looks sort of . . . cross.'

'Uh-oh,' said Kaz.

Her mother frowned as she got up. Kaz followed her to the front door. There stood Melvin Douglas, the farmer from Seaston, beneath a black umbrella. His face was scarlet, and he seemed out of breath.

'What can I do for you?' Kaz's mother asked in a level voice.

'I'll tell you what you can do – you can stop your antics, that's what! You can stop encouraging those hippies, that's what!'

Kaz was standing behind the door. She could not see her mother's face, but felt her own drain of colour.

'I – beg – your – pardon?' said her mother very slowly.

'I think you know what I mean! People in your road are sick of smelly hippies trailing backward and forward, lowering the tone of the whole place.'

'Is that a fact? Somebody telephoned you, did they?'

'As a matter of fact they did! People round here and over at Seaston want this bypass, and they don't want these protesters here, and the sooner types like you stop encouraging them, the better for the rest of us. I've seen your letters in the paper! You should be ashamed of yourself!'

Kaz heard her mother draw in her breath, and saw her knuckles whiten as they gripped the door. There was a tense silence in the kitchen behind them. When she spoke, Kaz's mother kept her voice as icily calm as it had been before.

'Well, Mr Douglas, I can tell you for a start that I am *not* ashamed of myself. I'm doing what I can to help those people because I admire what they're doing. Yes, I do! You call them smelly – well, how can they be smelly when I'm letting them have showers right now? Mm?'

'Oh, you are, are you?' he said unpleasantly.

'Yes, and I shall continue to do so. I shall have who I want, when I want, in my own home – and it's no business of yours or of anyone else in this street. Anyway, it so happens that there are a good many people round here who signed my husband's petition calling for the road work to be stopped, and who question the need for a so-called bypass this size. It'll only bring more and more traffic to the area . . . oh, but it won't matter to you over in Seaston, will it?'

'You don't care about our traffic,' he said sullenly, cowed by her tone.

'Yes we do! My husband wrote to the paper saying that a *small* by-pass for Seaston, a single carriageway, would have solved your traffic problems at a fraction of the cost, *and* left the hill alone. That's been said all along – but he that has ears to hear, let him hear!'

'You can tell them on the hill, we'll be seeing them off soon. By any means we can.'

'Is that a threat, Mr Douglas?'

'It's a promise, Mrs Armstrong.'

'Are you speaking for your parish council here?'

'I'm speaking for my neighbours. These people are criminal scum and they deserve to be treated like scum.'

'Well then, it's you who should be ashamed of yourself. A man of your age, with your position in the community . . . I advise you to say no more, go home and look in the mirror. Ask yourself if you're justified in casting stones at people you don't even know. I think you should go on your knees in the parish church and ask forgiveness!'

Kaz's mother stood up straight, to signal that the conversation was at an end. Melvin Douglas stood for a minute, shuffling his feet with uncertainty, whilst the rain ran off his umbrella. Then he muttered, 'You'll see . . .'

'See what, Mr Douglas?'

'Who's going to win. Who's in the right. We'll show you!'

'Well, we shall certainly look forward to that! Now, can I suggest you go home and have a hot toddy, before you catch cold?'

She closed the door and stood for a second with her eyes closed. Kaz hugged her mother. She felt her trembling slightly. 'Oh, Mum, you were so brilliant, you really told him, you utterly showed him . . .!'

There was a little burst of applause from the kitchen, and a subdued, 'Yip, yip!' from the top of the stairs, where Colonel had been sitting, listening. But Kaz and her mother were staring at Jamie. He was standing white-faced in the kitchen doorway, and as they moved towards him he smashed his fist against the door frame, his face working madly in the effort not to cry. At last he gave up, and rushed towards his mother like a child half his age. He threw his arms round her and burst into loud sobs that were more like groans, because he was trying so hard to control them.

'It's not fair, Mum. Everybody hates us! Everybody hates us!' he cried.

Fifteen

'Come up – go on, I dare you.'

'No!'

'Oh, please!'

Kaz looked up at Ash, peering down at her through the branches of her gnarled old oak, and smiled. 'I can't – I really can't. I've told you a million times I hate heights.'

'I want you to see my house!' he called. 'It's really great in here.'

'You sound like a proper little housewife,' she jeered.

'So what? Sexist! Hey, what do you think of my banner? Harmony made it.'

Kaz smiled. She knew he could not have done the neat lettering himself. FOLLOW THE RAINBOW, it said, in curly green script.

'It's brilliant!'

Mark put an arm round her shoulder and squinted up. 'How's your brother these days?' he asked.

'Oh, he's OK . . . but the whole thing's really got to him. He's very moody and sort of . . . obsessed about the road now.'

'Aren't we all?'

'Yes but, you know, Mark – he's only eleven, and it's like he's given up on schoolwork and friends and everything. I have too, but it's different with me – I'm older. I can sort of see an end to it. Next year I'll start the two-year GCSE grind, and I know I'll get back to normal. But Jamie just prowls about, as if he's not really with us. All he's interested in are his science books and his chemistry set.'

'Well at least that's something,' said Mark, fiddling with his climbing harness.

Ash was now lowering a bucket on a rope. 'Here, Mark – push Kazzie into this so I can haul her up!'

They laughed, then Mark turned to Kaz with that dreamy look in his eye she had seen before. 'It would be nice if you could just see what it's like in the trees – just once. So you can understand why we feel like we do about them . . .'

'I do understand!' Kaz protested.

'No, but I mean *really*. It's like another world, Kaz – you can lie back in your sleeping-bag and close your eyes, and feel every leaf trembling around you. It's like you become part of the tree – you're one of the branches and the leaves are sort of growing out of you.'

'Like the Green Man,' said Kaz softly, picking up his tone.

'Just like the Green Man,' said Mark seriously.

'You know about him?'

'Of course I do . . . Sometimes I think I *am* him.'

There was a swoosh and a flurry, and Ash was abseiling down the trunk. He jumped down next to them. His hair hung around his face, and

161

he had crowned himself with leaves. 'No, you're not – *I'm* him!' he laughed.

'I'll tell you one thing for certain about the Green Man,' smiled Mark.

'What?'

'He's in the process of waking up!' he cried.

Kaz stepped forward and stroked the trunk of the oak, tracing its ridges and channels and whorls with her finger. 'You are, aren't you?' she whispered. She closed her eyes and breathed deeply. She felt she could distinguish between the rich, loamy dampness of the earth, the dry, almost mouldy perfume of bark, the acid freshness of new green leaves, even the milkiness of the sap itself – all combining into the one, the life-force, the growing creature. The darkness behind her eyelids was tapestried red and green; her ears were full of whispering leaves. Without thinking she opened her eyes, and walked round the tree looking for a low branch. Then she reached up and plucked a small leaf to nibble. It tasted bitter, as if it drew sorrow up from the earth and into its veins.

'I *would* like to go up into the tree,' Kaz said aloud, surprising herself.

In the end her ascent was undramatic. Mark would not allow anyone to climb unless they had been trained to do so. To build the tree dwellings they had borrowed a ladder and tools, not to mention wood and nails from a sympathetic local builder. Since Ash's platform was one of the lowest, Kaz could climb up in a very conventional way. Mark held the ladder against the oak, and Ash went first. Kaz held on tightly,

162

not looking down, and the only really difficult bit was climbing out and up over the edge of the platform. Kaz moved very slowly, glad of Ash's hand. At last, she was there.

'OK?' Mark called from the ground.

Kaz allowed herself to peer down, dizzy, not with vertigo, but exhilaration. 'It's brilliant!' she called.

The tree colony looked totally different from this new angle. There were huge, square-mesh hammocks slung in many of the trees, in which one or two people could read and sleep. Across in a huge beech tree was the largest platform – a communal kitchen, with stores and a camping stove so that they could heat up soup and beans when it came to the siege. There was also sleeping space on this platform, and on another large platform, out of sight from the oak. A noise of hammering in the distance came from the construction of another wooden house, and amongst the leaves clear plastic sheeting, blue and green tarpaulins, and black plastic sacks (anything to keep out the rain) glinted in the dappled light. Large banners hung down like flags here and there, bearing slogans like, SAVE THE TREES and EARTH FIRST, in green and orange daubed lettering.

Ash pointed out the walkways: rope stretched from tree to tree at foot and chest level. 'You just clip your harness on, hold with both hands and go sideways along, like a crab,' he explained. Kaz saw Harmony bouncing and swaying across from one beech tree to the large kitchen platform.

'Now *that* I could not do,' she shuddered.

'So what do you think?' asked Ash.

Kaz felt like a child who has done something daring for the very first time, and wants the world to see. She waved across at Harmony, who had reached the kitchen platform and could wave back. Then, still standing, Kaz shoved a hand in her pocket, pulled something out, and held out a balled fist to Ash.

'Present!'

'For me?'

'Who else?'

She opened her palm to reveal Rizlas and a packet of Old Holborn tobacco. He snatched them up with a little whoop, and grinned up at her with the delight of a vulnerable little boy. Somehow it made her want to cry.

'I really don't approve of smoking, you know,' she said sternly.

'Yeah, yeah, Kaz – but up here if I didn't smoke I'd go mad.'

'*Go* mad?' she laughed. 'Maybe you smoke because you *are* mad! I mean you all bang on about pollution, yet you fill your lungs with rubbish!'

'OK Miss Goody-goody, so why the present then?'

'Because.'

'Because-type presents are the best.'

He started to roll a cigarette with quick expertise. A lick, a tap, and the sliver of paper was in his mouth. A spurt of match, then he waved his hand again. 'Well? You still haven't told me what you think.'

Kaz sat down just by the entrance to the shelter, where she could see a tattered paperback lying open on his sleeping-bag. Because she was thrilled to be there with him, yet not sure what to say, she pointed to the book.

'You read?'

It was one of those moments when you can almost see your own stupid words scrolling up on the screen before you, and want to reach for the delete key.

'Durr . . . uh . . . Yesh . . . Miss . . . oi . . . can . . . read . . . reel . . . buks,' he said.

'Oh, I didn't mean . . .'

'I know, Kaz, but you make assumptions, just like everyone else. Just because I had a lousy family and went into care, and ran away to end up with this lot, doesn't mean I'm thick, y'know.'

'No, I *know* that! Oh . . . I'm sorry,' Kaz said unhappily, wondering why, with Ash, she still managed to put her foot in it.

'Yeah, sure,' he said abruptly.

They sat cross-legged, each staring down at the wooden planks and not speaking, for at least three minutes. Then Kaz could bear it no longer.

'What is it, anyway?' she asked in a high squeaky voice.

'What?'

'The book, silly!'

'It's a fantasy – by John Christopher. You know him?'

'I've heard of him,' fibbed Kaz.

'He's a brilliant writer. You should have a go.'

'Maybe I can borrow it when you've finished?'

'Sure,' he said carelessly. He sprawled across to reach for the book, which he thrust at her almost aggressively, as if defying her to laugh at his choice of reading. 'It's not really a kids' book, even if it looks like it,' he said.

'*The Prince in Waiting* by John Christopher.' Kaz smiled. 'Is that you?'

'So what am I waiting for, then?'

'You tell me, Ash.'

'For . . . everything to be perfect,' he blurted.

'Yeah right! Won't you have to wait a long time?' she jeered.

He said nothing, so she opened the book anywhere and read aloud:

> '*I learned a lot, from the best way of sleeping on hard ground with only a single blanket to keep out the cold, to the techniques of filling and skinning and jointing a bullock: once we were out of our own territory we lived, as raiding armies always did, on the land we were invading . . .*

'Hey, Ash, it really is about you! Where did you get this?'

'I dunno – somebody gave it me. Do you think it's rubbish, then?'

'I just don't like this sort of historical fantasy stuff.'

'It's not! It's set in the *future*. What's happened is this: England's been destroyed by some great disaster – I think it's a nuclear bomb, myself. So they've only got legends about times past when people had machines and big buildings and could fly. Now they live in tribes in small settlements, with their own princes and that . . .'

She studied his face. It was alive with enthusiasm. Thin and keen, he looked rather like the picture on the front of the paperback: a craggy dark hero in a leather jerkin with Stonehenge in the background. All around were the busy sounds of Ash's own tribe in their small tree settlement. Ash was the prince of the trees . . .

Kaz could not help smiling. He asked why and grinned back when she explained. 'Yeah, but – like, in the book they're quite violent. Not like us . . . Apart from that, yeah, not too different from all this! It'd do a lot of people good to get rid of all their machines and live like us.'

'You wouldn't really want us to go back to a primitive life?' Kaz asked dubiously.

'Why not?'

'Oh, come on, Ash! We need progress. Hospitals, and technology, and . . .'

'Who says so? They do as much harm as they do good.'

'But women died in childbirth, people lived in muddy hovels with no decent food, no light, no water . . .'

'You get food and water from the land,' he said stubbornly, 'and use herbs for healing, like Skye says.'

'Come on, Ash! People like my mum bring you food. Mark's using a mobile phone over there, and anyway, you come round to our place for hot water. You've even watched TV, I've seen you! Come on, you've got to be honest – you wouldn't want to go back to the dark ages!'

His face was closed off now. He snatched the book back from her, and threw it back on to his sleeping-bag. 'How do you know it wouldn't be better? Sometimes I'd like a bomb to drop and *smash* all the roads and the cars, and make it so people couldn't sit gawping in front of their precious TVs all day and night under their stupid selfish roofs. I'd make them like us, so they could see how they'd cope! You know something? My mother always had the TV on – I mean, sometimes there'd be nothing for me except a slice of bread, but there was always enough for *his* beers and she always had her fags and she always had the TV on, didn't she? Sitting there by the gas fire, and saying things like all black people should go back up the trees, the gawping fat cow! And then – when *he* was . . . when *they* were . . . God! And I was *crying*, she'd turn the sound up, wouldn't she? Yeah, man, our Kev abused to the music of *Eastenders* – that's modern life for you! Effin' brilliant!'

His eyes were hard and glittering. Appalled, Kaz went to reach out and touch his hand, then drew back, afraid. She knew there was nothing she could say that could even approach this boy's damaged soul, and felt helpless before an abyss that was far more deep and terrifying than the drop from this tree. What was the point of saying anything?

The oak leaves rustled all around them. In the distance Mark was calling encouragement to somebody, 'Go on, go for it! You have to relax and feel you're a part of the tree . . . Don't tighten up, don't be scared . . . that's it, great!' Somebody was strumming a guitar. Smoke from the large campfire below drifted through the leaves, and there was a smell of onions frying. At least Ash had this, Kaz thought.

He was rolling himself a cigarette with exaggerated concentration, still with that closed-off look on his face.

'Do you remember you told me about the rainbow joining up

beneath the earth?' she asked quietly. He nodded without looking up. 'Well, I think about that a lot, you know? When I feel down about all this, or I think school's a waste of time, especially when the others won't talk to me or when they tease me, and Chris and Sally don't really bother with me any more – well, then, all I have to do is think about that thing you said, and that circle of light always down there in the darkness where we can't see it. It makes me feel better. I reckon it'll always be with me.'

Ash was looking at her now, his face illuminated by an expression of gentle amazement and pleasure. 'Do you? That's really nice. You can carry thoughts like that around and it doesn't matter if they're daft, they just keep you going. I've had another one just lately too – all that stuff your dad was saying about the Green Man? I was asking Skye and Colonel about it, and they knew it too. Skye's really into nature mythology and all that. She goes on about the Goddess and Mother Earth, you know? Anyway, sometimes I lie here at night, and listen to the owls, and the wind and the trees creaking all around me, and I think I hear the Green Man talking to me . . .'

'What does he say?' whispered Kaz, holding her breath.

'He says they can't cut down this oak. He says that they used to believe fallen oaks had bad powers – you know, they'd be revenged, and that. But he says it's all gonna be OK – we *can* save the trees. He says he won't let them cut the wood down, because he's been around longer than them. He promises me we can win. Anyway, that's when I feel better – I mean, I might be freezing cold and damp, but it's all worth it. Don't you think?'

Kaz nodded and looked around. Between the branches the view was wide and beautiful. In the sky, and in the trees, you could be free, thought Kaz; nothing could touch you. No wonder Ash wanted to be up here with the Green Man. Who could say that that was not just as real, just as meaningful, as his horrible memories of home?

'I sometimes hear him too,' she said softly. 'At first I used to think of him as scary, but not now. Sometimes he's friendly, but mostly sad.'

'Sad? What about mad – as in angry?' said Ash. He pulled her into a kneeling position, ducking his head beneath the spreading leaves to point. 'Look over there,' he said.

She followed the direction of his gaze, and gasped. From this height you could see the scar on the landscape like a razor slash across a face. The extent of it was barely imaginable at ground level; from up here the whole grandiose scheme became plain.

'When he sees *that*, I think he must get seriously mad,' said Ash gravely. 'Just like I do. The Green Man's got no time to be sad. I think he's about ready for a punch-up!'

Just then there was a noise, and as if on cue Mark's bearded face appeared over the edge of the platform, surrounded by leaves, making them both burst out laughing.

'It's the Green Mark!' called Ash.

'Are you two going to stay up here all day?' called Mark. 'I think we should help Kaz get down, and then there's work to be done.'

'Aw – what work?' moaned Ash.

He and Mark began to talk about the numbers of people and tree-house places, and whether they would need to build another one for the new recruits – one of the country's most experienced climbers, two university students and a trainee chef, who intended to cook for them all, plus a freelance photographer.

Kaz hardly heard a word they said. She looked over towards the scar, and Rowley's cranes in the distance, and brooded on the sheer *power* of the enemy. All those diggers . . . the age of machines . . . Kaz shook herself, willing herself back to the present sound of leaves and voices, and the guitar, picking out a plaintive melody. The present. You have to live in the present, she thought, because the future is too frightening. Maybe the world will all be destroyed – only not by some unnamed disaster, as in Ash's book, but by concrete and machines. Taking over, everywhere. The last few members of the tribe clinging to the trees, trying to save them . . . For some reason a line from one of her mother's records floated into her mind, sung by a sweet female voice, something about paving paradise to put up a parking lot.

Then she edged towards Mark and Ash, breathing hard at the thought of scrambling down the ladder. Imagine falling – the air rushing past you, the earth's force pulling you down and down, all the colours of the rainbow enfolding you in the speed of light: red, orange, yellow, green, blue, indigo, violet . . .

She clenched her jaw and peeped over Ash's shoulder. The ground seemed so far away. But she knew that the brown scar – and the war of the trees – was getting nearer.

Sixteen

'Can I have a word with you, Kaz?' Mrs Robinson murmured, as the girls poured out of the classroom, eager for break. Kaz glanced around anxiously. Her English teacher read that quick, rolling movement of the eyes correctly. 'I'm wondering why that piece of work was so much below par,' she explained, in a louder voice. 'It's time we had a little talk.'

When the last girl had left the room she said, softly, 'It's all right, Kaz – I don't think any of your friends noticed.'

'What friends?' said Kaz bitterly.

'Oh yes, I know. Don't think the staff haven't seen how hard it is for you.'

'Most of them disapprove of me too,' snorted Kaz.

'Well, some do, some don't,' said Mrs Robinson mildly. 'But none of us like to see you so quiet and withdrawn. I wish you hadn't allowed yourself to be quite so involved in the environmental issue.'

'Why not? It's all there is,' said Kaz.

'There's school; there's friendships; there's reading . . .'

'I do read – but as for the other two . . .' Kaz shook her head so vigorously her hair whipped about her face.

'What happened to your friendship with Christine and Sally? You used to be inseparable.'

'Well, none of my so-called friends are interested in the road, and as for school . . . frankly, French lessons and learning about the Victorians has got as much relevance to me as a . . . as . . . the tooth fairy!'

'Oh my dear, I expect you believed in the tooth fairy when you were little,' smiled Mrs Robinson.

'You believe in all sorts of things when you're little,' said Kaz shortly.

'What about now?' the teacher asked.

'Oh, I believe we can stop the road,' said Kaz stoutly.

Mrs Robinson looked at her with a mixture of affection, admiration and sadness. 'Can I just give you three pieces of advice?' Kaz looked at her without saying anything. Her teacher carried on, 'Well, first, don't set yourself targets you can't possibly achieve, not even in your dreams, do you understand, Kaz? Don't take it all on yourself, other-wise you'll blame yourself for not making everything perfect. Second, don't think everybody at school thinks the bypass is a good thing. There just might be some sympathy for you and your new friends, if you choose to look for it. And third – you're good at writing – so try to put down what you're feeling about all this. Keep a notebook or something. It will help you make sense of it – when it's all over. Will you do that for me?'

Kaz nodded. When she walked from the classroom into the empty corridor one girl lounged against the wall, waiting for her. She felt the old tingling along her nerve endings, waiting for the bullying to start. But this was not Debbie Mansfield or any of her cronies; it was Chris.

'Want to come to town this Saturday? I've got some money to spend,' said Chris.

'I'm not sure,' mumbled Kaz.

'Oh go on, Kaz – you've got to lighten up a little!' To Kaz's surprise Chris tucked her arm through hers, as in the old days before the road. They walked a few steps together. Pleased, Kaz did not know what to say, and so her voice came out hard and stiff.

'Do I? I'm not sure what there is to be light about.'

She heard Chris sigh. Then the arm was withdrawn, and her friend faced her. 'Where do I start?' she said, in exasperation. 'I mean, there's lots of things! More to life than a road protest, you know, Kaz! The way you go round, you'd think the rest of us were from another planet, or terminally thick or something. You're like one of those born-again religious freaks who's seen the light and thinks everybody else is blind!'

Chris ran a hand through her short reddish-brown hair, making it stand up in spikes. With a shock Kaz realised that she had barely noticed the new haircut, let alone remarked on it. In the old days she would have gone to the salon, joined in the discussions, squealed at the result . . .

Maybe Chris was right. Maybe she had created her own isolation.

'Debbie and the rest of them . . .' she began.

'Oh, I know about them! They think they're a real hard posse! But if you hadn't cut yourself off from me and Sal and the others, they wouldn't have been able to get at you so much.'

There was a short silence. Kaz could not prevent the tears from filling her eyes. 'I'm sorry, Chris,' she sniffed at last. 'I just didn't think anybody understood. You'd be talking about the disco and all that, and I'd think . . . I had nothing to talk to you about any more.'

'Well, why don't you try?' Chris demanded, as the bell shrilled for the next lesson.

Kaz thought about that as she got off the bus, and trudged wearily along Greenway Lane towards the Office Camp. The truth was, sometimes the road, and the passion of Ash, Skye and especially fiery Maria, wearied her. Soon it would be over. Life would go on. It had to. And in some ways it would be a relief.

The Office Camp was almost empty. Eviction notices had been served on this patch too; there was a sense of siege everywhere. Maria was in the caravan, on the phone as usual, Kaz saw that her face was scarlet with rage, as she continually hit her fist on the newspaper open before her.

'But who *gave* the interview?' she shouted. 'It says here it was a "protester at the tree-camp who chooses to be anonymous". So *who*, Mark?' There was a pause as she listened. Then she sighed and lowered her voice, 'Well, see what you can find out, OK? Tell Skye and Colonel too. What? . . . Oh, I bet he is! . . . OK, see you in half an hour. Bye!'

It did not take Maria long to explain. The *Solchester Echo* contained a big story asserting that morale amongst the protesters was at rock bottom, which is why they had decided to change tactics. It stated that there would be more acts of sabotage, that the people in Twybury Wood planned to spike the trees so that it would make it dangerous to operate chainsaws, and that one of their tactics would be to pour buckets of urine and excrement on guards and police. All this was attributed to an unnamed protester who said that he – or she – was anxious at the number of violent outsiders whose stated ambition was to cause injury to as many guards as possible. The article went on to quote the reaction of Mr Melvin Douglas of Seaston Parish Council, who said, 'This information simply proves what we have always known. These so-called protesters are not interested in the environment but in causing trouble. We'll soon have them all evicted, and they can go back where they came – and good riddance.'

'My God!' breathed Kaz, sitting on the caravan step in shock. 'But it's not true! None of it's true!'

'That's never stopped them in the past,' said Maria grimly. 'The thing is, they've either made it all up – which is unlikely really. Or else they've got somebody to say all this stuff – paid, probably. Oh, I don't know.'

'But who?' wailed Kaz.

'I wish I knew,' whispered Maria. She looked crumpled and beaten, and not at all the fearless warrior Kaz admired. They sat side by side on the caravan step, the eighteen year old and the fourteen year old, holding hands. For a while they did not speak. Then Maria fingered the grubby friendship bracelet Kaz still wore.

176

'Ash gave it me – ages ago,' Kaz said proudly.

Maria nodded. 'He's a great guy. One of the best.'

'I know,' said Kaz. Then she added, 'It's a rainbow – see?'

'What else?' Maria said, with no joy in her voice.

Two local women, one about forty-five, the other at least ten years older, arrived to bring food and to man the office. Then Maria and Kaz set off along the footpath, to walk to Twybury Wood.

'Colonel's called a meeting at Rainbow Camp,' said Maria. 'He's determined to find out which idiot's been talking to the press.'

'I think they made it up,' said Kaz.

Maria had filed in front of her at this point, approaching the stile where the Armstrong family first encountered Melvin Douglas. Now she stopped so suddenly Kaz bumped into her back.

'What on earth's going on?' muttered Maria.

Kaz could see and hear people ahead – a small group of police and security guards. Somebody was shouting angrily. Maria broke into a run, Kaz following hard behind, and almost fell over the stile in her rush. In the distance were the trees – and the bright, suspended banners – of Twybury Wood, and beyond them the towering earthworks of the hill itself. But immediately ahead they found the footpath filled by the bulk of a young policeman, who spread out his hands, genially enough, to bar the way.

'I'm sorry, Maria, the footpath's closed,' he said.

'What? You can't close a footpath!' she yelled.

There was a group of people ahead, one of them Colonel, who was shouting like a man possessed. 'Footpaths belong to everybody – that's the LAW! I'm gonna go and ring a solicitor and sort this out!'

'This footpath stays open until I see a piece of paper saying it's formally closed!' shouted Skye. With that she started to march backwards and forwards, backwards and forwards along a short stretch of footpath, like a lion pacing to and fro in its cage.

'Excuse me!' said Maria very politely to the young policeman, and to Kaz's amazement he did stand aside and let them pass, as if he was unsure about his instructions.

'Come on! Walk the footpath!' Skye screamed. 'If we're walking the footpath the footpath is open!'

Kaz and Maria and Colonel joined her, pacing to and fro, to and fro. Next came Janey Morgan, and three other local women. Then Mark and a couple of others came jogging down from the Tree Camp, and soon there was an extraordinary file of them, marching up and down. The policemen and security guards watched on, some amused, some clearly irritated.

After about ten minutes a Land-Rover bumped its way over the grass, and Inspector Lavery got out slowly. He was a pleasant man who had been given the job of policing the road protest and sometimes wished he had not. As soon as they saw him, Maria and Skye went running over to tell him their views. He held up his hands in mock alarm.

'All right, all right, girls – I know you want an explanation.'

'You bet we do!' said Maria. Skye just stood indignant, hands on hips.

'All that's going to happen is this: we are going to close this foot-path for a couple of hours to enable the contractors to bring up some heavy machinery. It's to ensure public safety, you see?'

'SAFETY! What you mean is, they want to start clearing the people out of the trees, and need the right stuff for the job!' snorted Maria.

'Will the footpath be open again after that?' Skye demanded.

There was a second's hesitation before he said yes. But it was enough to send a groan rumbling through the watching crowd, who had stopped their pacing to listen. Skye raised two hands to her hair and lifted it away from her face, as if to cool herself down. 'Please tell the truth, Inspector Lavery,' she pleaded.

He paused, then said in a quiet voice, 'You must be aware that this footpath is right in the middle of the route for the bypass. In time – er, at the right moment – it *will* be closed for ever. A new footpath will be routed alongside the road . . .'

'Oh, brilliant!' shouted Kaz. 'So people like me can come home from school and go for a nice country walk beside all the traffic and get asthma!'

'I know it isn't easy to get used to,' the inspector said gently.

'Too right!' yelled Maria, her face scarlet.

'People won't get used to it! People will be all over this hill when they find out!' Colonel shouted, shoving his way to the front of the group in such an aggressive way Kaz thought the policeman must step back. But he stood firm and did not alter his tone. 'Look, I respect the fact that all of you believe very strongly in what you're doing, and trust me, it isn't easy for some of us who've lived round here all our lives to see . . .

all this. But the law is the law, and the fact is that Rowley Construction is acting on the instructions of the Department of Transport, and all the proper procedures have been followed and . . .'

'Procedures, procedures!' shouted Maria. 'I hate all your procedures.' And she burst into tears.

It was so rare to see Maria give in that everybody was subdued. Kaz went to put her arm round Maria's shoulders. Colonel announced that they should go have their meeting anyway, leaving police and security guards clearly pleased – and a part of the old footpath temporarily closed.

'They can do *anything* when it's for a new road,' said Maria bitterly, when they were seated by the fire at Rainbow Camp. 'I mean, you try and cut down a tree when it's in your garden, and they won't let you. You have to get permission. But this lot can cut down trees with birds in them, close footpaths, destroy wildlife, tear out the badger setts – and all to worship the Great God Road.'

'No – it's the Great God Car,' Skye pointed out.

'Whatever,' sighed Maria.

People talked in an aimless way, Maria and Harmony huddled and whispered together. Dougie lay back with a can of beer and a thin cigarette, looking bored. Ash was whittling a stick, in a world of his own. Nobody said anything about the mysterious interview in the *Solchester Echo*; it was as if the footpath issue had stripped the group of all organisation. An air of dispirited, sullen idleness hung over the camp and Kaz felt bored and frustrated. When she looked at her watch and realised with horror that she was late, nobody bothered much that she had to leave.

As she raced down the hill, leaving the camps, the police and the security guards behind, Kaz said aloud, 'Stuff you!' – and realised that she meant everybody.

As she predicted, her mother was angry with her for being late. Kaz got round her parents in the end by telling them about the footpath, exaggerating the amount of time it had taken up. She knew her father would make tutting noises and shake his head. 'It's a bad job,' he said, 'and it makes you wonder what'll be left when they've finished.'

'They talk about new footpaths and all these new trees,' nodded her mother, 'as if it was so easy to replace the old ones that have been there for – what? A hundred years?'

'At least,' he said.

'They just don't care,' moaned Kaz. 'They can do anything they like. And it's like – the police, they're on the other side. Everything's against us.' Tears filled her eyes and she gulped, choking on her potato.

Jamie was looking from one to the other, his freckled face pale, his expression opaque behind his glasses. 'I hate them!' he whispered, with such intensity Kaz stared. He took his glasses off and rubbed at them as if he wanted the lenses to break, and his eyes were as round and cold as wet pebbles.

'Yeah, Jams – so do I,' said Kaz miserably.

'But you can't let it eat you up. That's not healthy,' said their father decisively. 'You have to get on with life.'

Jamie was shaking his head. 'But the animals can't, Dad – can they? Not when their homes are destroyed. And the birds won't be able to, when they chop down Twybury Wood, will they? What about all *that* life? It's not fair! It's just not FAIR!'

With that he jumped up from the table and ran out of the room, slamming the door behind him – as if it were all their fault. Kaz and her parents looked at each other with real concern.

'He's really taking everything to heart,' whispered their mother. 'He's too young to take it all on his own shoulders. I'll go and try to talk to him.'

She came down five minutes later to say that Jamie had locked his door, had shouted through that he was doing his homework and was perfectly all right, and that she was to leave him alone.

'Best thing, probably,' said Kaz's father heartily. 'Come on, Sue, there's that film on you wanted to see, starts on BBC2 in five minutes. Let's put our feet up and forget about the damn road, OK?'

'Veg-out time!' grinned Kaz. She began to clear the table.

The three of them were engrossed in the movie when Jamie came to the living-room door.

'Can I just go down to Tom's?' he asked. 'I feel a bit fed up and . . .'

Tom was a friend who lived at the end of their road, only about twelve houses away.

'Fine, lovey,' called his mother, not taking her eyes from the screen.

Kaz thought she heard the shed door being opened, and a bicycle being wheeled out, but she was not sure. Jamie would not need his bike to go to Tom's, so . . . she must have imagined it. She turned back to the film and joined in her parents' laughter. At last the titles scrolled up the screen, and her father stretched. 'Well, it was a load of rubbish and a complete waste of time, but I loved every minute of it,' he said.

'Me too,' said her mother. 'A bit of escapism never harmed anybody.'

'Yeah, and you always get at me when I say that!' laughed Kaz. 'You wait and see – you'll be watching *Gladiators* next!'

'Waddya mean, *watching*?' growled her father, flexing his biceps. 'After all that gardening, I'll be *entering Gladiators*.'

'What'll they call you – the Mighty Wimp?' giggled Kaz, putting out a finger to touch his arm as if it were a straw that might break.

'No – Strongarm, of course!' he said in a silly, deep voice.

They were all laughing loudly when the doorbell rang. 'Oh, dear,' gasped Kaz's mother, 'I hope it isn't old Melvin Douglas come back for another go.'

'Melvin Vermin, you mean,' said Kaz.

'If he ever comes back here he'll get the harsh end of my tongue,' said Kaz's father, rising.

'Ohh, listen to scary old Strongarm,' laughed her mother.

She and Kaz were still sitting on the sofa, smiling at each other, when they heard the door open, a shocked pause – and then three voices all at once.

'Oh! What . . .?'

'Mr Armstrong?'

'Dad . . .'

It took a second, and both Kaz and her mother were in the hall, gazing with disbelief at the sight on the path.

A police car was parked outside their gate, and a constable stood on the doorstep, one hand holding Jamie's bicycle and the other cupped with gentle firmness round Jamie's neck. Jamie looked as if he had been crying.

'W-what's been going on?' stuttered Kaz's father at last.

'If I could just step inside for a moment, Mr Armstrong,' said the policeman. 'I'm PC Whittaker, and I need to have a few words with you about this young man.'

'Jamie – are you hurt? What's happened? Where've you been?' blurted his mother.

Jamie just shook his head, his gaze moving from one to the other parent, and his mouth opening wordlessly.

'I'm afraid I have to tell you that young Jamie here's been a very bad boy. He's lucky somebody didn't get hurt,' said PC Whittaker seriously.

'*What*?' cried Kaz's father. 'What *on earth* . . .?'

'Well, your lad here obviously fancies himself as a bit of a scientist. He made an incendiary device – seemed to think he could blow up the Rowley Construction site single-handed, then make his getaway. Now, sir, if I could just step inside . . .'

In shocked silence they all went into the sitting-room. Eventually, Kaz's father found his voice. '*An incendiary device*? What do you mean? What – what incendiary device?'

'Maybe you should get your boy to explain, Mr Armstrong,' said PC Whittaker.

'I think we should sit down first,' said Kaz's mother faintly.

They were like people moving in a dream, thought Kaz. She saw her father and mother sit on the sofa, the policeman perch uneasily on the edge of a chair, and Jamie just stand there, his head and limbs hanging, as if the puppeteer had gone away.

'Come on, son,' said his father.

'Jamie? Tell us what happened, Jamie,' pleaded his mother.

Still he stood there in silence. They waited. PC Whittaker studied his polished toecap, and shifted his heavy thighs. Kaz chewed her nail.

'Jamie – please!' cried his mother.

At last the boy raised his head and said, simply, '*I hate them.*'

'Well what's that supposed to mean! What sort of excuse is that for . . . for . . .?' shouted his father.

'Don't yell at him, Peter!'

Jamie put his hands over his ears and sagged. Kaz was at his side first, cradling her brother and whispering, 'It's OK, Fleabag, OK, Jams, it's OK.' She led him to the huge armchair and fitted herself into it with him, just as they used to do, and he snuffled quietly against her – just the two of them against the world. Their parents seemed to be frozen, incapable of dealing with the eleven year old who had been transformed into some kind of terrorist.

'I think you'd better tell us what happened, since Jamie can't,' Kaz's mother said to the policeman, in a small, tired voice.

PC Whittaker was about Peter Armstrong's age and had children of his own. A part of him wanted to smile and treat the whole thing as a joke, for the sake of the parents. Yet he put on his professional face and told the story with the utmost gravity, for the sake of the boy – who had to learn that you can't do what he'd done and get away with it.

Jamie had managed to construct some sort of home-made incendiary device, had ridden down to the Rowley Construction site and lobbed the device over the gates. Bicycling off at speed he was caught by two guards off duty, on their way back from the Indian takeaway.

Meanwhile his little 'bomb' had caused minimum damage to the roof of the guard hut by the gate, before it was put out. The guards had called the police . . . and here they were.

The Armstrongs all gaped at Jamie, who refused to look up. He leant into Kaz for protection, twisting his hands over and over in his lap.

'*Jamie*!' their mother exclaimed.

'I can't believe it!' muttered their father.

'Will they charge him?' asked Kaz.

'Look, he's only a lad, and I'm sure this is the first time he's done anything like this. I think he should be made to realise he could have caused real damage, and if he'd managed to hit some fuel . . . well, serious injury could have resulted.'

'He might have hurt *himself*!' Kaz's mother exclaimed.

'Exactly. So given all the circumstances I think this is best sorted out within the family. I don't think Rowley Construction, or you, would want it to go any further.'

Kaz's father let out his breath in a rush. 'Look, will you say how sorry we are – to all concerned . . .'

'*I'm . . . not . . . sorry . . .*' snuffled Jamie.

'Jamie!' hissed his parents.

PC Whittaker sighed and rose, brushing down his trousers and squaring his shoulders as if preparing himself to meet the real world of proper crime.

'Look, if I can suggest . . . I mean, it's no business of mine . . . but the lad's obviously very upset, and I think a little talk . . . He obviously feels very strongly about the roadworks – these kids, they take things to heart.'

'Too right!' said Kaz harshly.

'That's enough from you, young lady,' said her father, with a reproachful look.

When the policeman had been seen out, Kaz's parents walked slowly back into the living-room and flopped down on the sofa like old toys with poor stuffing. Jamie's head was still down; Kaz looked over his head at them, as if daring them to be angry with her brother. There was a silence. It was broken by her mother's tears. 'Oh, Jamie, something aw . . . awful might have happened!'

'But it didn't, Mum! So there's no point in thinking about it!' said Kaz.

'I think we need to do some talking,' said her father, in a quiet, resigned voice, as if he realised that anger was useless.

'Come on, Jams – talk to us. Come on!' whispered Kaz, giving her brother a squeeze.

'I . . . wanted to set fire to the place . . .' he began.

'Obviously!' interrupted their father dryly. He was silenced by their mother's hand on his arm.

'*Why*, lovey?' she said.

'Because I hate them,' he said flatly.

'Yes, but . . .'

'They've spoiled everything,' he blurted, 'and they just get away with it. Everything! I read this road will only bring more traffic in a few years' time, so what's the point? Why do they have to cut down the trees? All the habitats will go . . . Nobody speaks up for the animals and birds, do they? All the government cares about is businessmen and lorries and making cars go faster. I hate them! I hate them all!'

'The thing is, son, there are ways of going about things . . .' his father began.

'Yeah, right! *Their* ways!' said Kaz.

Her father frowned at her. 'I can't help thinking, Kathleen, that if you hadn't got so heavily involved with all those people, Jamie wouldn't have been influenced.' Kaz felt her mouth drop open. No words would come.

'Darling, I don't think that's strictly fair,' her mother said, with an edge to her voice.

'Don't you?' he muttered.

'No – I don't. As a matter of fact I'm proud of Kaz's involvement – and mine too. I know we haven't got a chance of stopping the road, but maybe if we cause enough fuss and get enough attention we'll help the people trying to stop the next one. It's a drip, drip effect. To change people's minds. If I remember rightly, what really upset Jamie in a serious way was that foul man from Seaston coming to this house and berating me. And don't forget it was his unpleasantness that originally got your back up – so much so that you organised that petition. You can't back out now, Peter! You can't blame Kaz! You can't deny it all, for heaven's sake!'

Kaz and Jamie looked across at their parents, aware that the scene had shifted. This was not about Jamie's foolishness any more; it was about holding fast to a belief. Their mother sat erect – bright-eyed and fierce; her husband sprawled wearily, legs out, head resting heavily on one hand. He looked confused, somehow – and beaten. It was not a sight Kaz was familiar with, and it upset her. The last thing she wanted was for *them* to quarrel about the road.

'The thing is, you guys,' she said quietly, 'we are all on the same side! That's the thing to remember. That's what matters. We're a family – right? Old Fleabag here went a bit over the top, but that's only because he's a mad scientist and it's his way of expressing himself. Me, I'd rather write something. He won't do it again, will you, Jams?'

He shook his head vigorously. She went on, 'So there's no point in you two getting mad at each other, or you blaming me, Dad. The whole thing is horrible – I mean, Jamie heard that nasty old Melvin Vermin, and he got hurt at the walk – and that wasn't his fault or mine! It's not surprising he got upset. But if we don't *talk* to each other, and support each other, it's much worse. That's the trouble with you, Jamie – you bottle everything up and then go a bit mad.'

'They treat me like a baby,' he muttered.

'You trah being tray-eted like a teenayger, bu-oy,' she drawled in a deep Southern accent, knowing it would make them all smile.

She saw the unwilling capitulation of her father's rueful grin, and how he sat up, transformed once more into a father in control. She noticed how her mother threw him a glance that mingled reproach, forgiveness and triumph, then put out a hand to cover his; and how her brother leant forward too, no longer needing Kaz's embrace. It was at that second that Kaz felt very, very old.

'I vote we all have a cup of something and go to bed,' she said.

'Chocolate, please,' said Jamie, as if nothing had happened.

That night Kaz tossed around, sweating heavily. She dreamt that she was walking along the Western Road, and just as she reached the Rowley Construction site the ground was rocked by an explosion. She peered through the chain fence, and saw, to her horror, Jamie lying unconscious in the middle of the yard. Men in yellow jackets were running hither and thither, and Dougie and Ash were both climbing up the fence waving machine-guns and screaming, 'Let's get them!' But nobody took any notice of the boy. Kaz cried and scrabbled at the fence, but it was as if she and her brother were invisible, as the fire licked buildings, and somewhere deep within the site there was another *crump* of a following explosion. Then all the men, and Dougie and Ash, had disappeared. Now Kaz could not even speak, let alone move her arms. She was rooted and mute as a tree. Only her mind called, 'Jamie! Wake up, Jamie!' as the world seemed to fall apart around her. Then he was being lifted up by a shadowy figure, a man covered in leaves, with a beard, all green, who carried her brother up, up, up, into the Never-

190

Never Land, where Jamie would never have to grow up . . . And she was left down there, alone, invisible, immobile, as the fire crashed and crackled towards her.

Kaz woke, convulsed with horror and grief, her body as wet as her face. She sat up in bed and listened. Something had woken her, beyond her dream. Was it the telephone? Surely that was impossible. She looked round, confused, in the grey light of her room, and peered at her clock. It was just after four thirty in the morning. Yet she could hear voices from her parents' bedroom, then the sound of somebody moving about. Kaz jumped out of bed and stood by her door, listening. She thought she heard her mother say, 'I simply can't stay here . . . I have to go . . . You have to let me go,' but could not make out her father's words. Kaz shivered. Her mind began to splinter . . .

Then a bedroom door opened and closed and somebody was outside. Kaz quietly opened her bedroom door to see her mother creeping across the landing, dressed in jeans, rollneck-sweater and trainers. When she saw Kaz her eyes opened wide, and she put a finger to her lips, rolling her eyes in the direction of Jamie's door.

Kaz followed her downstairs and, safely in the kitchen, let loose her cross-examination. Unknown to Kaz her mother had put her name on the telephone tree, which was designed to gather as much fast local support as possible for the protesters at times of crisis. This was the first time her mother had been telephoned – and it was the occasion they had all been dreading for weeks. Maria had told her the first cherrypicker had arrived at Twybury Wood, accompanied by the bailiffs who would enforce the eviction from the trees. So the first attack had just begun, and people were needed to bear witness and give support, if nothing else.

'What did Dad say?' asked Kaz.

Her mother shrugged. 'He's not very happy. But I said I couldn't stay in bed whilst it was going on.'

'What about me?'

'You go back to bed, love.'

'NO!'

'Please, Kaz.'

'You can't expect me to go back to bed! Mum – they're my friends. Ash is in my oak tree! All these months, and now it's happening – and you can't think I can go back to bed as if it didn't matter to me.'

'Oh, Kazzie . . .' murmured her mother.

'Please let me go back upstairs and put my jeans on. Please let me come with you and help. Please!'

'But school . . .'

'So what?'

'Kaz! That's the wrong attitude and you know it!'

'I'm sorry.'

'Good!'

'But, Mum, this is *now*, and it's my *life*, and my *world*, and it's teaching me more than I learn in school – just lately, I mean. It's more important than *anything*. I've got years of school left – so what's one day? Oh, Mum – don't leave me behind! *Please!*'

The birds chirruped in the blue-grey garden, the sound trickling across their minds like water. Mother and daughter looked at each other. The tap dripped. Birdsong grew louder – as if the world outside was singing its own verdict. At last her mother sighed heavily, then nodded without smiling. 'Hurry up and get dressed.'

Seventeen

Kaz and her mother half walked, half ran down their road, across the empty A02, and set off up the footpath. In the blue stillness noises drifted down to them that were nothing like birdsong.

There was already a small crowd of spectators when they arrived. In addition, Maria had come up from the caravan, and Skye and her ground support team from the Rainbow Camp were standing looking up at the trees. Yellow jackets swarmed everywhere, and what seemed like a small army of policemen and women stood watching as the solitary cherrypicker raised its platform. Two men stood in its basket, documents in hand. Kaz's mother discovered they were the head of security and the under-sheriff of the county. They had to ask the people in the trees to leave, to give them the opportunity of obeying the law.

'They won't come down!' said Kaz.

'I know, love, but this way they're given the chance, and then . . .'

'Anything goes,' said a woman standing nearby, in a tone of foreboding.

The megaphone droned on. Kaz heard the phrase, 'at your own

risk' then strained her eyes to see if she could see Ash. But the oak was around the slight bend in the footpath, and the nearer trees were tall and thick. She could see Mark, though, and Harmony. Faces, some of them painted, bobbed amongst the branches yelling defiance. Colonel edged his way out along one of the walkways. He hung between two trees, resplendent in top hat and red braces, ignoring the cherry-picker and gyrating to the dull thud of a drum from one of the tree-houses. There was an insolent ease about him that sparked a ragged cheer from the onlookers.

Waiting. They were all waiting.

Then, trundling up the closed footpath from Greenway Lane, came the first digger, followed by another cherrypicker. The crowd let out a collective groan, and immediately people raced to lie down on the ground, ahead of the digger. The security guards raced too, to try to stop them. There was chaos, as the two groups clashed. But many of the women were lithe and fast enough to slip past the burlier men. Kaz and her mother had run with the rest, and found themselves in the middle of a scrum.

'Be careful of my baby!' screamed a woman's voice, high and panicky.

'You shouldn't have him here!' came a policewoman's loud reply. One of the girls from the Rainbow Camp was down on her knees, clutching a wailing infant.

'Come on, love, let's get you out of here,' said the policewoman, trying to help her to her feet.

'Leave me alone! I want to stay here!' cried the girl, hysterically.

Inspector Lavery raised his eyebrows, and the policewoman glanced across at a colleague as if asking for patience. 'Look, I don't think this is any place for a baby, do you? I suggest you get him as far away as possible.'

'I'm staying here. I've got a right to be here. This is a public path,' she said, her mouth set in a stubborn line.

'That's a bit stupid. This is no place for a baby,' whispered Kaz's mother to the young woman next to her, who shrugged.

'So what? It's a good tactic for holding them up.'

The policewoman, making a visible attempt to keep her temper, reached forward with both hands (far less gently this time) to help the girl to her feet.

'Get your hands off me! Police violence!' The girl lashed out with her free hand, knocking the policewoman's hat flying like a frisbee.

'That does it, young woman!' said the inspector, striding forward. 'You're under arrest!'

At that the girl's wails matched her baby's, women gathered round to protest, the inspector tried to reason with everybody, and security guards laughed. One of them shouted, 'One down, fifty to go!'

Suddenly the baby stopped his wails, and the relief was enormous. But a look of concentration was spreading over his little blotchy face. Then came the sudden, powerful, unmistakable smell – and a brown stain started to spread down the grubby beige leg.

'That's right, take him to the police station! Smell 'em out,' called a man's voice.

'Have you got any nappies down there?' the mother asked the

policewoman, who rolled her eyes to heaven. Then she flashed a black look at the young policeman standing by her, who was doing his best to suppress a grin. 'I don't believe this is happening,' she muttered.

'Take a sniff an' you'll know it!' he said, his face cracking. 'Go on, Trace, arrest the baby and change his nappy. Practice'll do you good.'

'Do it yourself then,' snarled the policewoman, unsmiling.

The mother had started crying again, joined by her baby. Then Skye pushed her way to the girl's side, and put her arm round her. 'You'll be OK, Jules,' she soothed.

'Yes, as long as she shows some sense!' said the policewoman briskly.

'Fascist police!' shouted a man from behind.

'Oh, for heaven's sake, shut up!' snapped Janey Morgan.

When mother and baby had gone, the security guards weighed in again.

'NO! NO! NO!' people screamed. Chaos, again chaos.

Somebody shoved an elbow in Kaz's eye, making her gasp with pain. She saw a huge guard pick her little mother up and throw her a distance of about two metres. She landed with a crash and a cry. Kaz saw Maria dragged by her legs, and a guard take a handful of the flesh exposed beneath her shirt and, under the pretext of pulling her to her feet, twist it viciously. She saw a man's head yanked back by his dreadlocks, and an ear bleeding where a ring had been torn out . . . There were screams of rage and pain and grief. It seemed both to go on for hours, and be over very quickly – or maybe that was just in memory.

At last they were all moved, and stood watching, held back by the vast army of guards and police, as the digger and the cherrypicker moved forward, growling like huge beasts. And all the time the under-sheriff argued with the tree people through his megaphone, and they boomed back defiance through their own, to the constant beat of the drum. Then, suddenly, there was a new sound – the most chilling of all.

Kaz watched in disbelief as the lowest branches of the first tree crashed to the ground. The whine of the chainsaw seemed to cut into her brain. Skye was standing next to her, face smeared with mud.

'See what they do? They cut all the branches off below them, so they're cut off. That's the tactic.'

'But . . . what about tonight? What about food and water?'

To Kaz's surprise Skye turned to her with a twinkle in her dark eyes. 'Oh, we can look after them,' she grinned, 'and they can get down. And we can get more people up the trees. There'll be reinforcements tomorrow.' Seeing Kaz's look of relief and astonishment, she added, 'Don't forget, a hell of a lot of us have done this before, whereas for this lot – ' she gestured towards the guards and police ' – it's probably the first time. They're protest virgins!'

People standing nearby heard this, and joined Kaz in loud laughter. Two security guards scowled at them.

'Somethin' funny?' asked one.

'Don't know what you losers have got to laugh at,' sneered the other.

Skye gave a little impromptu dance on the spot. 'Oh, there's always a bit of humour in a disaster area!' she said.

'Yip, yip, yip!' went up the ear-splitting cry from all around.

The light-hearted moment was cut short by the appearance of another digger trundling up the hill and a Land-Rover full of tree surgeons. How can we fight these numbers, with all their equipment? Kaz thought. Especially when they had the full weight of the law on their side.

The cry went up, 'The trees! The trees!' and again Kaz was carried forward, into the wood, without knowing what she was doing. Then she saw. Everybody was fanning out, and simply rushing to hug a tree – to occupy the wood so it would be too dangerous to use the chainsaws on the lower branches. Kaz saw her mother looking confused and hesitant, and rushed over to her. 'Mum, Mum! Let's stay together!' she cried.

'OK . . . Look, love – that one!' said her mother, stopping Kaz, who was bent on careering through the small wood towards her oak.

Kaz and her mother stood each side of the old ash tree, joining hands round the trunk. Kaz rubbed her face against the fissured, grey-green bark, feeling the life of it, the running richness of minerals and sugary sap within it, the unique and special *woodiness* of its existence – all hidden beneath that still, ordinary exterior. Just a tree. You see them all the time in parks and gardens and along the road. Not sacred at all . . .

'Oh, Mum – I love trees,' sighed Kaz.

'So does anybody with a soul,' said her mother.

Then they heard the heavy boots crashing towards them, and two yellowjackets, one a stocky woman with short blonde hair, were trying to prise them away from the tree.

'Keep hold of me, Mum!' Kaz called, then screamed as her fingers were bent back by the female guard.

Kaz allowed herself to drop down, making herself a dead weight. It was all she could do. But her mother had not experienced this before. She lost her temper, struggled, and was pushed to the ground. She fell heavily, and kicked out at the guards, catching the woman on the shin-bone, just below her knee.

'You . . . bitch!' shouted the guard.

'Bitch yourself!' yelled Kaz's mother. The male guard grabbed hold of her arms and dragged her roughly away from the tree. Kaz scrambled to her feet, and went to help, pulling at his arms and shouting, 'You leave my mother alone!' The female guard grabbed Kaz round the waist and pulled her away so violently they both collapsed in a tangle of limbs. Kaz grabbed the nearest bit and pinched it – hard. The woman bellowed; Kaz thought she would hit her.

But a voice from above called, 'Keep it fluffy! Keep it fluffy!' Kaz looked up from the ground and saw the tall figure of Harmony, edging her way along one of the walkways far above their heads. She waved down and called to the guards, 'Don't forget – God's watching you all the time. And if he's not, we are!' And she held up one hand in ironic blessing on the group beneath.

It was enough to burst the little bubble of rage that enclosed Kaz, her mother and the two guards. The two Armstrongs scrambled to their feet and allowed themselves to be marched out of the wood. The same thing had happened to the whole tree-hugging patrol – but somehow

Kaz felt that the exercise had not been pointless. It filled time. And time, passing quickly, was all they had.

As they reached the edge of the wood, and walked out into the sunlight, the trees above erupted with whoops and claps of pleasure.

'What's happened?' called Kaz to her mother, who just shook her head.

'Something stupid, if it's anything to do with you lot,' said the female guard, tightening her grip on Kaz's arm.

'Stupid yourself!' Kaz retorted.

'Little cow!' said the woman, shoving Kaz roughly into the open.

At first all they could see was the digger with something beneath it. Kaz caught her breath, imagining for a split second there had been an accident. But then she saw the reason for the applause from the tree people. At the same time, Colonel's voice boomed out mockingly over the megaphone, 'Now it's a victory for the Chief Pixie! Chief Pixie Maria locked on! Captain to base: Chief Pixie successfully locked on! Tree people to Earthlings: work over for the day. Repeat: work over for the day!'

Maria's hair splashed red against the dark underbelly of the machine. She half-lay like a rag-doll, her head bent at an uncomfortable angle – fastened by a black, metal, cycle D-lock to one of the pistons – immobilising the machine.

'Good God, how did she get there?' breathed Kaz's mother.

'Dived, of course,' said Kaz with studied casualness, as if people threw themselves beneath moving diggers every day. She folded her arms and watched with satisfaction. But it was then that she felt her wrist. 'My bracelet! Oh no!' The rainbow friendship bracelet Ash had given her had disappeared, torn from her wrist.

'I'm going to look for it in the wood,' she called. She began to retrace her footsteps, but there was a solid line of security guards between the protesters and the wood, who pushed her back with no difficulty.

'I can't bear it, Mum,' she moaned, flopping down beside her mother on the grass.

'Oh, I expect he'll make you another one, dear.'

It was impossible for Kaz to explain to a single living soul the significance of that bracelet. She hardly understood it herself.

'It's bad luck,' was all she said glumly.

The sun was high in the sky. People peeled off the layers they had worn for the early morning and lounged about, whilst police, under-sheriff and bailiffs clustered round Maria, who refused to disclose the combination of her D-lock. Kaz's mother set off home to make sand-wiches. She brought them back an hour later, together with a large bottle of water. More and more local people had arrived. The media disappeared, with no violence to film. At last the under-sheriff looked at his watch, and that section of the law withdrew, leaving the police to cope with the girl who could not be moved.

Kaz lolled back against her mother, full of sandwiches and relieved that the only victory for the enemy that day were a few lower branches off the nearest trees, which still stood, silent sentinels, proclaiming their strength. The wood rustled softly in the summer breeze, the voices receded . . . and Kaz, exhausted by tension and by the early rising, drifted off into a light, dreamless sleep. She felt herself floating in blue still air, as if in water, shot through with all the colours of light.

She was woken by a shouting and cheering. They had finally cut Maria free and she was being led off, under arrest, moving painfully, like a prisoner long kept in shackles. The police were leaving too, knowing that there would be no more work today.

'We've won!' crowed Kaz.

'Not really, sweetheart,' said her mother, gazing up at the trees, and the tree-houses and hammocks peeping through the branches. 'Come on, let's go home.' Her voice sounded flat.

'Why? I want to stay.'

'For one, I have to make my peace with your father. For two, I want to talk to Jamie. He needs attention right now. For three, Kaz, please just come with me because I asked you – just for once. OK?'

'But . . .' Kaz glanced at the wood, wanting – so much – to go and see Ash. But her mother was looking at her with that expression she found hard to resist.

Skye squatted down next to them. 'Didn't Maria do brilliantly?'

'Did you know she used to go to my school?' asked Kaz proudly.

'OK, so where's the rest of your schoolfriends?' retorted Skye. 'You should get them up here!'

'People don't care,' moaned Kaz, suddenly deflated.

'Oh, but they do,' said Skye serenely. 'It's just that they don't realise it at first. Everybody cares, in their hearts. That's the kind of awareness that goes back in our blood, right back to the goddess.'

'What goddess?' asked Kaz's mother with a smile that was just this side of patronising.

'The great goddess, the Mother Earth – who we all come from. All the myths of creation have a woman somewhere at the centre . . .'

'Yay!' said Kaz.

' . . . and I don't really think that sort of belief is buried very deep. What's the Virgin Mary but a goddess, after all? I think all beliefs, in all cultures, go back to the great fertility goddess. This is her hill we're sitting on!'

'No,' said Kaz decisively. 'I think it's the Green Man's hill. I think he's watching everything that's happening. I think when they cut a branch with a chainsaw he feels it like I'd feel a cut in my arm.'

'So – why don't your goddess and your Green Man *do* something?' asked her mother with a little smile.

'Do you know, there's a shop in Glastonbury called the Goddess and the Green Man,' said Skye, with her vaguest of dreamy looks. 'It's really cool . . .'

Perhaps because she had lost her bracelet, Kaz felt vaguely irritated with both of them. With everything. 'Oh, I don't know about her, but *he* will,' she said with complete seriousness, as if Skye had not spoken. 'I can sense it, I can! Just wait – he's starting to feel extremely angry!'

Eighteen

'You'll go to school as normal tomorrow,' said Kaz's mother as she kissed her goodnight. It was a statement, not a question.

'Oh but, Mum . . .!'

'Kaz, don't!'

'I'll be thinking about it all day. I won't be able to concentrate. What about when they try to cut down my oak? What about Ash . . .?'

Her mother held up a hand. 'Look, I'll go. I'll be there for you. And you can come up after school. They'll be working late, I know. They're so behind with the whole thing. They've just got to get the people out of the trees this week, no matter how. They'll probably bring the army in helicopters!' She did not smile as she said it.

So on Wednesday and Thursday Kaz raced up the hill after school, not bothering that she still wore her school skirt and blouse, to join the growing crowd who went to witness the war of the trees. School drifted by her, although for the first time girls began to show an interest in what was going on. They had seen it on the local television; it began to matter. National TV news sent reporters too, and the national press

205

covered the story with small headlines like, *Eco-war in Cathedral City* and *Hill Fort Sees New Battle*.

'I think I might come up and see,' said Chris.

'Yeah, sure,' said Kaz, her mind with Ash in his tree, wondering if the chainsaws were anywhere near.

Already Twybury Wood had changed, almost beyond recognition. The smaller trees at the edge had been stripped of their branches by the chainsaws, then bulldozed down. The guards and construction workers had dragged them into huge bonfires and doused them with petrol. Plumes of grey smoke drifted into the wood and over the hill, making the people in the trees cough. Still the tin whistle piped and someone played a jig on a fiddle, and the drums were played, so that sometimes it seemed as if the wood was full of music. Still the tall trees were occupied, and strung together by the walkways. There was a sense of Custer's Last Stand about the whole enterprise. Nobody believed that the tree people could hold out indefinitely with such a force against them; it was only a matter of time.

'At least they can't drag you out! It would be too dangerous,' Kaz had said to Ash, sitting around the fire at the wood base camp on Wednesday night.

'Don't put money on it, Kaz.'

'But what can they do? *How* do you get people out of trees?'

'Just wait and see,' he had replied, moodily poking at the fire with a long stick so that sparks flew up and Kaz drew back. She looked at his face, golden in the firelight, eyes focused with intensity on the flames as if he wished to enter them and be consumed. How could you ever know a person like Ash? How could you get close to him? Kaz reached out a hand and let it rest on his arm, without knowing why. He glanced sideways at her, met her eyes, nodded slightly, then went on staring at the fire, whilst the gentle sounds of talk and music receded all around them.

Kaz clasped her hands together, hating their sweatiness. It was too hot, yet they had to have a fire, even in June, for cooking. The pot of donga mush bubbled away, watched by painted faces. But Kaz knew now that the fire meant more than cooking: it was tribal – the flames keeping dark and danger at bay. For a while at least.

On Thursday the fences went up, effectively enclosing the small wood within a metal compound, so there could be no more tree hugging. When Kaz reached the site after school the deed was done, although she heard that the crowd had done its best to stop it. There had been violent confrontations. There were more protesters than ever, and many local people swelled the crowd, some of them drawn by the television too – and unprepared for what they saw.

'Now they're saying we're not allowed to get water up into the trees!' said Skye indignantly. 'That's inhumane.'

'We've got lawyers looking into it,' said Maria. She had not been charged after all; she said it was because she was a respectable local girl with good A levels and the police knew her well.

By Thursday night the scene looked totally different, more like a prison camp. Huge arc lights were trained on the fenced-off trees, powered by a generator, which thrummed away all night, banishing sleep. There were guards on duty, walking up and down in twos and smoking.

But although the security guards were supposed to stop anyone entering or leaving the wood, they had reckoned without the ingenuity of the tree people. 'Look at it this way,' Skye explained to Kaz, 'those guys on tonight are young and quite scared – they don't like being up here on the hill all night, they probably hate the job, and are only doing it for the lousy money – so if somebody slips them a smoke . . . know what I mean? What do they care? Whereas us . . .'

In any case, Ash's tree, and the ones at that end of the wood, were right by the next section of footpath that was still open, and so the experienced climbers found it easy to cross the wood that way and use the overhanging branches of oak as a means of exit. This time they gathered at Rainbow Camp (leaving their own guards in the trees), and Mark talked strategy.

'Make sure you've got plenty of water – all of you,' he said. 'And Ash, I want to check your harness later. Don't let me forget.'

'Yes, Dad,' Ash joked.

'I reckon they'll come in seriously tomorrow,' Mark went on, 'because it's Friday and they'll lose face if they haven't managed to remove a single person from the trees all week. That's what it comes down to . . . the under-sheriff's pride.'

'So – they'll hit us hard tomorrow?' said Harmony.

'I reckon.'

'We'll be ready for them,' said Dougie, shaking his dreadlocks back, then letting out an ugly cattleman's 'Eeh-hah!'

'You're always ready for something,' said Ash coolly.

'So would you be, man, if you didn't spend your time lookin' after wee girls,' said the big Scot, nodding to where Kaz sat between Mark and Ash.

Kaz was glad nobody could see her face flame. Instinctively she leant into Mark, as if he were her father, and the big bearded man put his arm round her and hugged her hard. 'Leave it out, Dougie,' he said quietly.

'So,' Kaz said brightly, as if nobody had spoken, 'what do you think they'll actually do, Mark?'

'More cherrypickers, more tree surgeons, maybe climbers . . .'

'Not climbers! They wouldn't do it,' said Ash. 'They wouldn't go on their side.'

'Some people'll do anything for money,' said Harmony.

The professional climbers sitting round the fire shook their heads and murmured together. Mark explained to Kaz, 'When you're climbing it's a real spiritual experience – that's why we can't imagine guys using their skill to destroy the trees. Sometimes I look down and get the feeling that I'm flying above everything – right above all the terrible things, all the human horrors – the suffering. It's pure and free. And I feel like I'm really young, and I've still got everything ahead of me . . .'

Ash said quietly, 'First time I ever had that feeling in my life was in the trees. Now, it's like I'm looking for it all the time. It makes up for . . . all that . . . in the past.'

Kaz looked from him to Mark. *I love you, I love you, I love you*, sang a voice deep within her, but whether the voice belonged to her or to someone else she could not say. It united them all: herself, Mark, Ash, Harmony, Skye, Maria and all the others around the campfire. And the ones still in the trees. And her parents and Jamie in their little house below. And Chris and Sally and the others in school. Yes, and even the hapless security guards who knew no better . . . All of them touched, just for that moment, by the rising sap of the Green Man, which proclaimed through her a universal love, which could not be touched by mere reason.

Yes, thought Kaz, focusing on Ash now, and most of all I love you.

Suddenly he grinned at her, his teeth white against his skin, and she wanted to dance down the hill, making it whole again through the sheer force of her happiness.

Later, Ash walked her down the hill in the mothy twilight, holding her hand lightly, casually.

'I'm going to try to get a good night's sleep, even with the lights and the noise,' he said, 'because of what Mark said.'

Kaz shivered. 'Tomorrow?'

He nodded, and they walked without speaking.

He insisted on walking her right to her door, but would not come in, even though she said her family would be pleased to see him. They stood looking at each other by the gate. Kaz felt eyes peering at them from behind twitching curtains but did not care. The neighbours could think what they liked.

'Well then . . .' she said awkwardly.

'Well then, little Kazzie.'

He looked down at her, with that odd, lopsided smile she could not begin to interpret. She wanted to know him properly, wanted to understand him and *console* him with such an intensity it took her breath away.

'I'd better go in,' she said.

'And I should get back to my tree. I mean – your tree,' he said.

'Yes,' she said.

'Goodnight then,' he said.

Kaz stepped forward, threw her arms round his waist and hugged him, hard, holding her face against his T-shirt. They stood like that for a few minutes, and then he said slowly, 'It's always strange . . . for me . . . real affection. I mean, sex and all that, it's different. Much easier. But just holding . . . Sort of, it never happened to me. I'm still learning it. You know what I mean?'

When Kaz looked up at last, he bent quickly to brush a kiss across her lips. It was a fleeting moment, and yet Kaz felt that time spiralled out of control for those seconds, leaving her dizzy.

Then he was loping off along the road, calling goodnight.

When Kaz came out of school on Friday afternoon, her mother's car was waiting, Jamie in the back.

'What's happening?' she asked as she scrambled in.

'It's worse than ever,' said her mother tensely, as she started the engine. 'We're going straight there.'

'Jamie too?' Kaz asked, surprised.

'Jamie too.'

'Don't worry, sis, I can take it,' said Jamie.

211

'I decided today that I want you both to see it,' said their mother, easing the gears. 'I know your father won't approve, but this is a once-and-for-all event, and I don't see why even Jamie shouldn't witness it.'

You could hear the noise from at least a kilometre away – as if a band of children had been piper-led to the hill, magically enclosed within it, and were screaming to be let out. Above the human cries, on a cruelly higher pitch, came the whine of the chainsaw, whilst the rumble of machinery gave a sinister undercurrent. The three Armstrongs raced up the footpath, as though their speed might change things.

It was four thirty. Guards and police stood in a line along the fence, whilst a crowd of about a hundred stood watching what was going on behind them, inside the compound. Kaz and Jamie bobbed about, glimpsing more police and guards behind the barrier, as tree surgeons wielded their chainsaws. Then the drums started up somewhere within the crowd, beating out a monotonous tattoo.

'Excuse me, excuse me, love!'

Kaz turned to see a television camera poking at her, as the cameraman attempted to get near the fence. She stepped out of the way, but glared at the news crew, and all the other reporters, with suspicion. She no longer trusted what any of them would say and knew that in many cases they could be relied on to make the road protesters look mad, bad or foolish. But later she was to see them as, in their way, protectors. Whilst they were present the security guards and road builders and under-sheriff's men had to have an eye to their public image. But once they were gone . . .

Kaz and Jamie wormed their way to the front of the small crowd and stood with their faces pressed against the metal fence. Now all the trees on this near edge of the wood were down, and the first of the big tree-houses was exposed to view. They had even cut down most of the branches beneath it. Above, Mark, Colonel and Harmony squatted on the platform, occasionally yelling defiance. Colonel still held the megaphone, and when one of the people outside the fence made a vain attempt to scale it or excavate a way underneath, he would shout out his humorous commentary as if it were a football match or horse race: 'Yes, yes, yes . . . Chief Pixie Maria is inside the compound, Maria's inside the compound, and she's running hard, but meatheads are coming up fast on the outside edge, and . . . ohhhh, yes, she's down! Chief Pixie Maria is down . . . but what a good try, ladies and gentlemen! . . . Oh, Mr Under-Sheriff, calling Mr Under-Sheriff, are you happy with what is being done in your name?'

Yelps and cheers echoed through the trees from all the other houses and hammocks. Kaz glimpsed Ash edging his way along the walkway back towards his own tree. Suddenly she wondered if Mark had checked his harness the night before, as he had said he would. But why would it need checking? She snatched in a breath suddenly, and a leaden weight rested at the pit of her stomach. 'God, it's so *high*,' she whispered to Jamie.

The two cherrypickers seemed dwarfed by the trees, their platforms kept down as the two men in each wielded their chainsaws on the lower branches. It all seemed half-hearted, and when, at a quarter to six, they stopped and rested, like huge insects with drooping heads, a little cheer went up from the crowd.

'They're giving up!' Jamie yelled.

Kaz looked round for their mother, to tell her, but the press of the crowd was too great. She bubbled with a surge of joy. The wood rustled ahead, still tall, still thick, with the tree houses still in place – unassailable. The afternoon sun was warm. The security guards were looking at their watches. Everybody wanted the weekend to come, and with it some respite from this tension.

There was a huddle of men under the trees – white hats and green hats and red hats clustered together, with Inspector Lavery's flat police cap taller than all the rest. The sudden silence wrapped round them all like a delicate gauzy scarf.

The national television news crew had already gone, and one by one the other journalists left. Even a few of the watchers decided it was time for tea. Six o'clock.

'Why aren't they all packing up and going home?' whispered Jamie.

'Dunno,' muttered Kaz, shaking her head.

At six thirty their mother tapped them both on the shoulder. 'Well, you two, I think it's time to go,' she said with a smile. 'Looks like they've finished work for the day.'

'Oh no, Mum – let me stay, please,' Kaz begged. 'It's Friday and I might get a chance to talk to Ash. He'll come down and we'll all go to Rainbow Camp. Oh, please!'

'Let me stay too!' Jamie cried.

'You know what your father will say!' she warned.

'Oh, who cares what Dad says,' snorted Kaz.

'Kaz!'

'Oh, I'm sorry. OK, you take Jams home, and let me stay.'

'Kaz!' protested Jamie.

'Why doesn't my family just leave me alone?' said Kaz sulkily, turning back to the fence and pressing her face uncomfortably against it.

She saw Ash again, high on a walkway, standing looking down. The trees were full of faces – like roosting birds. Kaz waved to Ash, but he did not see. He edged his way along to the main platform, but stopped just short of it, saying something to Colonel and Harmony. Kaz waved again, and could not stop herself from yelling his name. This time he saw her and raised a hand. Kaz felt the smile spread across her face and right through her body.

Suddenly, at six forty-five, there was a flurry of activity inside the compound. Guards ran to line the fence on the inside. Engines growled to life. Within minutes, the platforms of the cherrypickers rose and rose, above the heads of the guards, above the top of the fence, up and up, higher and higher . . .

'What are they doing?' said Kaz desperately over her shoulder. But her mother had no answer. Like all of them she was open-mouthed, taken by surprise.

There were two tree surgeons and a guard in each cherrypicker, and they advanced on the tree people in a way that was new: fierce, deliberate and determined. The first platform-basket was almost on a level with the main tree-house now; and the chainsaws were screaming. Kaz saw Colonel jerk out a foot and attempt to push the basket away, but the chainsaws did not stop. One was within half a metre of his leg. Suddenly somebody abseiled down and tried the same thing, swinging wildly on his harness. But the cherrypickers inched forward, and the saws did their work.

Kaz realised they were cutting at the branches beneath the main platform of the largest tree-house – where Colonel, Harmony and Mark had been sitting. By now Colonel and Mark were higher in the tree, but Harmony huddled resolutely on the platform, unmoved by the men who were getting closer and closer. At one point Kaz saw her cropped head drop on to her knees, as if she was praying.

There was such a noise of screaming from the crowd all round, and yelling from the trees, and the thunderous drumming that had started up somewhere behind her, and the terrible shrieking of the saws that Kaz felt her head must surely split in two, and spill her brains on to the ground as the sawdust of the living trees was being spilt in front of her eyes. Jamie was clutching her arm. Her mother was gripping her shoulders with both hands. All of them were transfixed.

The platform of the cherrypicker was nosing its way right into Harmony's beech tree. The tree surgeon stopped his chainsaw, and the two other men in the basket were reaching out for her. She was shaking her head and yelling abuse at them, while she attempted to fasten herself to the trunk with a length of rope. It was too late. One of them had her by the arm, and although she struggled, his strength was superior. They tugged at her, and she was dragged to the edge of the platform.

From above Colonel swung down, trying to cause a diversion. The crowd roared encouragement, although Kaz heard her mother's sharp intake of breath as his legs passed within a metre of the second cherrypicker's chainsaws.

Harmony was screaming now, with anger but real fear too. She was dragged to the edge, then held out over perilous space . . . and at last manhandled into the basket of the cherrypicker. How could she fight against strength like that?

As soon as the cherrypicker lowered Harmony to the ground she was bundled out and marched away, still weeping, by the police, whilst the crowd applauded her effort. Then the machine raised its head again, and the chainsaws started to attack the huge branches which supported the tree-house.

Kaz forgot to breathe. It was like watching some terrible surgical operation, where you felt each cut vibrate through your own body. First the smaller branches, then the ropes, then the large branches, until at last, with a sickening crash and a shower of food, blankets and possessions, the tree-house fell. A cheer went up from the security guards; a wailing from the crowd.

Meanwhile the second cherrypicker had nosed its way into another tree, and a struggle was going on in its branches. It took ten minutes, but at last the inhabitants, a man and a woman, were brought to the ground, and a few minutes after that their huge hammock dwelling slipped to one side and fell, as the saws cut through the ropes.

'This is so dangerous!' breathed Kaz's mother. At the same time Janey Morgan and two local men were running up and down, calling Inspector Lavery, calling the head of security, calling anyone who would listen.

'This is too dangerous – you can't operate chainsaws so near to people,' they cried. But backs were turned. Nobody wanted to hear.

Now some kind of madness seemed to sweep over everyone on the site. The idea of fluffy had long since disappeared; the rules had been cast aside. Janey Morgan had managed to get the attention of Jim, but he shrugged off her protestations and said, 'Well, they put themselves in danger by being up there in the first place, don't they? Not our fault.'

The two cherrypickers ducked, rose, ducked, and nosed forward, like living creatures, each taking a different tree. At the same time tree surgeons on the ground were tackling the trunks at that level. It seemed to Kaz that they did not much care whether or not anyone was in the branches above. The wood had crashed into a state of chaos.

Then she saw Ash. He had lost his temper and was abseiling down, swinging wildly, kicking out at the cherrypicker. The chainsaws went on operating. Kaz heard her own scream rise above the others, convinced as she was that he must surely lose a limb. Then she saw him grabbed by one leg. He kicked furiously with the other, and caught the guard in the face. At that the man lost his temper, and managed to grab Ash roughly round the waist. But Ash was quick, and wriggled free, kicking out again as he did so, and gaining a pendulum momentum to swing back towards the tree. The chainsaws started again. It was clear that he would swing back and then . . .

Kaz screwed her eyes tightly closed, losing her mind for a split second in a deep, reddish darkness, the colour of old blood. A voice in her mind was repeating, *please no, please no, please no, please no . . .*

She opened her eyes at the same time as she heard her mother yell, 'Stop the saws! Keep back, Ash!'

Suddenly there was a familiar bearded face in the trees, and Mark came in from the side, reaching out, trying to stop Ash swinging back. There was a flurry of arms and legs . . . Then Mark was falling, his heavy body turning like a rag-doll, crashing ten metres through the branches to hit the ground. The thud seemed to vibrate up into all their bodies – up into the trees too, and through the deep rock of Twybury Hill.

The chainsaws and machines stopped. Men rushed to where Mark's body lay amongst the stumps and fallen branches, a small pool of blood forming around his temples. A keening started high up in the trees. The watching crowd stood stunned, silent, then the screaming began on the ground. Kaz heard her mother start to cry and glanced sideways to where her brother stood, white-faced, grasping the fence with both hands, in shock.

Kaz stared in disbelief, but the noise rose to a crescendo all around her, accompanied by the tinny clamour of the fence being shaken in rage by scores of hands. The guards moved away nervously; one or two of them looked close to tears, others grinned with their customary callousness.

Then Kaz saw Ash coming down, tears streaming down his face. Nobody made any move to stop him, or even go near to him. He jumped the last metre or so and landed on all fours like a cat, scrambling over towards Mark's body. As he bent over the older man's head, touching it and stroking it, the crowd fell silent again, moved by the grief they shared. In the stillness Kaz could hear him clearly.

'Mark! Mark! You're gonna be all right, man! Hold on in there, OK? Do it for me, OK? Can you hear me, man? It's Ash. Oh, Jesus God, please let him be all right . . . Please! Mark? Mark? Please open your eyes!'

Then Jim knelt by Ash, and gently helped him to his feet. The word flashed through the crowd that an ambulance was on its way; that no more work would be done that day. They should go home. But nobody wanted to move. Jamie sat down with his back to the fence and held his head in his hands, curled like a foetus, rocking to and fro and crying quietly. His mother knelt beside him. The drum started up, beating out a solemn funeral tattoo. The wailing filled the trees.

Kaz could only look at Ash. He saw her through the fence and stumbled over, poking his fingers through the wire to touch hers, saying nothing. That was how they stood, for a long, long time, staring at each other wordlessly and weeping – as all around people called, 'We love you, Mark,' and, 'Don't give up, Mark.'

At last Ash managed to sob out one sentence.

'Kaz . . . He was . . . Mark was like a dad to me. He was.'

Kaz would always remember that on that Friday night she finally grew up. Nothing that had ever happened to her before seemed as bad as this; it was impossible to imagine that life could ever return to normal.

Ash slumped on the sofa in their sitting-room, desperate for news of Mark. Kaz's mother telephoned the hospital at eight, then at nine, to discover that he was not dead, as they had feared, but that his condition was critical. Kaz's father had to forcibly restrain Ash from jumping up and walking to the hospital. 'Listen to me, boy! They won't let you see him – nobody can see him!'

'Wait until tomorrow, love,' said Kaz's mother gently, 'and we'll go and find out what's happening.'

Kaz sat in dumb misery, holding Ash's hand. She even took a sip of the beer her father had given him, but screwed up her face at the bitterness of it.

'I'm going to make a formal complaint,' said her mother angrily. 'They were using those chainsaws with no regard for human life. None at all.'

The telephone shrilled, making them all jump. When Kaz's mother had finished talking her face was grimmer than ever. Janey Morgan and a group of witnesses had complained to the police, but the view of the authorities seemed to be that the people in the trees put their own lives at risk. There would be a police investigation, but . . .

'Waste of time,' said her father shortly.

'I get it,' said Kaz in a rage. 'People's lives are less important than building roads, that's it, isn't it?'

The second beer, on an empty stomach, made Ash start to talk. He spoke of Mark's gentleness, of his love of climbing and walking, of the way he just arrived one day with his equipment, to teach them about the heights. Then Ash began to weep again – the harsh, breathless sobs of a boy brought up to think men shouldn't cry.

221

'He treated me like a son, he really did . . . And, and it's all . . . it's all . . . my fault.'

'What's your fault?' Kaz asked.

'That he fell. He thought my harness was a bit dodgy, but I said it would be OK, and it got late . . . so he just said he'd swap with me. He was trying to look after me then, and he was trying to look after me in the trees. So it was . . . it was all my fault!'

'Of course it wasn't!' said Kaz and her mother together. But they knew he would never believe them.

The evening dragged on. Nobody wanted to talk much or do anything. They forced down supper with no appetite, then all went to bed early – Ash accepting the sofa despite a weak protest that he ought to get back to the oak.

On Saturday morning Kaz's mother telephoned the hospital early, whilst Kaz, Jamie and Ash still slept. She sighed heavily as she put the phone down, then turned to see her tousled daughter standing on the stairs, watching her.

'How is he?' Kaz asked.

'He's very, very ill. They're going to operate today . . .'

'Operate? What on?' cried a voice behind them.

Ash was standing in the doorway now, looking wild and dishevelled, his eyes smudged by shadows. Kaz's mother led him back to the sofa and sat Kaz down next to him. Then she explained that Mark had hurt his head, damaged his insides, and worst of all, suffered a serious spinal injury. 'They'll do what they can here, and then transfer him to the spinal injuries unit . . .'

'Will he be all right? What do they say? He'll walk again, won't he?' Kaz clamoured.

'Can we go and see him?' asked Ash.

Kaz's mother shook her head. 'Not for a few days. Then I will take you, I promise. For the moment, all we can do is ring each day and see how he is. But I have to be honest with you both – it'll be touch and go for a while.'

'What can we do?' moaned Kaz.

'I know what I'm going to do,' Ash said with a new strength in his voice. 'I'm going back to the trees. That's what Mark'd want.'

'Fine, but you can both eat a decent breakfast first,' said Kaz's mother firmly.

An hour and a half later Ash looked a different person. Kaz's mother had fed him and insisted he have a shower and put on clean clothes. Dressed in Kaz's father's old denim cut-offs and her mother's pink T-shirt with a dolphin on the front, he surveyed himself in the mirror and even allowed the trace of a smile to flit across his face. 'Well, I wouldn't say I look very cool,' he said.

'Take this for tonight.' Kaz's mother thrust a black sweatshirt at him. 'Come back here whenever you can, for a meal or a bath or whatever. We'll look after you.'

'I'll be OK,' he said. There was a short silence. Ash hesitated for a moment, then jerked his head forward awkwardly to kiss Sue Armstrong on the cheek. Kaz saw her mother's eyes grow bright, as she reached up and cupped his face with both hands.

'Don't try to do it all on your own, Ash,' she said gently. 'Let people care.'

'Come with us,' said Ash.

'No, I'm going to spend today with Jamie. He needs normality. He's very upset.'

Kaz and Ash trudged along the path to Twybury Wood without talking very much. Kaz wanted to, but he greeted her attempts with monosyllabic grunts, and so eventually she gave up. Why would he not let me *help* him? she thought. She was disappointed, frustrated and vaguely resentful too. Why should he think he was the only one affected by Mark's fall? Why didn't dramatic events draw people even closer together? Then she felt guilty, knowing she was placing herself at the centre again.

Plumes of smoke rose ominously over the wood, and as they drew near they saw the fires smouldering, so that the trees shimmered in the heat haze. An eerie silence marked the scene – no cherrypickers, no diggers, only a handful of guards and a gloomy group of protesters, eager for news about Mark. Colonel and Skye rushed to greet them, unsmiling, and when Ash told them the news Skye leant on her boyfriend as if her legs were about to collapse.

'I can't believe it,' she whispered.

'He knew it would happen,' said Colonel bleakly. 'I know he did.'

'He did it for me,' said Ash softly.

About an hour later they all sat in a circle, holding hands – local people and those who had come from afar to the hill, serious activists and those just along for the ride – and held an impromptu ceremony for

Mark. Skye stood in the middle, telling them in a ringing voice what Mark believed and how he had inspired them all. People spoke up then, if they wanted to, with little anecdotes about the man who was at that moment on the operating table. Ash started to speak but his voice choked into silence. Then Skye asked them all to stay perfectly still and quiet and simply wish Mark strength, each in his or her own way. Birds sang in the middle of destruction. Smoke drifted across, making their eyes water. And the earth continued its spin, as it had to – somewhere trailing rainbows.

At the end of that, without anyone giving an instruction, all raised their joined hands in the air and the hillside echoed to a long yelping call of faith. Puzzled, the guards watched – moved despite themselves.

When Kaz got up at last, reluctant to let Ash's hand go, she saw two familiar figures watching at a distance. Seeing her turn, they started to walk towards her – and with a shock of recognition she saw her school friends, Sally and Chris.

As they approached Kaz blinked, embarrassed by her emotion. But Chris put out an arm and hugged her without any self-consciousness, and Kaz was so pleased she could not speak at first.

'What are you doing here?' she asked.

'Sal was staying at my house,' Chris explained, 'and we heard it on the local news. About that man falling. We saw the trees on the TV last night and . . .'

'We just wanted to come up and see,' finished Sally.

'It's horrible,' said Chris in a quiet, shocked voice, looking round.

'Yes,' Kaz said.

225

'I wish we'd come up before,' added Sally.

'It's good you're here now,' said Kaz.

'We didn't understand . . . before,' said Chris.

'No,' said Kaz wearily.

She led them to the fence, and explained Rowley Construction's strategy, gesturing back down the hill along the gouged-out road, and feeling rather like a tour guide in a world of nightmare. It felt strange to be with her friends again, and she realised how much she had missed them. She had also faced the fact that you had to get on with things on your own, to survive. But at least Chris and Sally were here.

All the time she was looking for Ash, but could not see him anywhere. At last she asked Skye. The answer was what she expected: he had retreated to his tree.

'I think he just wants to be by himself,' she said.

'I know.' Kaz's hand moved instinctively to fiddle with the rainbow bracelet, but her wrist was bare.

A little way off, away from the fence and the ears of the guards, people had formed another group, sitting in a tight knot with Dougie and Colonel squatting in the middle. But when Kaz made as if to walk over with Chris and Sally, Skye put out a hand gently to stop her.

'I'm sorry, Kaz – it's private. I mean – we know you, and you're great – but we don't know them.'

'They're my friends,' Kaz protested.

'Yes, but . . . well, we haven't seen them before. You know? I'm sorry, Kaz. This is serious stuff.'

'Why? What's going on?' she asked, embarrassed and irritated at the same time.

'It's a council of war,' said Skye.

'What – today? Isn't it a bit soon? Shouldn't we be just, like, thinking about Mark?' Kaz asked.

Skye shook her head. 'We *have* to go on, Kaz. Whatever happens to Mark . . . this is happening too. Do you think he'd want us to stop all action because of him? *They* won't stop out of any respect. As if! They'll hit us again on Monday. You'll see.'

Nineteen

All through Monday Kaz wriggled in her chair, desperate for the day to be over, for news of Mark, for knowledge of what was happening on the hill. French, history, geography, maths . . . they all passed her by. She was oblivious to the frowns of her teachers.

At four her mother was outside with Jamie, and to Kaz's surprise, Harmony was in the back of the car. Kaz climbed in beside her, and the tall woman leant over to give her a kiss and answer her questioning look.

'I'm on bail. The master criminal's at large. Better be careful, Kaz!'

Sue explained over her shoulder that they were going to the hospital to leave some flowers for Mark, and beg that Harmony be allowed to see him for five minutes, to represent all his friends.

'Then are we going to Twybury?' Kaz demanded.

Her mother shook her head, and Harmony laid a hand on her arm. 'Why don't you leave it alone for today, Kaz? To be honest, not much has happened. The place is crawling with journalists, after Mark's fall, and Rowley Construction don't know how to handle it. They're terrified of bad PR.'

Harmony was allowed to see Mark for a while. They sat in the waiting-room until she came out again, with a serious, pale face. The doctor had told her that he would have to be transferred to the best specialist spinal injuries hospital in the south. It was his only hope.

'He was a decent bloke . . . He was quite honest and said . . .'

'What?' they asked in unison.

Harmony leant back and closed her eyes for a second. 'Well . . . he will get the use of his legs back, but it'll be months and months. And they say he'll certainly never climb again,' she said. 'Oh God, how am I going to break that to everybody?'

'It's just not fair,' wailed Jamie.

There was not much talking after that.

On Tuesday Kaz said she would take the bus home. 'All this stuff about the road . . . It makes you guilty to even be in a car,' she told her mother at breakfast. 'So don't embarrass me by showing up like yesterday.'

'Oh no – some people have to use cars. A lot of people do,' her mother said. 'The whole point is to *think* about the way you use the car, not be simplistic about it.'

'Exactly!' said Kaz triumphantly. 'So I should always take the bus from now on!'

'Always is a long time,' murmured her mother, giving in.

'I'm going straight to Twybury, Mum,' said Kaz, 'and nobody's going to stop me.'

'Easier to stop a tank,' said her mother.

Again school dragged, but there was a difference now that Sally and Chris were with her again, in every way. Something had changed: news that the man had fallen from a tree and nearly died put out a little hook to catch the imagination. Girls asked Kaz about it, but she shook her head and said she could not bear to speak. They nodded and seemed to understand. Kaz thought that maybe many more people would understand – if they could only see. You had to *witness*. Then you would remember for ever.

Chris and Sally told her that they wanted to go with her to Twybury after school. They telephoned their mothers to argue the case – and won. The dragging misery that clouded Kaz's mind was pierced, like a rainy sky by a rainbow.

When the three girls alighted from the bus they could hear the din echoing across the meadows. It seemed an unbearable length of time before they arrived, out of breath, at a scene of total devastation. Kaz stood and stared, unable, at first, to take in it.

There were mountains of cardboard boxes piled on the ground, and four cherrypickers this time – all packed with shaven-haired strangers: huge muscular men who were actually wrestling the people from the trees. There were cries, shouts and wails, all nearly drowned by the persistent screeching of chainsaws. The drums hammered out their rhythms, and the watchers (police and protesters alike) were statues frozen with upward-turning faces.

'What's happening?' gasped Chris.

Kaz shook her head and looked round desperately for somebody to ask. She saw a familiar mop of red hair in the crowd and rushed over. When Maria turned, her face was red, and streaked with tears, dirt and exhaustion.

'I've had to be at school,' Kaz panted, as if offering an apology.

'They came at four in the morning again, and we couldn't use the telephone tree because the office phone was dead.'

'What?'

'Yeah – coincidence, isn't it? Ash managed to get out of his tree and run down to tell me, and I got on my bike and went and knocked a few people up. There was nothing we could do anyway. By the time I got here they'd started making up the boxes and stacking them. They're supposed to break the fall – yeah? – if anybody else has an accident. Then these guys – she waved an arm at the men in the cherrypickers – arrive, and you know what . . .?'

'What?' Kaz almost screamed.

' . . . They're professional stuntmen and climbers. I mean, just look at them! They'll do anything, and they're not afraid of anything. It's a nightmare. But you've got to hand it to the old under-sheriff, he's pretty clever. Like – strongarm stuntmen and cardboard boxes – who'd've thought of it, eh?'

'Where's Ash?' Kaz asked, her heart in freefall.

'He managed to get back up, God knows how. I've never seen him so determined. He says they're going to have to kill him to get him out of that oak.'

'Oh my God,' whispered Kaz.

Chris and Sally were behind her, and she felt a hand snake through her arm, as if to give her support. But she knew she was beyond it now; there was nothing to say and nothing to do – except watch and wait, wait and watch. Because it was clear this was nearly the end.

Four forty-five, five, five fifteen, five forty-five, six . . . The hands crawled round the face of Kaz's watch, as the uneven struggle continued. One by one, despite D-locks and rope and retreating to the highest, thinnest, most dangerous branches, the people were removed from the trees.

One girl tore off her T-shirt in a gesture of defiance, as if daring security guard or stuntman to touch her, as if declaring by her semi-nakedness, that she was free. She climbed down alone in silence, and gave herself up for arrest – but not before an embarrassed constable had flung his jacket round her, whilst the young guards sniggered.

Dougie came down of his own accord too, but swearing abuse all the way. The cameras snapped him eagerly. With his fair dreadlocks flying about his head like ropes, and his red and white face paint, and his obscene gestures and curses and screams, he would make an excellent road protester picture – the very thing to disgust Middle England.

It took four of them the best part of forty minutes to remove Colonel from his tree; not that he fought, but because he had stripped to his underpants and covered his body with thick grease so they could not grip him. He still held the megaphone, and kept up a running commentary, which made even some of the police laugh: ' . . . Tree pixie to earth . . . tree pixie to earth . . . There's a nice strong man here trying to tickle me . . . oooh, ahhhh, oooh, aaah . . . Oo-oooh, that was nice, my darlin' . . . Ow! . . . Eeek! . . . Tree pixie being molested by four strong men . . . Please ring pixie-line . . .'

When at last he was pulled, with difficulty, into the cherrypicker basket, the people clapped and cheered.

The crowd grew thicker, as sympathisers came along after work. Apart from the drumming there was not much noise from that side of the fence, a sort of solemnity rather – as if everybody knew they were watching the trees' last stand. Something in Kaz she would not have confessed, wanted it to be over immediately. The torture of this drawn-out defeat was too much. Branches crashed and human voices yelled above the chainsaw – and when the butting digger smashed the trees down, they seemed to scream; high and unearthly, in that whistling second before they hit the ground. Kaz *felt* rather than heard the sound.

And it was the Green Man wailing too, keening with the trees in their death agony.

'They're determined to finish it today,' said a voice in her ear.

Kaz turned to find Skye standing next to her. 'Wasn't Colonel brilliant? They hurt him though – I saw one of them land a punch on him when they'd got him to the ground and they thought we couldn't see. You know what I hate most, Kaz? When I'm looking at that lot, up there – the climbers and stuntmen on their side – I want to *kill* them, you know? And that makes me just as bad as them. And I really hate that . . .'

'How do you know they want to finish today?' said Kaz fearfully.

'I heard them say so . . . Look, Ben's down . . . and look at Olly! . . . Oh, they've got him! WELL DONE! WE LOVE YOU BOTH!' she shouted.

233

Then she turned with swimming eyes. 'I think it's only Ash now, Kaz,' she said.

'I don't want to see,' cried Kaz.

'Come on!' yelled Skye, and she had no choice but to follow, with Chris and Sally behind her.

The wood was so thinned now that they could see the oak from where they had been standing, and the rest of the crowd realised too, that the old tree contained the last protester. The girls were swept along the curve of the path, to the point where the tips of the oak's branches overshadowed it, and they could see Ash's tree-house high above them in its fringe of leaves.

'Ash! Ash!' Kaz shouted, waving, but her voice was drowned by the chainsaws.

They saw his face, daubed with green face paint, bob over the edge of his tree-house platform, then retreat. Already two tree surgeons, expertly harnessed, were removing the lower branches, so that the platform was soon exposed. The banner proclaiming FOLLOW THE RAINBOW fluttered to the ground. The cherrypickers advanced on the oak at the same time as the chainsaw started to work on the main branch supporting the house.

'He's in there! You can't cut the branch!' people yelled. But the noise continued, and the old tree shuddered as the whirling chain bit deep into its wood. The platform shivered. A cherrypicker platform nosed its way into the heart of the oak, at the same time as the chainsaw severed two key ropes, making the tree-house lurch danger-ously to one side.

Ash was now crouched at the back, just by his shelter, like a man clinging to the deck of a sinking ship. Barefoot, with his dark hair in tendrils over his face, he looked like a skinny, frightened animal at bay, yet with the same determination to survive. When the men in the first cherrypicker reached out for him, all the crowd could see from the ground was a tangle of arms. Then they saw him dragged to the edge by his arms and legs, squirming and kicking, so that it seemed he must fall . . .

'Hold on! Hold on!' Skye shrieked.

'Give in, Ash! Don't get hurt!' Kaz yelled, her hand to her mouth – and she bit it hard without realising what she was doing.

Miraculously Ash managed to squirm free, twist away like a monkey, and somehow shin up over his shelter and on to the next branch up. Then he climbed on, up and up.

'He's not wearing a harness,' breathed Skye.

Kaz closed her eyes and held on tightly to Skye's arm one side, and Chris's on the other. Then a cracking roar made her look again, as the main branches were cut through completely, and Ash's tree-house crashed to the ground, in a shower of belongings. They looked pathetic: the sleeping-bag, the water carrier, the remnants of clothes, his boots, a packet of biscuits, the paperback they had argued over.

Then one of the men climbed out of the cherrypicker and started to pursue Ash, with the graceful, fearless ease of a professional. His scarlet singlet was easy to see amongst the leaves. The cherrypicker itself pulled back, and the arm was raised, all the time keeping pace with Ash's height, as if drawn to the fugitive like a magnet. The other cherrypickers had trundled there, and the four machines surrounded the oak, like strange space insects with long necks, preying on their quarry.

Ash was now at the top of the oak. He stood head and shoulders above the leaves, clinging on, but releasing one arm to raise a clenched fist. The crowd let out a collective sigh. The bailiff's climber was after him, branches shaking as he drew closer and closer, and because the chainsaws had stopped now, for a few moments, they could hear Ash shouting, 'No!'

'NO!' shouted Kaz.

'Hold on!' shouted a dozen voices.

Now the cherrypicker platforms moved in for the kill, just as the bailiff's climber reached Ash. There was a swift movement and then they saw him being hauled roughly over into the nearest cherrypicker basket, his captor following behind. The oak's branches shook, its leaves trembled.

As the platform was slowly lowered, the other machines following suit, the crowd cheered. Then people nudged each other, pointing up, making shushing noises, falling silent one by one.

Because Ash was crying openly. In the new, shocking stillness they could hear him sob, *'I couldn't do it, I couldn't do it! I'm sorry. I couldn't save the oak, I couldn't. Oh I'm so-orry.'*

Then the burly, shaven-headed climber who had caught him put his arms round the boy and hugged him. They heard him clearly. 'Ha-aey, you done just brilliant, man,' he said, as they reached the earth.

Now it seemed to Kaz that the universe was blotted out with rain, and would never be dry or fine again. She fell against Chris, who put her arms round her, and Sally put her arms round them both, so that the three girls stood crying like one entwined statue, listening to the wails all around. From somewhere behind them Kaz's mother stepped forward and laid a hand very gently on her daughter's head, her own face full of sadness. Jamie was crying openly, and holding on to his mother as if he were a little boy again.

They did not see Ash being led away by the police, nor Skye throw herself at the fence in rage, again and again, only to be arrested too. Kaz sobbed out Ash's name, knowing that her tears were for a mixture of things: grief that it was over, and relief that at least he was safe.

The deep rumble of a bulldozer made the girls break apart and turn their faces to the oak once more. The cherrypickers had pulled back; now the digger lined up to push the tree over. There was a sickening judder as it made its first hit, and the tree shook. Then it pulled back, gained speed again, and thundered forward. The lowered arm hit the strong wood like an enraged bull charging the fence in a Spanish bull-ring. The tree seemed to quake, but still stood. A third time the digger attacked, and this time there was a deep tearing sound as the roots gave way. Kaz whispered, 'My tree, my tree . . .'

The fourth charge was too much for the oak. The digger leant, and pushed, and leant . . . There seemed to be a second's pause before, slowly, slowly, the tree began to fall, in a shower of soil, stones and leaves. A deep groan rose from the crowd, as if they felt its death deep within their own bones.

Then something happened. As the tree fell it somehow began to twist anticlockwise. A huge bough was torn off, and smashed across the roof of one of the cherrypickers, whilst the rest of the oak continued to fall. Three of the bailiff's climbers were walking in what seemed to be a safe place, including the one who had captured Ash. They looked up in panic as the oak slewed towards them. They raced to get clear, but the man in the scarlet singlet was too late, and stumbled. One of the upper branches caught him on the back, and he lay still on the ground, motionless.

The silence was immense. Then people started to scream, and someone yelled, 'There's blood on your hands!' Kaz seemed to hear Ash's voice again, whispering to her that the oak trees have always hated being cut, that a felled oak had evil powers . . .

Men were clustered round the fallen climber. The cherrypicker damaged by the branch tried to start up and move, but its engine died.

'The oak killed the cherrypicker!' somebody shouted gleefully.

Security guards ran around in confusion. Through the arms and legs of police and guards they could see the climber move painfully.

'I'm glad he's not hurt badly,' whispered Chris.

Kaz shot her a fierce look. Her eyes burned and she hissed, 'Listen, Chris, *I don't care*! I never wanted to see anybody hurt, but this is the revenge – for Mark, and for everything. Yeah! And it's just like I wrote, don't you remember? My poem – the one Mrs Robinson read out? "*The earth will strike back like a sharpened knife*," it said. And now this has happened!'

It was over.

Twenty

The next day Kaz fell ill. She lay in bed with a temperature, listening to the birds sing sweetly in the garden, and glimpsing the coppery sheen of the beech tree as if through a mist. Drifting in and out of sleep she felt herself floating high above the earth, walking the rainbow so that its colours washed over her like waves. Then swooping down into the earth with a rollercoaster heave of the stomach, and searching for the light, searching for the light . . .

One day, then two, then three . . . hot, hot, hot.

The nights were the worst. It was then that she fell into proper, deep sleep, and inevitably awoke in tears, as the chainsaws hewed off her limbs and chopped her brain into tiny pieces, until at last all the parts of the creature that had once been her, living and breathing, were scattered in the desecrated woodland, to be wetted by soft rain . . .

She jerked awake, to find herself bathed in sweat. Then she clutched Rosie and stuck her thumb in her mouth for comfort, wanting so much to be little again, and not to have seen the things that she had seen.

239

Summer flu, the doctor called it, but Kaz knew more. That was like saying that the rainbow is merely the refraction of light in drops of crystal rain. Science did not have all the answers, she understood that finally now, and nor did reason. There had to be a world beyond science and reason, where the imagination was allowed to flower and where people revered the life of an oak tree beyond the speed of a lorry. If you lost faith in that, then you might as well give up, and sink into the darkness, discovering the hidden rainbow at last.

Kaz swallowed antibiotics knowing they could not cure what was really wrong with her. She told her mother, 'There aren't any medicines for sadness.'

'I know, my love,' she said, smoothing her forehead.

Kaz's mother was constantly in touch with Maria and Janey Morgan and the others, and reported back to Kaz what she thought she could absorb. The most important thing was that Mark was to be transferred to Stoke Mandeville Hospital in Buckinghamshire, the best place in the country for spinal injuries. Then the caravan had gone, bulldozed away, and the local paper reported the victory for Rowley Construction. They said that the detective agency which had been filming the protest was gathering files on key figures, who might be prosecuted in the future. All those arrested had been bailed.

'What will happen to them?' asked Kaz.

Her mother shrugged wryly. 'Oh, I think you know as well as I do that they'll just slip away,' she said. 'I think the police know it too.'

'Ash?' Kaz asked.

'Ash too,' said her mother, and bit her lip.

'What is it?' Kaz asked, trying to sit up.

'I wasn't going to tell you . . .'

'Mum! What?'

'He came to see you . . . *no*, don't protest, Kaz! You were fast asleep, and he understood. Anyway, he told me something terrible . . . Oh, Kaz, they *have* to go away now . . .'

Her mother took one of Kaz's hands, and an expression of great weariness crossed her face as she began to tell the story Ash had told her.

On that final day of the trees, when every single person was at Twybury Wood, all attention fixed on the last battle, a group of men had approached the Rainbow Camp. There were only a couple of dogs to guard it, and they were friendly, smelling the farm dogs on the clothing of the men and yelping around them in excitement. Melvin Douglas and his friends from Seaston carried cans of paraffin, and knew exactly what they were going to do. As they passed, they kicked down the rainbow arches, and the little grotto where Colonel and Skye were handfasted, and broke up the rough bench that held the cooking pots. Then it was a matter of minutes before the benders were ablaze, inside them the clothes, books, diaries, mascots, coloured hangings, crystals, letters, sleeping-bags, blankets and little objects that were the sole possession of the people who had arrived from nowhere to fight the road.

Nobody noticed the plume of smoke, because the trees were burning. Nobody heard the laughter, and the cries of, 'That should make them get out!' as the men surveyed their handiwork, before leaving over the hill the way they had come. When the first dejected protesters arrived back at the camp they found a smouldering wreckage. Luckily there were local people with them who took over and arranged shelter for the next two or three nights, for those who wanted it. But many chose to stay on the hill because the nights were warm, and they said they did not want to leave the wreckage of the trees.

'So that's it, pet. It was another revenge, and very wicked too. And now . . .'

'Those pigs! Those Seaston pigs!' cried Kaz in a rage.

On Saturday morning, feeling weak but much better, Kaz set off up the footpath to say her goodbyes. There had been a party on the hill the night before, funded by a local businessman, with music from a local band, but her parents had flatly refused to let her go, despite her protests and tears.

'There has to be an *end* to all this,' said her father, exasperated. 'You have to get back to normal life, Kathleen!'

'Life will never be normal again,' she wailed.

'Never is a long time,' her mother said.

Now she was strangely nervous at the thought of seeing Ash again, as well as the others. Kaz wanted to cling to what had been.

Ash came bounding towards her through the remains of the camp and the remains of the party, with the lolloping openness of a puppy.

'You came! I was going to come down to your house this morning. Didn't know whether you were better or not . . . Hey, this is brilliant!'

He enveloped her in a quick, tight hug. She smelt the woodsmoke on his clothes and closed her eyes briefly, loving its wildness, and trying to commit it to memory.

'Come and see Skye!' he said, dragging her along.

Harmony and Skye were trying to coax flames from the embers to boil a kettle; they looked odd and opposite, the tall woman in her thirties with cropped grey hair dressed in sombre black, and the tiny gypsy-like twenty-three year old in grubby purple and lime-green patterned shorts and a pink vest, with Colonel crawling about on his hands and knees, all feathers and silver earrings, picking up scraps of kindling. Others wandered about looking bleary and dazed. Kaz smiled broadly.

'What's so funny?' Ash asked.

'Nothing. I was just thinking . . . how you get used to things.'

'Get used to what?'

'You lot. I'm used to you lot. At first I thought you were scary – weird . . .'

'We *are* weird!'

'Yeah, I know that. Well, maybe I've got weird too.'

'Or maybe . . . there's not really any such thing as weird,' said Ash.

Kaz was assaulted by a babble of questions about her health, and roundly hugged, until she was short of breath.

'So, Kaz, you know the Tribe's moving on?' said Colonel at last.

She nodded.

'We lost this one, but it all helps, it all sort of chips away. People heard about it and they're asking questions. You know?' said Harmony.

Kaz nodded.

'People *will* wake up,' said Skye.

Kaz nodded again.

She looked around, letting her gaze travel from face to face. Most of the people here she remembered from the beginning. The outsiders seemed to have gone already. But then she realised someone was missing.

'Where's Dougie?' she asked.

A cloud seemed to pass over the sun. They looked at each other, and Colonel sighed.

'He went,' he said shortly.

'When?' asked Kaz, her suspicions aroused. There was such an odd expression on their faces.

'Let's put it this way, Kaz,' said Ash. 'Your old dad was probably right about Dougie. And we were wrong.'

'But . . .' Skye began, until he raised a hand to stop her.

'No, Skye, listen! You always want to believe the best about people, and you've always said we should accept anybody who comes along, but what if they're as dodgy as him?'

'I wish you'd tell me what you're talking about,' said Kaz.

The others stayed silent, watching with rueful expressions as Ash explained. The fact was, when Dougie came down from the trees he was the only one who mysteriously escaped arrest. Ash, from high up in the oak, had seen Dougie slipping away up the hill in the direction of Rainbow Camp. Was he there when the men fired the camp? Nobody would ever know. But there were no charred remains of his property in the large bender he had shared with five other men. He had clearly taken his things – and gone.

'But why? Did he know what they were going to do?' asked Kaz.

'I don't think we'll ever know. There's two ways of looking at it. Skye wants to believe that he decided to go and do his own thing. Leave, just like that. Most of the rest of us think . . . Well, look, he always had money, he was the one who always started the trouble, who's to say he wasn't doing the sabotage, just to bring it all down on our heads?'

'And there was that anonymous interview in the paper,' said Harmony.

'And the way somebody grassed on that Sunday march,' said Colonel.

'Do you think they were paying him, then?' gasped Kaz.

Skye shook her head vehemently, but Ash shrugged. 'Look, that kind of thing happens,' he said.

'They call it the fifth column,' said Colonel moodily, 'in a war – the guys who infiltrate the enemy.'

'Anyway, he came from nowhere and he's gone back to nowhere,' said Harmony, 'so we'll never know.'

'I never liked him anyway,' said Kaz.

'I think you have to believe the best of people,' said Skye stubbornly. 'He'd had a rough life in Glasgow, and . . . well . . .'

'Oh, Skye!' sighed Ash, with resignation.

He jerked his head to Kaz, and they headed off, towards the flat summit of Twybury Hill. The day was beautiful: tiny fluffy clouds dotted the bright blue sky and a slight breeze took the edge off the heat. They walked without speaking, holding hands with none of the old awkwardness. Kaz felt as if she was walking along the edge of the world, the sky above, and the green beneath her feet; her home somewhere behind her, and the hideous scar of the road to one side . . . But ahead – what?

'I can't believe you're all leaving,' she said in a small voice.

'Come with us!' he grinned.

'You know I can't,' she said indignantly, 'though sometimes . . .'

'I tell you what, Kaz, if I had a mum and dad and brother like yours I'd want to stay right here,' he said.

There was another silence. Ash bent down and swiped at a stalk, chewing at it as if it were the last meal he would have. He was frowning. Kaz stopped and faced him.

'What's wrong, Ash?' she demanded.

'Everything, really. Oh, we had a great party last night, and this geezer who'd paid for it, he made a speech and thanked us for all we'd done. And I was thinking – what have we done? The trees are down, and the road's being built, and . . . I couldn't save your oak, Kazzie . . .'

His voice broke off. Kaz put her hands on his shoulders and gave him a little shake. 'Of course you couldn't!' she said. 'I know you think you're great, but you're not Superman, Ashface! We just all did . . . what we could. And it was worth it. Just *trying* was worth it.'

'Yeah?'

'Yes!'

246

'You're great, Kaz,' he said slowly. 'You know that? Sometimes I wish . . .'

They were staring at each other now, and Kaz felt that those sharp brown eyes could penetrate right to the back of her mind and read all her vain little dreams and foolish insecurities. Ash cupped her head with his hands and pulled her close, bending to kiss her properly for the first time.

After a long while – during which Kaz abandoned herself to a feeling that was totally new, far beyond the odd, meaningless little episodes of getting off with boys at discos, which they giggled about in school – Ash pulled back and looked at her.

'Sorry,' he said.

'What for?'

'Sorry – for doing that. I always wanted to, but knew I shouldn't.'

'Why?'

'Because.'

'Anyway,' she said, 'I didn't mean "what for" about *that*. I meant – what do you wish?'

'I dunno. I suppose I wished I could kiss you!'

They both laughed then, still holding each other, quite naturally. Then Ash's face was serious again. 'No, I wish I could stay here, you know? I mean, I love the Tribe, but when I was in your house, playing the piano, and your mum gave me clothes, and that . . . Oh, it's like pressing your nose up against a window, yeah? And, like, you can see it all, but you know the door's locked and you'll never find the key.'

'Never's a long time, Ash,' said Kaz.

'You know what I'm saying,' he said.

'Yes, I do.'

He pulled up her wrist to glance at her watch, then made a face. 'We gotta go back down. We all walk to the bottom and somebody's organised transport.'

'Where are you going?' she gulped.

'Up north. There's a big ring road going through six sites of special scientific interest. Haven't you heard about it?'

Kaz shook her head miserably. He saw her expression and put a hand in his pocket, pulling out a little purple and black paper bag. 'Here,' he said thrusting it at her. 'A present.'

'For me? But why?' she gasped.

'Because,' he said.

Kaz opened the bag and took out a necklace threaded on fine leather: small wooden beads, the colour of the sky after rain. At the front were six slightly larger resin beads – red, orange, yellow, green, blue and purple. She held it, speechless, and looked at him.

'Harmony took me to this bead shop yesterday,' he said, shuffling his feet. 'D'you like it?'

Kaz could only nod, and smile like an idiot. Ash took the necklace from her hand and held it up to her neck. 'It fastens at the back like this, see? So the rainbow joins up, Kaz, see? You can wear it, and think about me.'

'I w-will,' she choked, not trusting herself to say more.

They took a last look down at the terrible view of the road-to-be, then turned and walked back to what had been the Rainbow Camp.

Their pace was swift. They both wanted to get it done with – the promises to write that would never be kept, the attempt at jollity, the hugs, the goodbyes.

The small procession trooped down the hill in the direction of Greenway Lane. There, a little knot of local people waited with packages of sandwiches, and plastic bottles of water. To Kaz's surprise, her parents and Jamie were among them. A couple of women carried small bunches of flowers, which they distributed cheerfully. But there were many tears, hidden behind too-bright smiles.

'Will you write to me, Ash?' Kaz asked, with some desperation.

'I'm not much of a one for writing, Kazzie,' he said gently.

'I don't suppose I can write to you?'

'Who knows where I'll be,' he said. 'Look, sometimes you have to just take hold of a time in your mind, one special time, and keep it there, hold it fast – like it's glowing in the dark, for ever, you know?'

Kaz nodded, because she had no choice but to agree. She stood with her mother's hand on her shoulder and watched him follow Skye and Colonel and the rest of the motley crew, on to the ancient, battered green coach that had somehow been rustled up to take them on to the next place. There were multicoloured flags at the windows, and flowers painted with some skill along its sides.

As it started to slowly pull away Kaz was blinded for a moment, but blinked furiously to see Ash waving. She made a conscious effort to pull her face into a grin, and waved back, pointing to her necklace with the other hand. She saw him grin, nod and make the thumbs-up sign.

The small crowd clapped as the bizarre old bus completed its three-point turn to face in the right direction.

It was only then that they noticed the enormous paper banner that stretched across the top front windscreen, announcing to the world who it was – travelling onwards.

JUST PEOPLE, it said.

'*I'm really disappointed in you, Kaz,*' *she is saying.*

Kaz hangs her head, but in truth she does not care. Well over a year ago now, she is thinking, a year ago, and it was all happening. Life seemed dull after that: a routine of school and a road being built. Everyday life in modern Britain. Progress. Looking to the future. But what future? I don't want it, I don't want it . . .

'*The thing is, Kaz, you have to get your act together. You're such a promising English student – do you think that's what you'd like to go on and do?*'

Kaz shrugs, and feels guilty immediately because Mrs Robinson sighs.

'*The thing is, the coursework folder really matters. It's your chance to do really well. I've talked to some of the other members of staff . . .*'

Now it is Kaz's turn to sigh.

'*. . . and they're quite worried, some of them. Ever since . . .*'

Kaz looks up. '*Ever since what?*'

'*Ever since the dreaded road protest your work has gone off. But I*

251

don't know why, Kaz! I'd have thought you'd have wanted to do really well . . .'

'What for?' asks Kaz, jutting out her jaw.

Mrs Robinson slaps her own thigh in her old expression of frustration. 'WHAT FOR? Honestly, girl, I used to think you had a brain under that blonde hair, but now I know you're just a bimbo! What for? So you can go and get a degree, and have a voice, that's what for! When I was at university I was proud to call myself a feminist, and I used to tell people that the suffragettes had chained themselves to railings for people like me. Now I get some of you lot in front of me, and you just don't want to bother, and it drives me crazy!'

Despite herself, Kaz looks up. This is interesting. She is unused to teachers talking like real, breathing human beings who feel things. Mrs Robinson hasn't finished; she's in full flood. 'I mean, you've got a clear choice. You can just drop out and die your hair pink and sell The Big Issue on the streets for all I care. Nothing wrong with the people doing that, but I don't know if they made it their life plan at fifteen. Or you can be the kind of person who thinks and who can argue – then, when you say no to things, people will LISTEN, for heaven's sake! Simple as that.'

'No, it isn't,' Kaz says sullenly.

'Yes it is, trust me,' says Mrs Robinson firmly.

'So?' says Kaz.

'Get yourself together – do some work, you ridiculous girl! And start with that piece of coursework.'

'I don't know what to write,' moans Kaz.

Mrs Robinson smiles now, and Kaz thinks, again despite herself, that any kid would be lucky to have her for a mother. (Ash said she was lucky to have Sue as a mother . . . so long ago, it seems.)

'We've been here before, haven't we? Remember once I told you to keep a notebook about the whole road thing. Did you?' Kaz shakes her head. 'Oh – pity. Well, write from memory. Isn't there something you can get out of it all?'

'There was something,' Kaz begins, very slowly. 'I mean, like, there were so many things, but I heard about this sort of mythological guy, called the Green Man . . .'

Mrs Robinson nods enthusiastically, 'Yes, I know.'

'But I don't know what to put . . . it's so HARD.'

Mrs Robinson claps her hands. 'I know, Kaz – why don't you BE him?' Kaz looks up sharply.

Kaz can't sleep. She broods about the Green Man, and starts to see the world through his eyes. She winces with the pain.

Meanwhile, far away, a boy who once painted his face green and crowned himself with leaves is sleeping in a bender beside a girl. He is dreaming about a woman who puts both her hands up to his face and tells him softly . . . What did she tell him? He can't remember. It has gone. But not the gentle, loving, motherly face of Sue Armstrong.

Now Kaz is up and writing. Yes, they have been here before, all of them: her room, her table, the tree creaking outside, Rosie flopped on the bed, the empty page – and the Green Man, his voice echoing off the hillside. Yes, she knows what to put, at last, and the words tumble almost as fast as a man falling from a tree.

Awakening *by Kathleen Armstrong*

All around me I see my children dying. I feel their pain. No more does my gentle water nymph sing happily as she slips over the stones; she has been poisoned and only moves slowly, her silvery colour dulled to murky brown. My meadows have been robbed of their beauty, the delicate flowers churned into oblivion. I cry as the tree gods are murdered, cut at their roots, crashing, falling, screaming, parted from their life source, all their secrets exposed to the world, and the animals they housed left without guardians, left to perish. Even the wind isn't safe: great dragons belch terrible, poisonous smoke into his powerful lungs until even the raindrops, that used to sparkle as they fell from the wind's eye, hiss and burn – filled with the earth's pain.

Who am I? You may see my leafy face carved on church benches, allowed by the Christian fathers – although I am far older than their belief. Sometimes people will notice me staring at them through the bark of a gnarled tree-trunk; they see me, tendrils curling round my face, my hands made of leaves. I am everywhere, and have been, throughout time. I remember when I was worshipped, thought of with awe. But now things have changed. People have lost touch with their old ways, trapped in their self-built prisons. I still see them in their cities, too busy to care even for their own kind. They no longer see the beauty in a tree, and are deaf to the sounds of nature.

It's not all lost though. Some people still care enough to have plants growing in windows, carefully fed and watered each day; to plant tree saplings and to try to save damaged hedgerows. Others even care enough to give their whole lives working for me.

One day I saw it – a group of people fighting for me, trying to stop a monstrous snake from weaving across one of the most beautiful parts of the country. There was one part of the snake's destination filled with beautiful trees, all of which would be crushed by the grey serpent. These people, all of whom have been touched by nature, turned the trees into their homes. Huge huts were built high in the branches, nets were strung up, creating giant hammocks. Many other homes were built from bare branches, on the ground. This Tribe was happy to share with nature and not take more from the trees than was needed. The trees were soon all linked and the Tribe prepared to use their own bodies to stop the snake's huge army of slaves from destroying the trees.

Then the terrible day came; the men in the yellow costumes, who worked for the snake, arrived – bringing with them evil monsters that they controlled. These creatures had massive teeth that tore into the earth, or long necks that reached up to the trees' highest branches; another had nothing but teeth that ripped into the trees' flesh when held by the yellow men.

Then the war began. The Tribe moved across the trees

perilously high – trying to save the branches from being cut. A few trees were lost, and as they fell the people screamed. But only I could hear the tree gods screaming. The grounded members of the Tribe were helpless. I could see the pain in their eyes. A few of them tried to run into the fenced area, only to be flung back roughly by the yellow men. Some, in desperation, tried to climb the metal barriers, tears streaming down their faces. As the day wore on people began to grow weary – the Tribe jumped with less precision from branch to branch; the yellow men controlling the monsters with less care. A terrible sense of dread fell over everyone as more and more trees died. And then suddenly a Tribe member was falling. Time stopped as his body twisted in the air. His friends were screaming, clawing at the fence, trying to reach him. I longed to be able to help him, but all I could do was make him land on some soft moss, and ask the tree gods to part their branches and guide his fall. He lay there, his body broken. I watched as even the yellow men cried.

Night came, the trees were down, they lay scattered like corpses. The Tribe walked around dazed. Someone decorated a tree, hanging the message, 'The battle is over, but the war has just begun.' The owls hooted in mourning for their lost homes; the small creatures who had sheltered in the roots had nowhere to hide. The wind howled over the newly bare hillside.

Now my Tribe has gone. There are other battles to be

fought all over the land. But one man remains who cannot move. My warrior. I watch over him as he heals in hospital. He offered his life for my children; I will not let him die. Outside his window is a tree and he passes the hours watching the ants who scurry, oblivious to his gaze.

The evil snake will soon be settled and the beetles begin their pointless journey along his steely grey back. The fields, the trees, the hedgerows, the brockways, the wild flowers – all these will never come back. But their silent grief and the wails of my Tribe have been heard. Man is starting to realise what he is doing. He must awaken or else the concrete jungles will take over all that is real, and the machines Man created must destroy him. Slowly, I am beginning to touch people with my leafy tendrils. They are seeing and hearing things they never have before.

It is a beginning.

I know.

For I am the Green Man.

And I am waking up.

Twybury Hill, Solchester.

8th September (I think)

Dear Ash,

Yes, I know it's ridiculous, but here I am writing to this guy I haven't seen for two years, and will never see again. But I want to, so there. I guess I always thought there'd be a ring on the doorbell and you'd be there, but that was silly too. You told me we all have to hold things precious inside our minds, and I do. So I knew you wouldn't really come back to visit. Thanks for the postcards, by the way! There was one from Preston and one from Newbury, and all you did was draw a little tree, but I knew they were from you. OK, sure – you told me you weren't into writing!!!!!!

Talking of writing, Mum had a letter from <u>Mark</u> a couple of weeks ago. Yes, we kept in touch! When he was in Stoke Mandeville he liked people to write to him (obviously), and so we did. We even went to visit him, about six months after you'd all left, and I saw him stand up by his wheelchair for about five minutes, with this big grin on his face. He's back in Nottingham now, and gone back to his old partner and they're having a baby! Isn't that cool? He wrote to Mum that the doctors told him he wouldn't be able to do things like that any more!! Dad says he can't imagine having a baby at that age – not if it was going to be like me and Jams. (By the way, Genius Jampot and the parents are all fine.)

I suppose I should tell you all the news. Well, next week I'll hit seventeen and tomorrow I'll be in the lower sixth, and doing A levels: English, Theatre Studies and RS. So it's a new start. My GCSEs were a pleasant surprise – I got seven in the end, and As for both English and RS. The rest Bs and Cs. Yeah, yeah, I know it's boring. You never cared about any of that, did you?

But maybe you might have. Actually, to tell you the truth, I think you'd have loved to have been nagged to death like I was, especially by Dad. Sometimes I really hated him for it, but I know they both want the best for me. And you know what I want? I want to be a journalist one day, so I can tell the world where it's going wrong! As I was saying, I know you wanted to have a family, sort of ordinary, like mine. I'll never forget all that stuff you told me, and how I wanted to do something for you – knowing there was nothing in the world I could do. That and the road made me feel so helpless. I suppose that's all a part of growing up.

I'm sitting on the hill writing this. It's as warm as that summer, but there's yellow in the leaves. The bypass has opened, and I can see the cars and lorries whizzing along it. There's so much traffic! The terrible thing is, I'm getting used to how horrible it is, and I have to close my eyes hard to remember what it was like – Twybury Wood, and the meadows, and all down to Greenway Lane. To get here from our place I have to cross a sort of concrete bridge thing. We all hate it like anything. A lot of people round here have said that if they'd only known what it would be like . . . etc, etc, etc, yawn, yawn. How can people be so slow? Mum says they can never picture things until it's too late. By then they're so done in, they just accept the next monstrosity.

Looking back, I'm quite glad it all happened – yet that seems such a bad thing to say. The thing is, I wouldn't have met all of you, and I wouldn't have got so angry with everything. Mum said it was bad for me to be so angry at my age. I told her I didn't trust anybody any more – politicians or police or anybody. It's not so bad now, but I learnt a lot, you see? I don't think I'll ever take things lying down. (Unless I lie down in front of a digger!!) I read about all the roads they want to build, and those out-of-town shopping malls, and Dad told me that food for supermarkets travels miles and miles by lorry when you ought to be able to grow stuff nearby – and I want to scream like the Green Man in his hill, and terrify them all so they STOP. 'Cos we can't go on, can we? We have to get off our backsides and tell them we want a future. Mum says we have to think of the earth as a library book we've borrowed for a while, and have to take good care of, to hand on to the next borrower – having really enjoyed it, and learnt something from it. That's good, don't you think?

Anyway, I'm rambling on. I was trying to work out how old you are now – must be nearly twenty, is that right? Maybe you've gone and got yourself handfasted to some beautiful girl on a hill somewhere!!! But I hope you sometimes think about Solchester and remember me. I think about you ever such a lot, even though it's stupid. There's a group of boys me and Chris and Sally have got friendly with, and the one I like is called Alan. I'm sort of going out with him, and I like talking to him. But he's not as nice as you, Ash – seems a bit ordinary in comparison. Mind you, when I think about it, you could be a real pain – always taking offence. No, I don't mean it really. I remember you as my own green man.

I've still got my rainbow necklace, I'm wearing it now, of course, it goes with Twybury. I've only got to touch it to get all the memories. So it's a magic necklace . . . Shall I tell you a secret? (I know you'll never read this so I can!) I really loved you a lot, Ash. You were so special and so different, and I wanted to hold you in my hand so that the world couldn't hurt you any more. Isn't that a sort of love? I don't think I realised it at the time, but it's like – the rainbow went on shining inside my mind, you know?

Now I've got that off my chest I feel better. I'll go on feeling better too, because I'm going to do really well this year – work hard and play hard, because life isn't a dress rehearsal, is it? Wherever you are, catch a thought from me – NOW! And I'm gonna rip this into little bits and push it under a bush to be recycled. Maybe the real Green Man'll pick it up and put it together and read it, and say, 'There, I knew that girl was mad!'

I'm being silly, because I'm embarrassed. But there's no one here to make me embarrassed, and anyway, I loved Skye and Colonel and

Harmony too, and Mark and everybody (well nearly!), and I loved the trees, and it's all joined into one, really.

So I'll stop, and just say – LOVE YOU LOTS, and take care of yourself, and be happy.

> Lotsa hugs from
>
> Your friend (yes, always)
>
> Kaz
>
> xxxxxooooxxxxx

Author's Note

When I visit schools and libraries, usually to talk about my Kitty books for younger children, but also to discuss the whole business of writing with older readers, the issue of fact versus fiction comes up again and again. 'Where do writers get their ideas from?' is the question, and the answer is as big as the world and as small and familiar as your own toothbrush. Writers, I say, use all kinds of inspiration, and yes, they do draw on their own experiences, but no, they don't only write about their own lives . . . and so on. So, what about this novel?

In 1994 by daughter Kitty, who was then fourteen, and I were deeply involved in an active protest against the Swainswick/Batheaston bypass, just outside Bath. It would be absurd not to be open about the experience that inspired this story. Yet this is not *about* that one protest – it draws on accounts of others too. Nor is it set in Bath, although the geography of Twybury Hill bears a strong resemblance to the landscape I know. Some of the characters are imaginative creations (Ash and the Armstrongs), some composites (Melvin Douglas and Dougie), others (Harmony, Colonel, Skye, Maria and Mark) based on actual people I like. The real 'Mark' did fall from a tree, and the story of his recovery after a long time is true, I am glad to say. Much of this happened but I've made it less nasty.

Kaz is (no one will be surprised to hear) very like my Kitty; in fact I owe my daughter a huge debt of gratitude for allowing Kaz to take over her own writings: the poem on page 101 was written in fact long before the road, and the essay on page 254 written as GCSE coursework when the protest was over. I owe her so much for every-thing else too: she is always my inspiration as well as one of my best friends. There are other acknowledgements: thanks to Kathy Jordan and Josephine Slater for hauling me in, to the local people in the SOS group who were so brilliant and brave, to family and friends for moral support, and to all the active environmentalists ('wild' and conventional) who taught me that you can't stand up for what you believe and expect to be liked for it. Thanks for the good times.